READY OR NOT

ALEX LAKE

HarperCollins*Publishers*

HarperCollins*Publishers* Ltd
1 London Bridge Street,
London SE1 9GF

www.harpercollins.co.uk

HarperCollins*Publishers*
1st Floor, Watermarque Building, Ringsend Road
Dublin 4, Ireland

First published by HarperCollins*Publishers* 2021
2

A catalogue record for this book is available from the British Library

ISBN: 978-0-00-837358-0 (PB b-format)
ISBN: 978-0-00-837359-7 (TPB)

This novel is entirely a work of fiction.
The names, characters and incidents portrayed in it are
the work of the author's imagination. Any resemblance to
actual persons, living or dead, events or localities is
entirely coincidental.

Set in Sabon LT Std by Palimpsest Book Production Limited,
Falkirk, Stirlingshire

Printed and bound in the UK using 100% Renewable Electricity by CPI Group (UK) Ltd

MIX
Paper from
responsible sources
FSC
www.fsc.org FSC C007454

This book is produced from independently certified FSC™ paper to ensure
responsible forest management.
For more information visit: www.harpercollins.co.uk/green

To Ross and Fleur, and other Lakeland friends

PROLOGUE

The Baby

The damn baby is crying again. As always. It never stops. Never stops screaming, its fists clenched, red face ugly and hateful and accusing.

There is something wrong with it. Some problem inside. Some failure in how it works. But how are you supposed to know what it is? How are you supposed to fix it? You can't take it apart and find the faulty piece of the mechanism and put it back together, repaired and working again.

You can't do anything. Change its nappy, put the fresh, warm bottle to its lips? That was what people said: they just need their bellies full, their nappies empty, and to be warm and safe, and they'll be fine.

Not this baby. This one has all those things, but still it cries. Because it is faulty. Broken.

Useless.

Stupid.

Every night. Every single one. Why? Why is it doing this? It's just a baby, you know that, but still. It is as though there is a malevolent intelligence at work. It seems malicious, deliberate. Why would it not want to sleep? It must want to sleep. It must be tired. So why doesn't it?

3

Does it intend to be infuriating? Does it want to provoke you?

No. It is a baby. There is something causing this. Some pain or distress that can't be alleviated.

The thing broken inside it.

Not that you care. The stupid thing can be in as much pain as it wants, provided it shuts up. Provided it gives you some peace.

And it has to. It has to stop. You can't take any more.

The baby's arms lift above its head as it cries again. It is a piercing, loud, angry wail.

Does it like having its arms up? Hold them there, then. See if it settles.

It doesn't. It simply wails louder, its arms struggling against your grip.

But you are much stronger. You squeeze. Pinch with your right hand.

Not hard. But hard enough.

It looks at you, and stops wailing. Stops making any noise at all.

You let go. So that was *all it took.*

The wailing starts again.

You pinch again, harder this time. And again, it stops crying, eyes wide. It looks shocked, if a baby can be shocked. Good. It is quiet. And that is all that matters.

But it does not last. Seconds later the wailing is back and it is twice as loud. It is like an ice pick in your brain. Right now you would bash its head on the floor, shake it, do anything to make it stop.

Footsteps on the stairs. You cradle it and make gentle soothing noises, sounds that mean this crying is not your fault.

The bedroom door opens.

'Everything OK?'

Stan Davidson

He should have taken a taxi. The rain that had been threatening all evening was here and instead of being inside an Uber, five minutes from home, he was walking along the road, water running down his face.

He hadn't wanted to spend the money, not after all the cash he'd pissed up the wall in the pub. He'd only had four or five pints; it was the drinks he'd bought for Carl and Andy and Ben and who knew who else that had emptied his wallet and, as the night wore on, worn out his credit card.

And it was a fucking waste. They were using him, but he couldn't help himself. It had been the same at school; they were the cool kids, the football players, the ones with fake IDs and pretty girlfriends. Most of the other pupils let them get on with it – they were happy to be the geeks or the nerds or fill whatever social niche they found themselves in, but Stan wasn't. He wanted them to like him. He wanted to be cool. To be the best player on the team. To walk with the swagger they walked with.

They knew it. They dangled membership in front of him, taunted him with the prospect they would welcome him into their group. At parties they goaded him into doing stupid stuff: *Hey, Stan, drink this* or *Stan the Man! You'll take on the dare, right? Go and pull Marj's thong up from the back of her jeans.*

He did it, every time. He couldn't stop himself. And every time the drink made him vomit, or the girl – rightfully enough – slapped him and told him he was – on one memorable occasion – 'a no-balls wanker who could fuck right off'.

And here he was, doing it again. Since they left school he'd created a carefully curated image on Instagram and Facebook. Anyone looking at his social media would think he was a successful financial adviser with a burgeoning private practice – *Another happy client! #DavidsonFinancial* – and a brand new Audi A3.

In fact, he had one client, his uncle Tony, whose total portfolio was worth a tick shy of twenty-five thousand quid, two thousand of which he let Stan invest for him. The Audi in his photos was rented; he and his dad had gone to visit some dying relative in Edinburgh and his mum was using the car. The rental clerk, bored, had upgraded them.

So when Carl had seen him in the pub and said *Looks like you're doing well for yourself, always knew you'd make it, Stan the Man,* he'd nodded nonchalantly. And when Andy had said *Drinks on you, mate* and Ben had added *Mine's a pint of Stella* he'd replied *Only too pleased, lads, go for it.*

Which was why he was walking home in the fucking rain.

He turned left onto a road that ran alongside a patch of waste ground. There was a sign up declaring it to be the property of some development company and warning people to keep out. That was how to make money. Property. Not advising your bloody uncle.

As he walked he saw a car, no lights on, parked by the road. It was a strange place to leave a car and he looked around for an owner. Maybe someone pissing in the bushes. There was nobody, and he carried on walking.

He passed the car. Up ahead was a railway bridge, then a left turn, and a few hundred yards to his road. He walked under the bridge, the darkness sudden after the moonlit street.

Behind him, he heard a footstep and he spun around. His eyes were not adjusted to the light but he was able to make out a silhouette. It was hooded, and, as he decided it was time to run, it raised a hand.

A hand that held something he recognized.

A hand that held a hammer.

Once the boy was dead the hooded figure worked quickly. The body was rolled onto its back, the arms were folded over the chest.

The figure knelt by the body, as though in prayer, then raised a finger, encased in a blue surgical glove, and dipped it into the gaping wound on Stan Davidson's temple.

It contemplated the blood, then slowly – almost reverently – it opened its mouth and sucked the finger clean.

It gave a low moan, and then took something from the pocket of its jeans and placed it delicately in the hand of its victim.

PART ONE

Friday, 16 July 2021

Tom

He'd been back at work for two weeks, and he wasn't sure he could survive much longer. His employer, a Scandinavian engineering company, had an enlightened parental leave policy, so he had stayed at home with his daughter Joanna – or Jo – for the first four months of her life. Alice was a self-employed journalist and, if she was to have any income at all, had to work, so initially the role of primary carer had fallen to him.

It had been hard. Jo wasn't much of a sleeper and he and Alice were in a state of constant exhaustion, but his dad had said something to him that had stuck with him.

I never had this chance, he said. *When you and your brother were born I had two days off work, then I was back in. I wish I had – so make sure you enjoy it. You might never get the opportunity again.*

So he had tried. It was hard at 2 a.m., eyes heavy, Jo's cries cutting through him, but he had forced himself to pause and try to enjoy the moment.

At least when he was home he could find time to nap in the day. Now he was back at work, and Jo was home, either with Alice, or Martha, a retired teacher who was helping look after her.

He studied the CAD model of an oil cooler housing on the screen and yawned, a deep, full yawn. Only 10 a.m. It was going to be a long day. At about 9.30 the night before, Alice had gone to bed. Jo – as usual – had no interest in following suit and he'd stayed up with his daughter, walking around the house in endless circles with her nestled against his chest in a papoose. It was the only way she'd go to – and stay – asleep. At a pinch he could stop walking, but as soon as he sat down – and heaven forbid he lay down on the couch – she would wake up and make a quiet whimpering sound.

It was the precursor to the full works. The full, red-faced, open-throated, screaming works.

And then he'd have to stand up and start walking again, trying to soothe her to silence for five or ten minutes until she settled down, if she ever did. It wasn't worth trying.

Then, at 2 a.m., Alice had come down and taken over. She had a different strategy. Jo would sleep for her, provided she was in constant motion, so Alice would strap her into the car seat, and go for a long drive, listening to an audiobook she wanted to read. They'd tried to replace the motion of the car with a bouncy chair, but that was not remotely acceptable to their daughter. Jo needed to be in something with wheels. Perhaps she'd be a racing driver when she grew up. He hoped so. It would at least make this into a funny story. At the moment it wasn't funny at all. It meant their nights had become a combination of him walking around wearing the floors out, and Alice driving around the streets.

His mum hadn't said as much, but he could tell she thought it was a situation of their own making. Their bedtime routine – when she would go to bed – involved various bounces and pats before they laid her gently in her bed, the room dark and silent. Then they had to remain in the room, bent over

12

the crib, one hand on her back. If they moved too soon or if someone made a noise or if it was too light, Jo would wake up and they would be back to square one.

He had explained all this to his mum when she had come to babysit so they could go out to eat. She had listened, and nodded, and then kissed him on the cheek and said *We'll be OK, love.* He tried to explain how important it was, but she ushered him towards the door and told him to have a good time.

They were home an hour later. At the restaurant, with no Joanna-related tasks to do for the first time in the ten weeks since she was born, free to do and talk about whatever they wanted, they had talked about nothing other than their daughter. By the time they had eaten their main courses, Tom was worried that something might have gone wrong.

I think we should go, he said.

We'll be OK. Call your mum and check.

He shook his head. He had been gripped by the sensation that he had to get home, right away, or something awful would happen.

When they arrived home his mum was on the couch, watching old episodes of the *Great British Bake Off.* She looked at her watch.

Were they closed? she said. *You just left.*

How was it? How's Jo? he asked.

She's lovely. Fast asleep. She was no trouble at all. Why don't you two go to the pub and have a drink. She'll be fine.

Tom started to say no, but Alice grabbed his elbow. *Good idea. Thanks Margaret. We won't be late.*

Later, when his mum was leaving, she hesitated on the doorstep. *You know, Tom, it might be worth letting Joanna learn to go to sleep herself.*

What do you mean?

I don't want to interfere, love, so you do as you see best, but if you always create the perfect sleeping conditions then

13

you'll teach her to expect those. It might be better to let her develop a bit more – flexibility.

That was it. She'd not mentioned anything since, but he could tell she thought they – he in particular – were overprotective.

So be it. Better over than under. It was no bad thing for a father to protect his daughter, after all. And she needed him. She was a baby.

He stared at the CAD model again. It was hard to concentrate, and he closed his eyes. Even a few seconds would help.

'Not getting much sleep?'

Tom jerked upright and opened his eyes. Carol, his boss, was standing by his desk, a paper cup of coffee in her hand. Her nose and mouth were concealed by a mask, but her eyes were smiling.

'Sorry,' he said. 'I was just – I needed a little rest.'

'That's fine. I've been there.' She handed him the coffee. 'Take this. It's fresh. I'll get another. Joanna still not sleeping?'

'Not really. She's up all night, for the most part.'

'How old is she?'

'Five months. She's at the doctors for a check-up today. Alice is going to ask if there's anything wrong.'

'I doubt it,' Carol said. 'Some babies aren't great sleepers. My second was a holy terror. I still have nightmares about it now. I'm sure she's perfectly healthy.'

'I hope so,' Tom said. 'But one way or another, I need some sleep.'

Alice

THIRD VICTIM RAISES FEAR OF SERIAL KILLER
By Alice Sark

The body of a 23-year-old male was discovered yesterday, at 9 p.m. The corpse had been concealed under a tarpaulin on a piece of waste ground near Appleton Thorn, in Warrington.

The victim – who has not been named – suffered serious head wounds which were confirmed by police as the cause of death. It is being treated as a suspicious death. No other details were forthcoming at this time.

If confirmed as a murder inquiry, the victim will be the third person killed in this manner in the Warrington area in the last four months. The body of Jane Kirkpatrick, 21, of Moston, Greater Manchester, was found under a bridge in Sankey Valley Park in April of this year. In June, the body of Amy Martin, a 31-year-old mother of two, was found in a field in Walton. Both were killed by blows to the head.

Although the latest victim is male, this has not stopped speculation that there is a serial killer at work.

A spokesperson for Cheshire Police did not confirm or deny whether the force believed this to be the case, saying only that at this stage of the investigation 'all possibilities are being considered'.

Alice read through the story. It had already had – in the hour since she had posted it – more comments and likes than any story she had ever written. People evidently loved serial killer stories, and they had a lot to say about them.

No doubt this is a serial killer. Has all the hallmarks.

Puts me in mind of the Ripper. Yorkshire variety, that is.

Bloody police need to find this bastard. Instead they're too busy arresting parents for taking their kids on holiday. Typical.

None of them knew the first thing about what was going on, of course, but that didn't stop them speculating; in fact, it had the opposite effect. It made them speculate more.

As she read the comments, more appeared. There really were a lot of people interested in this. She glanced at the clock. It was later than she'd thought; she was going to be late for Jo's appointment at the doctor's office.

She closed her laptop. She could read the comments later.

The doctor – Freya Quinn, Joanna's paediatrician – pressed her stethoscope to Joanna's chest. Alice watched as her daughter – already five months old, a fact that prompted everyone who met her to marvel at how quickly babies grew up – pawed at the instrument.

'Now, now,' Doctor Quinn said gently. 'I need to listen to your heart. It won't take long.'

Alice held Jo's hands away from the stethoscope. The doctor concentrated for a few moments then smiled.

'Sounds good,' she said. 'So. How is she?' She consulted her notes. 'Is she sleeping better? When I last saw her, your husband said she was struggling to settle at night?'

That didn't quite cover it, but it was a start.

'Not really,' Alice said. 'She goes down for a while but then she's awake all night.'

'All night?'

'Pretty much. It's like we're in a movie. That's what I say to my friends – we have the kid that you hear the nightmares about. I can't believe it when I'm out at 2 a.m., driving her around' – Alice shook her head – 'it's crazy.'

'Have you tried letting her cry it out?' the doctor asked.

'We did. But she just cried. After an hour we – well, me mainly – couldn't take it.'

'Does she sleep during the day?'

'Yes. I had to wake her up to bring her here. It's really frustrating!'

The doctor nodded. 'I went through the same,' she said. 'I have three, and the last one was allergic to sleep. At night, anyway. She was like a vampire – up all night and dead to the world all day.'

'How did you cope?'

'She eventually grew out of it. But not entirely. She's sixteen now and she's still a night owl. Children are who they are. You have to work with them.'

'So we wait? It's been a while. Some of the other mums I've met have babies who slept through the night from day one, which I can't even imagine, but even the ones whose babies didn't sleep well at first are through it now.'

'Don't compare yourself to other parents, if you can help it,' Doctor Quinn said. 'As I said, children have to find their own path, even at this age.'

17

'So there's nothing we can do? You don't think there's a problem?'

'Not a serious one,' the doctor said. 'There could be something. Colic, maybe. An immature gut that causes her pain when digesting food.'

'Someone suggested lactose intolerance?' Alice said.

'I don't *think* so,' Doctor Quinn replied. She consulted her notes once more. 'Her weight gain is normal. But we could check.'

'If it is colic, or an immature gut, what would we do about it?'

'There's not a lot you can do. It's her digestive system developing. It can cause discomfort.'

'And will it just get better?'

'Normally it does.' She reached for some plastic gloves and snapped them on, then adjusted her face shield. 'But I'll examine her.'

Doctor Quinn placed her right hand on the baby's pale abdomen and gently palpated it with her fingers. She moved her hand around, her face fixed in concentration.

'I don't feel anything abnormal,' she said. 'And Joanna doesn't seem to be experiencing any discomfort when I press on her stomach. She has normal movements?'

'What's normal?' Alice said.

'Same as for you, more or less. Not explosive, or persistent diarrhoea.'

Alice paused. Joanna's nappies were hardly things of beauty, but she didn't think they were anything to worry about, at least given what the doctor was saying.

'Normal, I think,' she said.

'Then I think we can simply monitor her for now.' Doctor Quinn started to popper up the onesie. Her nails were short and neat, her hands nimble and quick.

As she did up the second button Joanna twisted and

18

her arm became exposed. Dr Quinn paused, and ran her finger along Joanna's upper arm, then frowned and looked up at Alice.

'Hmm,' she said. 'What's that?'

'What's what?' Alice said.

Dr Quinn leaned forward, slid Joanna's arm out of the onesie and nestled it in her palm. She studied it for a moment, her expression watchful and concerned.

'A bruise,' she said slowly. 'On her upper arm.'

She tilted Joanna into a sitting position and lifted her arm. She examined it, her forehead creased in a slight frown. There were two bruises, one on each side of her arm, dark against her pale skin. There was a long pause before she spoke.

'Well,' she said. 'That's a little unusual.' The smile was still on her lips but the warmth was gone from her face. 'It's on both sides of her arm. Do you have any idea where it came from?'

Alice wanted to snatch her daughter from the doctor's hands and run from the room. 'No,' she said. 'I have no idea.'

'Hmm.' The silence settled between them. Dr Quinn studied Joanna's arm more closely. She pushed her chair back to her desk and opened her notes. She flipped through the pages, then took a pen from a mug with *World's Best Aunt* on it and started to write.

'What is it?' Alice said.

'Just making a note,' Dr Quinn replied. She scribbled some more words, then put the pen back in the mug and folded her arms. 'You can dress her now.'

Alice put Joanna's arm back in the onesie. She buttoned her up and held her on her lap.

'So you have no idea how this bruise came about?' Dr Quinn said. She picked up a cloth and wiped her face shield; there was a smudge on it where Joanna had grabbed at it.

'I don't,' Alice said. 'But – I mean, it's a only a bruise.'

'Bruises have causes,' Dr Quinn said. 'I'm wondering what that might be.'

'Maybe she was falling and someone grabbed her,' Alice said.

'Did anyone mention something like that happening?'

'No,' Alice said.

'And you don't remember doing that?' The doctor picked up the pen and wrote some more notes.

'No. I would remember. I could ask Tom. He spends a lot of time with her. Or Martha.'

Dr Quinn glanced up at her. 'Martha?'

'She's been helping out with child care. Now Tom's back at work.'

'Is she a nanny?'

'Kind of. She's a retired teacher. A ten-pound pom.'

'A what?'

'Her family emigrated to New Zealand in the sixties, when she was a teenager. They paid ten pounds – so they were called ten-pound poms.'

'I see.' Dr Quinn's pen scratched over the paper. 'And she's been taking care of Joanna?'

'Recently, yes. It's possible there was an accident when she was with Jo. If that's what happened, I'm sure it *was* no more than an accident,' Alice said. 'Or do you think—' She left the question hanging, unasked.

'I think the same as you. An accident. But you might want to check with your husband. And with Martha. Just to be sure.'

'Thank you,' Alice said. 'I will.'

Tom

He had headed for the door at 4 p.m. It was – at least – two hours earlier than he would normally have left work, but his eyes were closing and he could barely concentrate. He felt like he'd pulled an all-nighter and was leaving at dawn; when he walked across the car park the warm afternoon sun felt bizarrely out of place.

At least his boss was OK with it. Carol had walked past his desk and asked how he was.

Hanging in there. Good, actually.

She'd laughed. *I'd hate to see you when you're in a bad way. Why don't you wrap it up for the day? Go home and see that daughter of yours. And try to get some sleep.*

He'd muttered something about finishing up before leaving, and then, about sixty seconds after she left his resolve broke and he shut down his laptop.

He approached the roundabout that fed onto the motorway. There were four lanes; it was confusing at the best of times, but his mind felt like it was gummed up with treacle and he struggled to process the information coming at him. He had driven home from a friend's house once when he was drunk and it reminded him of that.

He blinked and forced himself to concentrate. It was easy to see how he could have an accident. Now he was back at work he really needed to get some rest.

He just didn't think Joanna was going to care too much about that.

When he pulled up outside their terraced house he saw Alice's dark blue Astra already there. He felt a surge of excitement at the thought he would see Jo – and Alice, too – in a few seconds. It was crazy that he had missed her so much when he'd seen her at eight that morning – and for most of the preceding night – but he did.

He opened the front door. The house was quiet, but he didn't want to call out in case Jo or Alice was sleeping. He walked quietly down the hall and into the living room.

Alice was sitting on the couch, her phone in her hand.

'Hi,' he said. 'Good day?'

'Yeah, not bad.' She patted the couch and he sat next to her. She leaned over and kissed him on the cheek. 'You?'

'A bit rough.' He put his head on her shoulder. 'I missed my girls.'

'We missed you, too.'

She stroked his head and he closed his eyes.

'God, I could go to sleep right now,' he said. 'At least I got out early. Carol told me to call it a day.'

'That was nice of her.'

He looked around the room. 'Where's Jo?'

'Sleeping. I put her down.'

'I might have a nap myself.'

'Me too.' She held up her phone. 'Big day tomorrow. I heard there's a press conference I have to go to at nine. It's about the murders. I think they may be about to confirm it's a serial killer.'

'Can you ask your buddy in the police? Get the story early?'

'Nadia? I did. She wouldn't confirm or deny. That's what makes me suspicious. If there's no news the police force is a like a sieve. They only stop talking when they've been told to.'

Tom crossed the room and went into the kitchen. He poured a glass of water. 'That's at nine?' he called into the living room. 'What's the plan for Jo? Martha?'

Alice appeared in the doorway. 'Yep. I called and she's free.' She hesitated. 'We had the doctor's appointment today.'

'How was it? What did she say about the sleeping?'

'She had a daughter who was the same. She thinks it'll pass. But we should keep an eye on it.'

There was an awkwardness in the way she was speaking, a stilted, uncertain tone that made him pause.

'Is everything OK?' he asked.

'There was one thing.'

His stomach clenched and his throat tightened. What was she going to tell him? His mind raced to a series of catastrophic conclusions in an instant. Some rare form of childhood cancer? A fatal disease with no cure? Some awful reason his daughter couldn't sleep that would ruin her – and her parents' – lives?

'What is it?' he said.

'She – the doctor noticed a bruise—'

'A bruise?'

'—on her arm.'

'Where on her arm?'

Alice touched the top of her bicep. 'Here. On the front and the back. Like she'd been grabbed hard. Or pinched.'

Tom stared at her. 'Pinched? How bad is the bruise?'

'Not terrible. But it's noticeable. Enough for the doctor to comment.'

'Jesus. How did it happen?'

'I don't know. Dr Quinn asked me the same. I said maybe she'd been falling off a bed or couch and someone had

23

grabbed her arm to stop her. I don't remember anything like that, but I thought you might?'

He shook his head. 'Nothing.'

'Are you sure?'

'Are you saying I hurt her?'

Alice shook her head. 'No! Of course not.'

'It sounds like you might be.'

'I'm not.' She stood up and put her hand on his forearm. 'I know you would never hurt her. I felt the same when the doctor was asking me. Like she was accusing me.'

'It's her job to look out for this stuff.'

'I know. But it did make me wonder. The bruise came from somewhere, and if it isn't you or me, then who?'

Tom leaned against the kitchen counter. 'Not my mum. She would have said.'

'No. Not her.'

He took a deep breath. 'Martha?'

'It could be. I mean, I'm sure it's totally innocent. I'm sure there's an explanation, but—'

'We don't know anything happened yet. Let's not jump to conclusions.'

'We know *something* happened. There's a bruise. On both sides of her arm.'

'I need to take a look.'

'Let her sleep. You can look later. But trust me. It's not nothing.'

'Then what do we do?' Tom said. 'I don't want to leave her with Martha if there's any risk of something happening to her.'

'Could you ask your mum?'

'Not tomorrow. She's taking Dad to the hospital for his chemo.' He sat on the couch. 'You think there's any risk leaving her?'

Alice shook her head. 'I'm sure she'll be fine. If it was Martha there'll be a simple explanation.'

24

'You want me to talk to her tomorrow morning?'

'I think so. I have to leave early. She'll be here at 7.30.'

'OK,' Tom said. 'It could have been from anything. I can't believe Martha had anything to do with it. She would have said.' He paused. 'Maybe we're being overprotective. Everyone's still on edge after eighteen months of mask wearing and hand washing.'

'It's times like these I miss my parents,' Alice said. 'It'd be so much easier if we had them around to help.'

'I know,' Tom said.

'I mean, they never even met Jo,' Alice said, her eyes welling up.

They never even met me, Tom thought. *But I don't suppose the grief ever leaves you, however long ago something like that happened.*

'I miss them,' she said. 'I really miss them.'

'I know,' he said. He hugged her close. 'But it's going to be OK. Really, it is.'

Ambleside, July 2013

Alice

Alice laughed as Hendrik – a tall, Dutch student from Rotterdam – finished his story about a hapless hiking trip he and his friend, Donny had taken that day. It had been a mess from start to finish; they'd brought the wrong map, forgotten to pack rain clothes, got lost in a sudden fog, and then ended up miles from where they expected to be, and had to hitch-hike back to Ambleside, to the relative comforts of the youth hostel, where Alice – and Ned, her boyfriend – had met them.

'But anyway,' Hendrik finished. 'That's what I like about England. Whatever happens, every day we finish in the pub!'

'Remind me not to go walking with you.' The speaker was a girl, Clara. She was blonde and athletic and had a strong Yorkshire accent and went everywhere with her friend, Lizzie. 'Although it does sound like an adventure.'

Donny nodded. He was shorter than Hendrik and very muscular, with a round, freckled face and cornflower blue eyes.

'Tomorrow we go hiking again,' he said. 'It will be even more fun. You can come. And Lizzie, of course. Has anyone ever seen you two apart, by the way?'

'No,' Clara said. 'Never been done. Where are you going?'

'We're going to that one you guys call Hell.'

'Helvellyn?' Ned, Alice's boyfriend, leaned forward. 'You're going up Helvellyn?'

'Yah. That's it.' Donny said. 'That's the one.'

'You might want to be a bit better prepared. It's a serious mountain.'

There was a brief, uncomfortable silence around the pub table. Alice and Ned had come to the Lake District for a holiday after graduating from university in Nottingham. On the first night they had met Hendrik, Donny, Clara, Lizzie, and a host of others in the youth hostel, and over the past few evenings had met up with them to eat or go to the pub. Alice enjoyed their company, enjoyed hearing the stories of their home countries, but Ned was less interested. The night before she had bumped into Clara and arranged to meet up, but Ned had insisted they go to a restaurant to spend some time together – after all, that was why they had come away.

They had found a place and had a formal, three-course meal, during most of which Alice had wished they were in the pub. Tonight, though, they had come out with the group.

'Well,' Donny said. 'Maybe we will be more careful. Or maybe not! It is fun to have risks in life, no?'

'It's not fun for Mountain Rescue when they have to come and pull you off the mountain.'

'Pull us off on the mountain?' Hendrik said, deliberately choosing to misunderstand. 'This Mountain Rescue service sounds very appealing.'

Ned didn't reply. Alice watched his jaw clench and unclench. She could almost hear the grinding of his teeth above the din of the pub. She felt a growing exasperation. What was his problem? He was a great guy – loving, considerate, warm – so why did he have to behave like this? Why couldn't he just relax? It made everyone uncomfortable.

27

And it wasn't the first time. They had been together for two and a half years and it had been great for the first twenty-four months, but a few weeks before last Christmas a student on her course – Michael Tatler – had asked her out. When she explained that she had a boyfriend, he had said they could just be friends, and he had stuck to his word.

Although not according to Ned. According to Ned, the text messages and emails – all related to their course work – were cover for an attempt to prise her away from him, and her replying to them was encouragement. Eventually he had badgered her into telling Michael not to contact her again. Nellie and Madeline, her best friends at university, had told her she should inform Ned that it was none of his business, but she could see that – maybe – he had a point, so she did what he asked and moved on.

Since then, though, he had become increasingly jealous and suspicious.

'Well,' she said, aiming to break the tension. 'Mountain Rescue certainly aim to please.'

Ned flashed a glance at her, his lips pressed together. She knew what was coming: he was going to ask her why she had said that, why she had sided with Hendrik.

'Yes,' Hendrik said, with a broad grin. 'They aim to please! Anyway, what shall we do tonight? Maybe finish these' – he lifted his pint glass – 'and then move to a more lively place?'

Lizzie nodded, and Clara followed. 'We're in,' Lizzie said, and looked at Alice. 'You guys?'

Alice was about to say yes – a change of scene would help to dissipate the tension – but Ned jumped in.

'I don't think so,' he said. 'But thanks for the offer.'

'You have other plans?' Donny asked.

'Yes,' Ned replied. 'We do.'

They did not have other plans, but Alice knew there was

no point in mentioning this. Ned was not going to go with the group.

'OK,' Donny said. 'Then maybe we see you tomorrow, at the breakfast table?'

'Maybe,' Ned said. 'Maybe.'

'So,' Alice said. 'We have plans?'

They were alone, the others' empty glasses still on the table. Ned finished his pint.

'Another?' he said.

'Is that the plan? To stay here?'

'Look,' he said, 'I didn't want to hang out with them. We came here to spend time together.'

'We spend plenty of time together. We hiked all day together. We sleep together. We could spend a few hours with other people.'

'We could. But not those people.'

'What's wrong with them?'

'I don't want to listen to their stupid stories about how irresponsible they are. It's infuriating. People come here and blunder about on the fells with no idea what they're doing, and then inevitably they get lost and have to be rescued.'

'That's what Mountain Rescue is for.'

'It's not. It's for real emergencies.'

'Fine,' Alice said. 'Maybe it is. But why's it your problem?'

'I don't have a problem, Alice.'

'Why don't you like them?' she said. 'It seems to me that's what this is about.'

He shrugged. 'You're right. I don't really like them. And so I don't want to spend time with them.'

'Why? They're nice guys.'

'I don't agree.' He paused. 'Although I'm sure you think so.'

'What does that mean?'

He sniffed. 'I think you know.'

29

She almost laughed. 'Is that was this is about? You think I'm interested in them? I've got the hots for the Dutch boys? Ned,' she said. 'I don't know why you would think that. I'm here with you. You're my *boyfriend*.'

'I've seen how they flirt with you.'

'They don't!' She shook her head. 'And even if they do, so what?'

'It annoys me.' Ned frowned. 'Forget it. Let's forget it and move on.'

Alice found that she didn't want to. She wanted to air this out. Otherwise it would fester. This uptightness was a recent thing, and it was unlike Ned. He'd never been exactly happy-go-lucky, but he was warm and fun and committed to his friends and family. When they'd met she'd been struck by how he listened to people – to her, mainly. He was attentive and interested and cared about what people said and how they felt.

'This is because of Michael, right? You're still worried about that?'

'No!' he said. 'Not at all.'

'After everything we've been through together – after all that shit with my parents' deaths – I can't believe you're insecure about us. I mean – think about it. Think about what happened.'

'I'm not *insecure*,' he hissed. 'God, I'm so sick of it. You think I'm some weak, second-rate, pathetic—'

'I do *not*,' she said. 'That's just not true.'

'Forget it,' he said. 'You know where they are. Go and join them. I'm going to bed.'

He stood up, picked up his phone, then walked towards the pub door. As he reached it, he glanced over his shoulder, as though expecting to see her following him. For a brief moment she almost did, but she caught herself. This had to stop. She had to take a stand, so she folded her arms and stayed in her seat.

He gave a slight shake of his head, then left.

Alice exhaled, puffing out her cheeks. She had no idea what to do next. Go and catch up with the others? There'd be some awkward questions about where Ned was, but she wasn't going to run after him now, partly from pride, but mainly because she simply didn't want to.

Her wine glass was still about a third full. Maybe she'd finish it and see how she felt after that.

'Excuse me?'

She looked up. A girl of her age, with long, blonde hair and a deep tan, was hovering by the table. She smiled a broad and welcoming smile.

'Hi,' Alice said.

'Mind if I sit here?' the girl asked. Alice realized she had a strong Australian accent. 'Join you for a beer?'

'No problem,' Alice said. 'Feel free.'

The girl sat down. She was holding a half-pint of lager and an iPhone.

'I'm Brenda,' she said.

'Alice. Are you from Australia?' A few days earlier Ned had offended a New Zealander by assuming he was Australian, so she added, 'Or New Zealand?'

'Oz, mate,' Brenda said. 'Perth.'

Alice had, for a while, been contemplating a post-graduation trip to Australia and had read a couple of travel guides.

'That's the west of the country, right?'

'Right. Surrounded by a whole lot of nothing much. Fun city, though.'

'I was thinking of going there.'

'To Perth?'

'Australia. But I could have ended up in Perth. Passed through.'

Brenda raised an eyebrow. 'You don't really pass through Perth,' she said. 'It's the kind of place you have to really want to go.'

'Maybe I'll get there someday.' Alice sipped her wine. It was good to have some uncomplicated company. She gestured at Brenda's glass. 'Can I get you a drink?'

'You sure?' Brenda said.

'I'm sure.'

'Then yeah, thanks. Half a pint of Stella, if that's all right.'

When Alice got back from the bar, Brenda was typing something on her phone. 'It's amazing,' she said. 'All I need is a wireless signal and I can FaceTime my friends on the other side of the world for nothing. Or message the mates I came over here with.'

'You came with friends?' Alice asked. 'Are they here?'

'There's three of us, but the other two wanted to go to Durham. I'd heard the Lake District was spectacular, so we split up. We'll meet up again in a week or so.' She sipped her beer. 'Are you here alone?'

'No. I came with my boyfriend.'

'That was the guy who just left?'

'Yes. Ned.'

'I wondered if you were together. You were having a pretty intense conversation.'

Alice nodded. 'It was more of an argument, but yes.'

'He stormed out?' Brenda raised a hand. 'Sorry. None of my business. Tell me if I'm being nosy.'

'That's fine,' Alice said. 'I don't mind. We were supposed to go – or at least I thought we were supposed to go – out with a group of people we met at the youth hostel, but he turned against the idea. He was quite hostile to them.'

'Why?'

'I don't know. He can be a bit overprotective. A bit jealous.'

'You been together long?'

'Since the first year of university,' Alice said. 'We just graduated, so like, two and a half years.'

'That's a long time.'

32

'And we've been through a lot together.'

'Really?'

'Yes.' Alice hesitated. She didn't want to pour out her life story to a stranger, but she found Brenda easy to talk to; there was a breeziness to her which put her at ease. 'My parents – both of them – died in the summer after my first year at university.' She bit her upper lip. Even though she had told this story many times it still struck her afresh, still left her struggling to believe it had actually happened, still caused a deep pain that she was certain would never end.

'How?' Brenda said. 'You don't have to talk about this if you don't want to.'

'It's OK. It was a car accident on the motorway. Broad daylight, normal weather.'

'Jeez. I'm so sorry.'

'Thanks. I was at Ned's parents' and I got a call. I couldn't believe it. He's been there for me ever since.'

'You have brothers and sisters?'

'No. Only me.'

The silence that followed was awkward. Alice was used to it, but people didn't know how to react when they found out what had happened to her parents. There wasn't much they could say.

The quiet was broken by her phone buzzing. It was a message from Ned.

Hi. Are you coming back?

She hesitated. The anger she'd felt at him had subsided, but even so she didn't want to go and sit in their room in the youth hostel and argue about how she had encouraged Hendrik or sided with Donny. It was exhausting, and she wanted a break.

She typed a reply.

33

In a bit, I met an Australian girl and am having a drink with her

He replied immediately.

Right. An Australian girl. Enjoy your night out

She closed her eyes. She just wanted this to stop.
'Your boyfriend?' Brenda said.
Alice didn't even want to talk about it. It was embarrassing.
'Forget it,' she said. 'Let's finish these and go somewhere else.'

Monday, 19 July 2021

Alice

MURDERED MAN IDENTIFIED
By Alice Sark

The body of the man found on Thursday, 15 July has been named as Stan Davidson, of Lymm, Cheshire. Mr Davidson, 23, was last seen at the Thorn Inn pub in Appleton Thorn, which he left some time before midnight on Wednesday, 14 July. He shared a flat with a friend, Mr Nick Taylor, who confirmed he did not return home on the evening of the 14th. Mr Taylor said he was not alarmed by his flat-mate's failure to return home and did not mention his absence, as he often stayed with his girlfriend.

The police confirmed that the case is being treated as a murder inquiry. The spokesperson did not respond to questions regarding any links to the murders of Jane Kirkpatrick and Amy Martin, who were both killed recently in similar circumstances. However, it seems increasingly likely that the three murders may be linked – and if so, there is a serial killer operating in the Warrington area.

There will be a press conference today.

Tom

Tom sat on the couch, his legs flat on the cushions. Joanna was lying with her head on his knees. He looked down at her and held out a finger. She grabbed it and squeezed. Her grip was surprisingly tight; he'd heard from another dad that babies' grips were strong enough that they could hang from a bar.

Try that in your CrossFit gym for a minute or two, the dad, who was squat and heavily built and had tattoos all up one arm, had said. *We're all weaker than babies*.

Joanna smiled, her eyes wide. They were an unusual grey-green colour; she'd inherited them from Alice. It was amazing to him how much he loved her, how strong the instinct to take care of her was. The lack of sleep and loss of free time melted away in moments like this, moments when he sat, peacefully, with his beautiful baby daughter.

A daughter who had been a surprise. They'd talked about having kids, but not for a few more years. They were both twenty-nine now – Alice had been twenty-eight when Jo was born – which was young, at least by the standards of their friends. Alice was on the pill, but had somehow mixed up some dates when they were on holiday in Greece, and nature had taken its course. It was unlike her; she was normally very organized, and he could tell that she was more annoyed about the fact that she had messed up than that she had got pregnant.

It had been a happy accident, though. There was no question they would keep the baby. They had always wanted kids; all that had changed was the timing.

The doorbell rang and he glanced at his watch. It was a vintage Omega his dad had given him when he was twenty-one. At first he had thought it was old-fashioned and only worn it out of a sense of duty, but it had grown on him over the years and it was now his most treasured possession. It was only going to increase in sentimental value, as his father, still only sixty-three, had late-stage bladder cancer, which left him with no more than a year to live.

At least his dad had met Jo. That was another reason to be glad Alice had made the mistake with her pills. If they'd waited, his dad would never have met his first grandchild. Tom's younger brother, Roland, was unlikely to have kids any time soon; he was unlikely to do much of anything. He'd had a hard few years; after dropping out of music college halfway through his first year he'd developed a punishing drug habit. He'd always smoked weed and taken various pills, but at some point he'd started taking heroin, which had pushed him into a deep, dark hole.

There had been some serious consequences, family-splitting, relationship-wrecking consequences, and no one had heard from Roland for a couple of years, which was, in some ways, for the best.

No one other than his mum. She had tried to get him off it on numerous occasions, but nothing had worked. She'd talked to every doctor and addiction counsellor she could find to see what she could do to help, but the answer had been clear: not much, at least until Roland wanted to be helped.

That time had come six weeks ago when Agnes, Roland's girlfriend, had died of an overdose, after which Roland had turned up at their parents' house and declared he wanted to get clean.

He had succeeded, to a point. There had been a few relapses – one occasion he had gone missing for two days, before arriving one morning on Tom's parents' doorstep, filthy, pale, thin and exhausted. Tom was there with Jo, and he had left in disgust. His parents were free to welcome Roland back, but Tom had no intention of doing the same. He was not planning on Jo being cradled in her uncle's pipe-thin, needle-scarred arms.

The doorbell rang again. He laid Joanna in her Moses basket and went to let Martha in. She had short, tidy hair, and a lithe, muscular build, even in her sixties.

'Good morning,' she said. She came from Yorkshire, and had retained the fat vowels of her childhood accent, although there was also a hint of New Zealand in her voice. 'How's Jo? Did she sleep?'

'Not much,' Tom said. 'About the same as usual.'

'Oh well,' Martha replied. 'It's tough, but it'll pass. They all get there in the end.'

'If you say so,' Tom said. 'I don't dare hope.'

He followed her into the living room. A slow, warm smile spread over Martha's face when she saw Jo. She bent over the basket and made a quiet kissing noise.

'Well, she's asleep now,' she whispered. 'She's beautiful, Tom.'

'I think so,' he said. 'But I'm biased.'

'No. You're right. She's a darling.' Martha put her bag on the couch. 'Well,' she said. 'If it's OK, I'll make myself a cup of tea while she's sleeping. Alice is back around noon, she said?'

'Yes,' Tom said. 'There's a press conference this morning.'

'About the murders?'

'Yep. She thinks the police are going to say there's a serial killer.'

Martha looked genuinely shocked. 'That's terrible. The

streets aren't safe. You won't find me out alone, especially at night.'

'I don't blame you.'

'Anyway, you go off to work. I'll be here until Alice gets home.'

'Before I go,' Tom said. 'There is one thing I wanted to mention.'

'What's that?' Martha said.

Tom faltered, momentarily. He was not looking forward to this conversation.

He took a deep breath. 'Alice took Jo for her check-up yesterday.'

'At the doctor's?' Martha's smile faded. 'Is she ill?'

'No,' he said. 'It's nothing serious. It's . . .' he paused. Looking at Martha he could hardly believe she would have hurt Joanna – any child, any *person* – deliberately. She radiated calm and kindness. He always felt he was rushing to feed or dress or change Joanna; she always seemed to be moving at the perfect pace. She had the gift of infinite patience.

'What is it?' Martha said.

'It's her arm. There's a bruise on it.'

Martha frowned. 'Really?'

'Yes. On her bicep. It's on both sides, like a pinch mark. The doctor noticed it.'

'The poor thing,' Martha said. 'How did it happen?'

'We don't know. Alice doesn't remember anything that could have caused it, and I don't, either.'

'Could I look?' Martha said.

'Sure. Of course.'

Martha bent over Joanna and carefully lifted the blanket from her. She was wearing a short-sleeved onesie, and Martha examined her arm. The bruise was clearly visible on her pale skin.

'Gosh,' she said. 'It must have happened this weekend. I didn't see anything on Friday. I would have noticed this.'

'We were wondering,' Tom said, 'if maybe on Friday morning, when you were with her, before Alice took her to the doctor' – he realized he was rambling and stopped. He could barely bring himself to ask the question.

He didn't need to.

Martha sat back on the couch, her expression first wounded, then fixed and angry, then finally composed. She put her hands, palms down, on her knees. 'I know you have to ask, and I'm OK with that. But let me be very clear, Tom. If you're asking whether I did it, the answer is no. If you're not asking – if you're accusing me of doing something – then the answer is still no, but you need to know this will be the last time I come here.'

'I'm not saying that,' Tom said. 'I'm not accusing you at all, but like you said, I have to ask. Maybe there was an accident. She was falling and someone grabbed her. Or she banged herself against something. I didn't see anything, but maybe you did. That's all. I'm just asking.'

'I understand,' Martha said. 'And if I had seen anything like that, or done anything like that by accident, I would have told you on Friday. I wouldn't have waited for you to find out and come and ask me. But there was nothing for me to tell you.'

'OK,' Tom said. 'I'm sorry, Martha—'

'Don't be. You're a father. It's your job to take care of your daughter.' She looked at Joanna, then back at him. 'She's a baby, Tom. I would never hurt her. I *couldn't*. I need to know you believe me.'

He studied her. There was no way she would have done anything to Jo. 'I do,' he said. 'Really, I do.'

'I hope so. But that still leaves the bruise. Did anyone else see her in the days before you noticed the bruise?'

'Only my parents. We went there for dinner. Roland was there, but I didn't see him.'

'Roland?' Martha said. 'Who's that?'

'My brother. He lives with Mum and Dad.'

'I didn't know you had a brother.'

'It's a long story,' Tom said. 'For another day.'

'And he didn't see her? You're sure?'

'I don't think so.'

'There is another thing to watch for,' Martha said. 'If nothing specific happened, it's possible she bruises easily. I don't know what that means, medically, but I have heard it can happen to some kids.' She leaned forward. 'But whatever it is – something or nothing – I had nothing to do with it. I would never harm Jo,' she said. 'I promise you that. I would never harm a hair on her head.'

Alice

The room was only half full, but it was much busier than at any time since before the pandemic. The vast majority of the journalists present wore masks; plenty of others were taking part virtually. Alice was pretty sure that it would be some time before the days of everyone attending in person returned, in part because of a lingering fear of catching something, and in part because it was cheaper and more convenient to attend by video.

She preferred to be there in person. She found it almost impossible to work at home. Even when Joanna was asleep she had half an ear – and half her attention – on whether Joanna was starting to wake up, or was actually awake or just making some noises in her sleep. And if she was awake there was no way she could work at all.

The room fell silent as three people took their seats at the table. Alice recognized Detective Superintendent Marie Ryan in the middle. To her left was a woman with short dark hair; to her right was a man. Alice recognized neither of them.

'Thank you for being here,' Ryan began. 'As you know there was a body found the evening of Thursday, July 15th. That body has since been identified as Mr Stan Davidson.

Mr Davidson was twenty-three. We are treating this as a murder inquiry, but not' – there was a long pause – 'as a standalone murder. I'll hand it over to Detective Inspector Wynne to give more details.'

There was a noticeable tightening of the tension in the room. If it was not a standalone murder that meant only one thing: the police thought they had a serial killer on their hands. Although there had been plenty of speculation that might be the case, to have it confirmed – or to think it was about to be confirmed – was still a significant moment.

The short-haired woman to DSI Ryan's left – Detective Inspector Wynne – looked out over the room. Her gaze was flat and expressionless, and there was a stillness to her, a sense that she was taking in every detail before she spoke.

'Welcome,' she said. 'And thank you, DSI Ryan. I'm Detective Inspector Jane Wynne. As you know there have been three murders in the last four months in the Warrington area. Mr Davidson is the most recent. Ms Amy Martin and Ms Jane Kirkpatrick were the first two. There are certain similarities between all three that lead us to believe they may have been committed by the same person. In particular, the cause of death is a heavy blow to the head. We are aware there has been speculation to this effect, and although at this point I am unable to reveal any details, I *can* confirm that we are now operating on the assumption that this is indeed the case.'

'So you're saying it's a serial killer?' The question came from a tall man with dark hair who ran an online news site.

Wynne nodded. 'That's correct.'

The tall man spoke again. 'Any suspects?'

DSI Ryan leaned towards her microphone. 'We have some leads we're following.'

Sue Brown, a journalist on one of the Liverpool papers,

raised her hand. 'It's unusual for a serial killer to target women and men,' she said. 'Mostly they have a type. Does the fact that in this case the victims are men and women lead you to question whether it really *is* the same person?'

It was a clever question, Alice thought. Sue Brown knew the police wouldn't have said it was a serial killer if there weren't significant links between the murders – beyond the blows to the head – links that would remove the doubts they would have had at the victims being female and male. She was hoping, by asking the question, to find out what those links were.

Wynne gave a wry smile. 'I'm afraid I'm not able to expand on our reasons. You'll have to make do with the information that there are links.'

'Then do you have a profile of who it might be? Who he is?' she said.

'You used the word "he",' DI Wynne said. 'We aren't certain it is a man, but—'

'In most cases it is,' Brown said. 'And the manner of these killings – a blow to the head – would suggest a level of violence that would indicate it's more likely to be a man. No?'

'More likely,' Wynne said. 'But at this point we can't rule anything out.'

They'd be looking for a man, though, Alice thought. They always were in these cases.

DI Wynne scanned the room. 'Any further questions?'

No one spoke up.

'Then we can end,' Wynne said. 'Thank you all for coming.'

Alice wanted to know more about what the police knew. Fortunately, she had a contact.

'Hi,' she said. 'It's me. Alice.'

Nadia Alexander was a Detective Sergeant – newly minted

in the past six months – and best friends with Manjit, Alice and Tom's neighbour. They had met her at Manjit's house-warming party, and since then Alice had been out with her on a number of girls' nights.

Alice dialled her number.

'Hi,' Nadia said. 'How's it going?'

'Good, Nads. You?'

'Busy.'

'Are you working on the murders?'

'We all are.'

'Must be interesting,' Alice said.

'It is,' Nadia replied. There was a guarded tone in her voice. 'But you know I can't talk about it.'

'Of course!' Alice said. 'I wouldn't expect you to. I'm working on my story from the press conference. I wanted to check a few details.'

'This isn't really the right process for that,' Nadia said.

'I know. But it's nothing much. It'll be quick. So, it's two female victims and one male, right?'

'Right.'

'And there are enough similarities to say they're linked?' There was no reply, so she continued. 'Any details on the similarities?'

If Nadia told her something she could use it in her copy. Serial killers were always of huge, morbid interest to the public, so any new information or angle was gold dust, but right now everyone had the same information: three bodies, two female, one male, police treating them as linked. If she could come up with something extra she'd be ahead of the game – and this story would soon be the biggest in the country.

'None,' Nadia said. 'Come on, Alice, you know better than this. I'll see you soon, OK?'

The phone went dead. Alice stood up and walked over to

45

the window. She yawned and glanced at the couch. It had been another long night.

Jo was sleeping in her basket. It had been twenty minutes, so she'd be asleep a while yet, with any luck.

Alice lay on the couch, and closed her eyes.

Wednesday, 21 July 2021

Alice

Alice walked into the London Bridge pub. It was a few minutes past 5 p.m. but it was already busy, full of early drinkers, or the people who were still working from home and needed to get out of the house and away from their computer screens.

She looked around for Nadia. It had been two days since the press conference and there had been no more news, but an hour earlier Nadia had called and asked if she was free to meet up.

I have something to share, she said. *About the murders. Are you free?*

Now? Alice asked.

Yes. We could meet in the pub?

I have Jo with me. Tom's at work. She paused. She could ask Tom's mum to come. *I'll call you back. Give me a minute.*

It turned out – thank God – Tom's mum was free, and she had come to the house to take care of Jo. She scanned the pub again. Perhaps Nadia hadn't arrived; then she saw her, at a table in the corner, a glass of wine in front of her. Alice headed over.

'I decided it was too late for coffee,' she said. 'Good to see you. How's Joanna?'

'She's great.' Alice sat down. 'Not sleeping, but other than that, she's lovely.'

'And Tom?'

'He's fine. It's hard work, but we're OK. You? Busy with the case?'

'Flat out. I'm glad to have an excuse to get away.'

'So, you had something to share?'

Nadia nodded. 'We do,' she said. 'Something you might be interested in.'

'What is it?'

'It's a detail we've been holding back. If we get a false confession we can tell if they don't know the details – if all they've read is what's in the press.'

'People do that?'

'All the time. We've already had a handful of people claim they're the perp. If we didn't have a way to weed them out we'd have to spend valuable resources checking them out.'

'Why on earth do people do that?'

Nadia shrugged. 'God alone knows, Alice. Attention, maybe? But they must know we'll figure out they're bullshitters in the end. And then charge them with wasting police time.'

'It's weird.'

'Yeah. But perhaps they just want to be part of it.'

'A bad case of FOMO,' Alice said.

'Very bad. And very annoying.'

'But you have a detail in this case?'

'More than one. So I can share this one with you. It's pretty out there.'

Alice paused. 'Why me?'

'There'll be a press release shortly. But someone has to be first.'

'Thank you,' Alice said. 'What is it?'

'The killer leaves a sign at each scene,' Nadia said. 'They fold the arms of the victim across their chest and insert a crucifix in their right hand.'

'Jesus,' Alice said. 'Is there some religious connection?'

'Could be. But what it might be is hard to tell. There are plenty of Christians around. And it doesn't even have to be a Christian. It could simply be someone who likes crosses.'

'What do I do with this?' Alice said.

'Run the story,' Nadia replied.

Tom

Tom opened the front door. His mum's car was outside, and Alice's wasn't. She hadn't mentioned she was going out, so presumably something had come up.

'Hello?' he called. 'Mum?'

Her voice came from the living room. 'In here.'

He walked down the hall. His mum was sitting on the couch, holding his daughter.

His brother, Roland, was in the armchair opposite them. Tom stared at him.

'Tom,' his mum said. 'Is everything OK?'

'Why's he here?'

'I came with Mum.' Roland held up his hands. They were thin and pale, the fingers long. 'But if I'm not welcome, I'll leave. I don't want any problems.'

'See you later, then.'

Roland shrugged. 'See you later.'

'Wait, Roland,' his mum said. 'Tom. I'd like you to consider changing your mind.'

'No way.'

'He's your brother.'

'He gave up any claim to that years ago.'

His mum shook her head. 'It's time to forgive,' she said.

'I can't.'

'Really?' She folded her arms. 'Because your dad and I have. And it was worse for us.'

It was worse for them. It was a *lot* worse. But still, it was too much to ask.

'No.'

'Tom,' his mum said. 'Please.'

Tom shifted uncomfortably. 'I can't.'

'I'd like you to try.'

'Why should I?' he said.

'For your father. He'd like to see his two sons reconciled.'

The subtext was clear: he wanted to see it before he died. It was not the kind of request you could refuse.

Tom waited a long time before he replied. He'd do it, but only for his dad.

'Fine,' he said. 'He can stay. For now.'

Tom settled onto the sofa. 'Where's Alice?' he asked.

'She went to meet a friend,' his mum said. 'A police officer, about the case. You look tired, Tom.'

'Tired doesn't come close.'

'I'll make a cup of tea, then Roland and I can mind Jo. You can have a rest.'

Tom wanted to say *No, I'll be fine*, but he simply nodded and watched her walk into the kitchen. Roland was sitting by Joanna's Moses basket, looking down at her.

It was the first time he had met his niece.

'They're like little aliens,' Roland said. 'How do you know what to do?'

'I don't,' Tom said. 'Sometimes I feel like I have no idea.'

Roland grinned at him. His teeth were still stained, but he was starting to look less gaunt. A small pot-belly was establishing itself above his belt.

Joanna gave a whimper, then started to cry. It was amazing to Tom how she could go from peaceful to screaming in a matter of seconds.

'Uh-oh,' Roland said. He poked a long finger towards her. 'It's OK,' he said. 'No need to cry.' He tapped her on the chest a few times and she started to wail.

'What did I do?' he said, a look of mild panic on his face.

'Nothing. She just woke up.'

'So what do I do now?'

'Pass her to me.'

'You want me to pick her up?'

'Yes.'

'How?'

'Put your hand under her neck and back and gently lift her.'

'I can't,' Roland said. 'I don't know how.'

Tom walked over and took Jo from her basket. He sniffed her bottom.

'Needs a change,' he said. He pointed to the side of the couch. 'Can you grab that mat for me? Lay it on the floor.'

Roland picked up the mat and placed it next to Tom, who laid Jo down and unclipped her onesie, then snapped off her nappy.

A look of disgust passed over Roland's face. 'Jesus,' he said. 'That's foul. It stinks.'

Not as bad as the crack den you were living in, Tom thought. 'She's a baby,' he said. 'They poop.'

'Man,' Roland said. 'I sometimes wonder why anyone would put themselves through this.'

It wasn't just what you went through when they were babies. Tom thought of his parents and what they had been through with Roland: the worry, the heartache, the despair. He wondered sometimes whether it had contributed to his dad's illness, built up inside him and poisoned him from within.

52

He had to put that thought aside, though, or he would not be able to have any kind of relationship with his brother at all, whether his dad wanted it or not.

'Good question,' Tom said. 'But it's worth it. I hope you find out someday.'

'No chance,' Roland replied. 'There's absolutely no chance of that.'

Alice

Alice drove home, writing the story in her mind. She had the name already; it had come to her immediately.

The Crucifix Killer.

She yawned. It had been a long day. A long few months, but she'd write it that night. It couldn't wait.

When she got home Tom was on the couch, Jo asleep in his arms. He appeared to be on the verge of sleep himself.

'How was Nadia?' he whispered.

'Great. We talked about the murders. She gave me a new thing to write about.'

'What was it?'

'It's horrible. The killer folds the victims' arms over their chests, and puts a crucifix in their right hands.'

'Holy shit. That's crazy.'

'I know.'

'People are going to lap it up, though. They love this kind of stuff.'

'I *know*.' She smiled. 'And I have a name.'

'Which is?'

'The Crucifix Killer.'

'My wife,' Tom said, 'is an evil genius.'

'Just genius will do, thanks.'

'I had a fun evening,' he said. 'I got to see Roland.'

'I met him when your mum came. I wasn't sure whether to invite him in, but—'

'That's fine,' Tom said. 'It's not your problem.'

'You didn't throw him out?' Alice said. 'You said once he was no longer your brother.'

'Mum asked me not to. For her and for Dad. She said they'd forgiven him, so I should be able to.' He looked away, tears in his eyes. 'And with Dad's condition—'

'Isn't that emotional blackmail?' Alice said.

'I suppose it is, but what choice did I have?'

'You don't have to forgive him,' Alice said. 'It's up to you.'

'Maybe he's genuine,' Tom said. 'Maybe he's quit heroin for good.'

'Maybe.' She shrugged. 'You're probably right. At least you can give him a chance. Treat him as though he's turned over a new leaf. If your parents did, then you can.'

'That's it,' Tom said. 'I'm surprised they forgave him. Dad hasn't said his name for years. And now he's letting him live in their house.'

'Maybe his illness has changed your dad's priorities,' Alice said. 'And everything's forgivable, in the end.'

'Not everything.'

'Tom,' Alice said. 'What did Roland do? You've never told me.'

'You never asked.'

'Perhaps now's the time,' she said.

Tom looked at her. 'It's a long story.'

She gestured at Joanna. 'Well, as long as she stays asleep, I've got nothing better to do.'

Summer, 2012

Tom

In the summer of 2012 I was twenty-one; my baby brother was eighteen. I was working a summer job after university, looking for something permanent, the older more responsible brother. Roland was about to start music college, doing his thing. Tall, slim, handsome, with long hair and long legs that perfectly suited the jeans he wore, which were tight around the thighs and flared below the knee in a throwback to the 1990s which were themselves a throwback to the 1970s.

He was also charming and funny, and a talented musician. He'd won a place at the Royal Northern College of Music, but wouldn't last the first year of the course. That was Roland's problem; he was feckless. For all his talent, he never seemed to achieve anything, because he never stuck at it for long enough. It was almost as though he was too scared to really apply himself in case he failed.

Is that true? Or is it just my attempt at a post-facto pop-psychological justification for what he did? Either way, what's undeniable is that he had talent, and he wasted it. A large part of the tragedy of Roland lies not in what he became but in what he could have become, but then perhaps that's true for all of us.

He lived with three friends in a tiny flat in Manchester city centre, not far from the pub he worked in. Worked is perhaps putting it a little strongly; between the four of them I think they shared a full-time job, but they did enough to get by. Roland spent the rest of his time hanging around with a group of friends who, supposedly, were members of his band. They called themselves The German Genius, which now makes little sense to me as a name but back then, in a country where 52 per cent of the people were a few years off voting for Brexit, was quite provocative.

He was also still a presence in our family home. I often saw him there, particularly around mealtimes. He'd be in the yard with a cigarette, pacing back and forth, talking on the phone. We were still – just about – a family.

That all changed one Saturday. I went around to my parents' to pick up some paperwork I wanted. When I arrived, Dad's car was parked on the street. He wasn't supposed to be there – he was supposed to be at a cricket match at Old Trafford. Perhaps he'd left his ticket, or his wallet.

It was neither.

I could hear Dad shouting from outside the front door. I glanced up and down the street to see if anyone else had heard; Mum would have hated the neighbours to witness a family argument.

I cracked the door and slipped inside.

From the door to the living room I could see into the kitchen. Dad had Roland's shirt bunched up in his fist and was holding him against the kitchen cabinets. The tap was running; one of them must have knocked it on. On the counter top, in between Roland and the sink, was a twenty-pound note. It was not a lot of money, but then that wasn't the point Dad was really concerned with.

'How long have you been stealing from me? Eh?' Dad shouted. He was a big man, and Roland was puny next to him.

'I've not been.'

Dad pulled him forwards and then slammed him back against the cabinets. I jumped; I'd never seen this kind of physical aggression from my father.

'Don't lie to me. You think I don't know how much money I have? You think I haven't noticed some of it disappearing?'

'It might have been Tom.' This time Dad slammed Roland so hard against the cabinets that the house vibrated. Good, I thought, pinning it on me, the bastard.

'Don't you dare blame your brother. He has a job. So what's it for?' Dad said. 'What are you spending it on?'

'Stuff.' Roland's voice was strangled. 'Let me go. You're hurting my throat. We've got a gig tonight and I've got to sing.'

Dad's knuckles whitened as he gripped harder. 'Don't worry. You can say you're trying to sound like Rod Stewart. So what did you piss it away on? The money I went out and earned for my family?' I think that was the worst thing for Dad. Not the theft or the lying or the betrayal but the waste.

'Stuff. Food. Living.'

'You must think I'm fucking daft.'

I don't think I'd ever heard Dad swear. Some part of me thought he probably didn't know words like that, that maybe our generation had invented them.

'I know what you spend it on. You spend it on bloody drugs.' He pushed his face close to Roland's. 'What drugs, I don't know. Heroin, is it? You tell me. Either way, you can do what you want, lad. But don't bring that shit into my house. You got a house key?'

Roland nodded down to the left. 'In my front pocket.'

Dad tried to reach into the pocket, but, bunched up against the counter, the jeans were too tight, so he grabbed the lip of the pocket and pulled it off. The jeans were button-fly, and the force was such that the buttons scattered on the kitchen floor.

Key in hand, he shoved Roland towards the door. 'Now get out.'

I ran back to the car. From the window I watched as Roland left the house, clutching his jeans to his waist to stop them falling down. I didn't see him again for nearly a year.

That was the first I knew that Roland was taking heroin. I never discussed it with my parents, but looking back it seems clear to me that they'd known – or suspected – something for much longer. There was the disappearing money (and who knew what else), but more than that there was the grapevine. In Warrington, people knew what other people were up to, in particular if it involved scandal. And hard drugs were scandal.

That was nothing on what was to come, though.

About a year later I was walking home from the pub to the flat I shared, when I saw a skinhead leaning on a lamp post. He was wearing scuffed black boots, a pair of loose-fitting black trousers, and a faded check shirt. He started to walk towards me.

I bunched my fists in my hand. *Wallop him, then run*, I thought. And shout. Draw some attention to yourself.

'Hey,' he called.

I started to run in the direction I'd come from.

'Hey! Tom! It's me! Roland.'

I slowed to a stop and turned around.

'Roland?'

He grinned and ran his hand over his skinhead. His teeth were yellow and seemed long. I realized it was because his gums had receded. 'Look a bit different, don't I?'

He looked terrible. Thin, gaunt, red-eyed.

'Sorry I haven't seen you for a while,' he said. 'I've been busy.'

I shrugged. 'It's all right.'

'How's Mum?'

59

'She's all right.'

'And the old man?'

'All right.'

'Everybody all right, then?'

'Yeah.'

He laughed and punched me in the shoulder. There wasn't much force behind it. 'Look at you. Typical engineer. One word answers for everything.'

'Fuck off,' I said. 'That's two words.'

'Anyway,' he said. 'I need a hand.'

I tensed. Whatever Roland was going to get me into, I probably didn't want to be involved in it.

'I've got to get home,' I said.

'Relax,' he said. 'I don't need you to do anything. But I need some money.'

Of course. What else would it be? 'No way.'

'Please,' he said.

I put my hand in my pocket. 'I've got three quid.'

His left eye twitched. 'That'll do.'

I handed it over.

'Hey,' he said. 'We're playing a gig on Saturday. Upstairs at the Lamb and Flag in town. Chrissy's singing with us. Come along. Entrance is a fiver, but you can come in for nowt.' He jangled the coins in his hand. 'You've already paid.'

My dad had a sister, Maureen – or Mo, as everyone called her – who had a daughter, our cousin Chrissy. Mo had raised her alone after the father had skipped town when she was pregnant. Chrissy was two years younger than Roland, and – in my view as well as everybody else's – pretty amazing. She was pretty, with a snub nose and curly red hair, and a wicked, hoarse laugh. She was also a gifted singer – somewhere in our family was a musical gene, which I hadn't inherited, but which Roland had in quantity and which Chrissy had in abundance.

But more of her later.

On the Saturday of the gig, I decided to go. There was a sandwich board outside the Lamb and Flag. I read the words chalked on it.

Upstairs
Tonight Only
The German Genius!!

At the bottom of the stairs a shaven-headed fat man in a dark suit stopped me.

'Ticket?'

'It's my brother's band. He invited me.'

'Oh aye?' He squinted at me. 'Did he now? That'll be a fiver, mate.'

I handed over the money and headed up the stairs. The room was large, with a bar at one end and a platform at the other. I bought a pint and found a table in a dark corner.

Some people near the door started to whistle, then cheer, then clap. I turned around. Roland, Chrissy and the other band members were walking through the crowd, guitars and drumsticks in hand. Roland didn't have his usual guitar, the one in his hand was beaten-up and cheap. I wondered where the old one had gone; looking back, it's obvious. He'd turned it into heroin.

'All right!' Roland said from the centre of the stage. He looked as bad as when I'd seen him a few days back, the only difference being that now his eyes were bright – black and shining. 'We are The German Genius!'

The pub-goers gave an ironic cheer.

'And we have a special guest tonight. On bass guitar and vocals, Chrissy McLellan!'

There were a few non-ironic wolf whistles. Chrissy gave a half-bow.

I didn't know many of the songs in their set, and to be

61

honest I didn't enjoy them. The German Genius were heavily influenced by punk and I had no idea what they were trying to do. I wasn't the only one; after fifteen minutes of their set the punters were getting restless.

'Play something by the King!' someone shouted.

Roland rolled his eyes and muttered something to his bandmates. They started making a discordant noise and then Chrissy, eyes closed, started wailing.

Someone booed.

'It's Teddy Bear,' Roland said. 'Our version. You ignorant fuckers.'

'Get off,' someone else shouted. The boos grew louder.

A short man in a brown suit pushed his way to the front and stepped onto the platform. Roland leaned down and listened to him; they evidently knew each other.

'All right,' he said, when the man in the suit was gone. 'The landlord says we'd better play something you lot like if we want to get paid. So, any suggestions.'

'"Sailing",' a woman shouted. 'By Rod Stewart'

Roland shrugged. '"Sailing" it fucking well is, then.'

I have to say the set improved from then on.

I knew better than to tell Roland that, though. Halfway through he spotted me and gave me a wink; when they were finished he came over.

'What did you think?'

'It was great. Especially at the start.'

'Yeah. Well, these ignorant fuckers don't know what's good for them. They just want to hear the same old shit and get drunk on Friday and Saturday nights. Not the life for me, man.'

No, I guessed it wasn't. He preferred to be strung out on heroin seven days a week. It may have been more glamorous, at least in his mind, but it was hardly a way to live.

'Here.' Roland handed me his drink. 'I get free drinks. That – and the money – is the only good thing about doing this.'

62

'Is Chrissy in the band for good?'

'Sure is. She just joined. She's an amazing singer. Too good for this shit. She could really do something. Go places, you know?'

I looked around. I wanted to talk to her, but she was nowhere to be seen.

'Where'd she go?'

'Back home. She's got a curfew.' He shook his head. 'Pain in the tits, that is. She's old enough to do what she wants, and Mo's going to have to swallow it.' He punched me on the arm. 'Gotta go. I've got shit to do, man.'

'When are you playing again?' I suddenly missed Roland. I wanted to see him. 'I'll come and watch.'

'I dunno. Not for a while. I'll let you know.'

'Cool.'

'Hey,' he said. 'Can you do me a favour?'

'What?'

'There's a watch in the top drawer of the chest of drawers in my bedroom. Can you fetch it for me?'

I didn't answer; my unease must have shown on my face.

'You won't be doing anything wrong. It's my watch. Grandad left it to me.'

'Are you going to sell it?'

He wrinkled his forehead. 'Sell it? Are you messing around? I love that watch. Since I don't live at home any more I want to have it with me. That's all.'

I believed him. I wanted to believe him. Besides, it seemed a reasonable enough explanation.

'OK. I'll get it. Do you still live in the same flat?'

'Yeah.' He smiled. 'Bring it whenever.'

So I agreed. And in doing so – although I didn't know it at the time – I set in course a chain of events that would bring family life crashing down around me – and all of us.

Wednesday, 21 July 2021

Tom

They heard a cry from upstairs and Tom paused.

'I'll get her,' he said. 'You stay here.'

Alice put her hand on his knee. 'There's more?' she said.

'A lot more.'

'And it gets worse?'

He nodded. 'A lot worse.'

She squeezed his knee, then leaned over and kissed him on the cheek. 'I'm so sorry you went through all that.'

He shrugged. 'It is what it is,' he said, and stood up. 'I don't think about it too often. But it does make me – not nervous, exactly, but vigilant – when it comes to Jo. I don't know what pushed Roland down the path he took – or if anything even did. Maybe it is just who he is, or some chemical imbalance in his brain that drugs helped him with. I don't know. But I do know I need to do whatever I can to protect Jo from it. I can't go through that again.'

'You won't. *We* won't.'

Jo cried again, louder this time, and Tom moved towards the door.

'I want to know the rest,' Alice said. 'What happened next.'

'I'll tell you,' Tom replied. 'But I have to get Jo.'

'OK,' Alice said. 'I can't believe you never mentioned any of this.'

'Well,' Tom said. 'I guess we all have our secrets.'

The Baby

Who would choose to have one of these? Who would want a baby?

They do nothing. They give nothing. They just take: money, time, attention. People with babies are no longer themselves. They live for the child. It cries: they come running. It wants something: they provide it.

Wiping up puke and shit and piss.

It's degrading.

An adult human, reduced to wiping up puke and shit and piss.

Animals don't do that. Unless their mother protects them, a lion will eat his cubs. They are mere prey to him. He feels nothing for them.

They are food.

At least that is useful. Human babies are not even that. They are nothing but a burden. Yet people have them. It is a mystery. Are they so in thrall to some animal instinct to reproduce that they cannot see clearly? All the evidence is there. They can see others going through it. That should be enough to put them off.

They cannot act like the lion. The lion has its needs and it fulfils them.

People are required to take care of their offspring. Once they are born they are there until the day the adults die, draining them of everything that makes them special.

So who would choose this? It is unfathomable. But they do it anyway. Some are mistakes, of course, but they can't all be.

You know what people say. It's the wonder of being a parent, a father, a mother. The awe at having created a new life. The sensation of having some purpose beyond yourself.

This is nonsense.

There is no awe in creating a new life. There is nothing to celebrate in that.

Any fool can do it. It is nothing special.

And to think otherwise is weakness. There is nothing special about a baby simply because it has your DNA. If it was switched in the hospital for another one – provided it looked roughly similar – people would have no way of knowing.

It is just another person.

And other people – all of them – are either rivals or tools. Tools are there to be used for whatever you want. Rivals are there to be destroyed.

A baby is a rival. It competes for your resources. This is nature's trick: you think it is somehow part of you, so you care for it. It is not part of you. You have been tricked.

But not everyone falls for the trick.

Not you. You don't fall for it.

Not at all.

Ambleside, July 2013

Alice

They found them in a pub a few streets further into town. Donny, Hendrik, Clara and Lizzie were sitting at a table by the window; they waved as Alice and Brenda approached and beckoned them inside.

Inside it was dark and loud and smelled of beer. It was the kind of place Ned would have hated.

'Hey,' Donny said. 'You made it. But Ned looks different.'

Alice laughed. 'This is Brenda,' she said. 'Brenda – meet Clara, Lizzie, Donny and Hendrik.'

'Hi Brenda,' Hendrik said. 'Nice to meet you.'

'You're not from round here,' Brenda said. 'Let me guess. Swedish?'

Hendrik shook his head.

'German?'

He raised his hands in mock offence. 'Please. Do Donny and I look German? We are handsome, and funny. We are from the Netherlands.'

'Sorry,' Brenda said. 'I didn't mean any offence.'

'That's OK,' Donny said. 'None taken. You are from Australia? Or New Zealand maybe?'

'Australia.'

'Ah,' Donny said. 'Shame.'

'Why's that?' Brenda asked.

'It was us Dutch who gave them the name New Zealand. When did you arrive?'

'Today,' Brenda said. 'I met Alice in the pub.'

'Are you staying at the youth hostel?' Clara said.

'Yep. In one of the dorms.'

'Us too,' Lizzie said. 'Alice has her own room, but we're in the cheap seats.'

'Only because Ned wanted it!' Alice said.

'Where is Ned?' Hendrik asked.

'He went back to the hostel. He wasn't feeling well.'

'Oh,' Hendrik said. 'I hope he's OK. Does anyone want a drink?'

Before she could answer, her phone buzzed. She glanced at the screen.

It was a message from Ned.

Where are you?

She typed a reply.

Having a drink with the group

With your Australian friend?

Yes. And Donny and co

I'm sorry I stormed off. Why don't you come back? Remember we're getting up early to go to Grasmere.

For a second she was on the verge of replying *yes, I'll leave now*, but she caught herself. She realized she didn't want to. She had no interest in leaving the pub and walking back to the hostel so she could sit in a room with Ned and answer his questions about Brenda and Donny and Hendrik.

It wasn't fun. Ned wasn't fun.

She felt unmoored and slightly giddy, as if she'd suddenly seen how large and full of possibilities the world was.

She typed decisively.

Back later. Don't worry. Go to sleep. I'll see you in the morning

His reply was a rapid-fire staccato of messages.

Fine

Enjoy your night out

Glad I know where – who – your priorities are

And by the way, fuck you, too

She rubbed her temple. Maybe there was a way not to go back at all. She could sleep in a spare bed in the dormitories. Or on the floor. Or by the lake.

'Is that Ned?' Donny said.

'Yes.'

'Is he feeling better?'

She shook her head.

'Not really.'

Ambleside youth hostel was actually in Waterhead, a small town on the north end of Lake Windermere about a mile from Ambleside itself. Alice and Brenda walked along a road by an open field, the lake glistening under the moonlight to their right.

It was a warm, bright night – this far north it hardly got fully dark in summer – and Alice felt alive with the glow of the evening. She would remember it as one of the funniest nights she had ever had; it was hard to say why it was so funny, and it would have been impossible to explain to someone else. It was one of those nights where you simply had to be there.

'Well,' Brenda said. She sucked on a Marlboro cigarette she had bummed from a guy outside the pub. 'That was a laugh.'

'Yeah. Donny's a riot.'

'Good-looking too,' Brenda said.

'I have a boyfriend.'

'Not a happy camper, though?'

'No. He was pretty pissed off when I said I was staying out.'

'What did he say?' Brenda said.

'That my priorities are wrong – hanging out with you lot instead of him.'

'He should have come.'

'He should.' Alice hesitated. This felt like a betrayal. 'And he ended with a "fuck you".'

Brenda frowned. 'There's no need for that. That's just fucking rude.'

'I know. He gets a bit overwrought.'

'Violent?'

'No,' Alice said. 'He's never like that. Ned's not a nasty person. He's very sensitive. Over-sensitive, really. It makes him emotional.'

'Still a pain if you have to deal with it,' Brenda said.

'I know. But he's OK.'

'How long are you here for?' Brenda said.

'Three more nights.'

'Then you go home?'

'Back to Nottingham. I share a house with two friends, Nellie and Madeline. They're on a trip in Australia, as it happens. I was planning to go, but Ned talked me out of it.'

Talked was not quite the right word. He had badgered her about it until she gave up on the idea.

This is our last chance to spend a summer together before we get jobs and settle down. Then it'll be normal life – marriage, kids, two weeks away in summer. He'd grinned. *That'll be great, but this is the last opportunity to really be together before it happens.*

It sounded to her like there was plenty of time to be together later, which was all the more reason to go away with Nellie and Mads. She had pointed this out, but then he had told her he had plans, specific plans for her and him. It was supposed to have been a surprise, but that was ruined now.

A week in the Lake District.

And if she went away she would spoil it.

In the end it wasn't worth it, so she had waved Nellie and Mads goodbye, and packed up her hiking boots.

'You live in Nottingham?' Brenda asked.

'I've recently finished at uni there. The lease on my flat runs out in a few weeks actually, so I'll have to move my stuff out.'

'Where will you go?'

Alice shrugged. 'Get a place with Ned somewhere, probably. He's got a job in London in accounting. I want to be a journalist, so I can do that anywhere.'

They were approaching the hostel.

'Maybe I'll see you tomorrow,' Brenda said.

'We're walking to Grasmere over some mountain Ned knows,' Alice said. 'So we can visit Wordsworth's house and grave.'

'Sounds fun. I'll be mooching around the lounge getting

72

over my hangover,' Brenda said. 'Then I was thinking of taking the boat down to Bowness. Find a pub for lunch.'

'Jesus,' Alice replied. 'Sounds like heaven.'

'Well, enjoy your day. And maybe we'll catch up when you get back. Goodnight.'

Their room contained a double bed and a bunk bed. There was a family of four at check-in who were split between dormitories and had asked if there was a family room available; Alice had suggested to Ned that they swap, but he had shrugged and said they should have booked earlier.

She sat on the edge of the bed and slid her jeans off, taking care to be as quiet as she could. The last thing she wanted was to wake Ned and have to talk about the night.

She crossed to the bathroom and eased the door open, then sat on the toilet. When she was done, she grabbed her toothbrush – no flush, that could wait – and spread some toothpaste on it.

'You're back.'

Ned was standing in the doorway, arms folded. His eyes were red and swollen.

'Hi,' she said. 'Did I wake you up?'

He shook his head. 'I couldn't sleep.'

She felt a pulse of anger. 'You were lying there, watching me?' she said. 'It's a bit creepy, Ned.'

'I didn't know what to say.'

'Well,' she said. 'I'm back now, so I'll brush my teeth and we can go to bed.'

He didn't reply.

'Ned. What's wrong?'

'What's wrong?' he said. 'You're asking me what's *wrong*?'

She nodded. 'Yes.'

'What's right?' he said. '*That's* the question. What's *right*?'

'I don't understand.'

'We came here to be together, and you prefer to spend time with a bunch of random people we hardly know.'

'We were in the pub with them and you left,' Alice said. 'It was your choice.'

'And then you meet someone new – an Australian "girl"' – he made air quotes around 'girl' – 'and decide even she's more important than me.'

'What do you mean, "girl"?' Alice said, mirroring his air quotes. 'Are you worried I was with another man?'

'I'm not worried about anything.'

'Ned, ever since the thing with that guy Michael you've been insecure about us, even though nothing happened with Michael. I don't know what to do about it. We're together. You're my boyfriend. I don't know what else I can say to make things better.'

'I'm not insecure,' he said, his jaw clenched. 'You just spent the night in the pub while I was alone here. We're on holiday, together.'

'My God,' she said. 'I wish I'd gone to Australia with Nellie and Mads.'

'You should have!' he shouted. 'You should have fucking gone with them if that's what you wanted.'

'I tried,' she said. 'I tried, but you stopped me.'

'I didn't stop you,' he said. 'I offered you an alternative.'

'No,' she said. 'You made it so awkward for me to go that I stayed.'

As soon as she'd said it, she realized it was the wrong thing to say. His mouth dropped open.

'So you only stayed with me because I made you?' he said, his voice low. 'That's good to know, Alice. Good to know how you truly feel.'

He turned away, and walked back into the room. Alice brushed her teeth. This was not going well. Their holiday was rapidly falling apart.

74

Their relationship was rapidly falling apart.

She rinsed her mouth and followed him into the room. He was lying on his back, his eyes closed.

'Ned,' she said. 'We need to talk.'

He did not reply.

'I know you're awake,' she said. 'Stop playing games.'

'What do you want to talk about?'

'Us,' she said. 'Our relationship.'

'What about it?' he said.

'I don't think it's working out that well.'

He paused, and she saw his mouth twitch.

'What do you mean?' he said, a quiver in his voice.

'Things aren't great between us.'

'It's fine,' he said. 'It's all fine.'

'Are you happy?'

'Yes.' He sniffed. 'Perfectly happy.'

'I don't think I am,' Alice said.

He sat upright. 'Are you trying to break up with me, Alice? Is that what this is?'

She didn't reply. She didn't know how to. The only answer she could think of was *Yes, I am*, but she wasn't sure she wanted to see his reaction, especially with nowhere to go.

His eyes narrowed, and he shook his head. 'You'll regret it,' he said. 'You think life is about having fun and doing what you want and being free' – again, he put a word in air quotes – 'but it isn't.'

'It is,' she said. 'That's exactly what it is.'

He ignored her. 'So dump me, Alice, but that'll be it. Once you do, it's over for good. Got that? For good. So go ahead, and say it's over. I dare you.'

She saw, in that moment, who he would become. She saw the seeds of the sanctimonious, arrogant husband, the distant father, the man frustrated at the world and filled with self-hating anger.

75

And she wanted no part of it.

'Go ahead,' he said. There was a small smile of triumph dawning on his lips as he saw her hesitation. 'Say it's over.'

So she did. She surprised herself, but not as much as she surprised Ned. His mouth fell open.

'No,' he said. 'Alice, please. Don't do this.'

'I'll sleep in the bunk bed,' she said, too tired to care any more. 'Goodnight.'

Alice was woken by his warm breath on the back of her neck. Her head was throbbing and her mouth was dry, and the feeling of him breathing on her made her feel sick.

She opened her eyes and saw the light coming in through the curtains. So it was after dawn, but this far north in the summer the dawn was early. From the birdsong she could hear, it was *very* early. From the feeling behind her eyes, whatever time it was, it was too fucking early.

He nibbled her ear and slid his hand onto her hip.

'Darling,' he said. 'Are you awake?'

It was, she thought, a fucking stupid question. There was no answer. If she was asleep she couldn't answer. If she was awake but wanted to be left alone she'd have to say no – but that was ridiculous.

She grunted and shifted her hip away from him. Her stomach felt delicate, and she needed to pee.

More than anything, though, she wanted to be allowed to sleep.

That was clearly not Ned's plan. He nestled closer, spooning her. He had, she realized with dismay, a hard-on, which he was pressing into her buttocks.

His slipped his hand under her T-shirt and moved it up to her breasts. She fought the urge to gag. She had had too much to drink and eat and she would not have wanted this at the best of times.

And the best of times were gone for her and Ned. She felt no desire for him at all; in fact, she felt a vague – and growing – revulsion.

'No,' she said. 'Not now, Ned.'

He ignored her, and pressed himself harder against her.

'Ned,' she said, louder. 'I said no!'

'Don't be like this,' he said. 'We had a stupid argument. We can move on. And this is the *perfect* way.'

'Ned,' she said. 'I'm serious. No. I'm tired. I want to go back to sleep.'

'When you wake up, then?'

She didn't reply. She didn't think he would like the answer, and she didn't want to discuss it at that moment.

'I'm sorry,' he said, his voice breaking. 'I'm sorry I was mean. And jealous. It was stupid of me. I won't do it again, I promise.'

'OK,' she said. 'That's good.'

'Why are you being like this, Alice? I said I'm sorry.'

'Ned,' she said. 'We can talk about this later. But it's too early. OK?'

'OK,' he said. 'Later's fine.'

The conversation did not go well.

She wasn't sure which of the emotions he thought would change her mind. There was sadness (*I can't live without you, I really can't, you don't know what you mean to me*), withdrawal (*fine, I'm fine, I'll just sit here in silence, staring out of the window*), being a selfless martyr (*I'm happy, as long as you're happy, if you love someone set them free, go well into the world, I'll always love you but I'll never hold you back*), hopeless sobbing (*it's – sob – I love you – sob – and if – sob – you don't love – sob – me, I'll never – sob – understand*), arrogance (*you'll be back, though, I know you will, when you realize what you've thrown away, people like me don't grow on trees you know*), and anger (*you fucking bitch, how could you do this? That's what you are, you know, a fucking bitch. As long as you're happy you don't care about anyone else. You're a bitch. And a slut. You were fucking that guy, Michael, I know you were*).

None of them worked. All of them confirmed her decision.

Most of all the threats.

That's what he ended with, standing by the door, his rucksack on his back, basketball cap on his head, his eyes red-rimmed.

'You'll regret this,' he said. 'One day, you'll regret this.'

'That's a risk I'm ready to take,' she said.

'It's not a risk. It'll happen.'

'You seem very sure, Ned.'

'You want to know how I'm so sure?' he said, his face twisted in anger.

'Not really,' she said.

'I'll tell you anyway, Alice.' He leaned forwards and jabbed a finger at her. 'Because I'll *make* you regret it. I'll damn well make you, if it's the last thing I do.'

Brenda was sitting at a table by a large bay window reading a book. Windermere glistened in the morning sunshine behind her, swans bobbing on the water.

She looked up as Alice approached. 'Hey,' she said. 'Aren't you supposed to be visiting the grave of some dead poet?'

'I was,' Alice said. 'But there was a change of plan.'

'Your boyfriend – Ned, right? – went on his own?'

'Not exactly. We had a bit of a relationship chat when I got back.'

'A 2 a.m. relationship chat. Nice. Just what you want.'

'Right?' Alice said. 'Anyway, a few things got said and a few feelings got hurt and in the end – we sort of broke up.'

'Sort of?'

'I'm not sure he fully believes it's over.'

'Is it over?' Brenda gestured to the chair opposite. 'Feel free.'

Alice sat down. 'I think it is,' she said. 'It's weird, but when I got back here and he was waiting up ready to *unload* all this shit on me – I saw it there and then. I didn't want to be with him any more. It was like I knew it all along, but I couldn't see it.'

'Sounds pretty terminal.'

'I know. I'm shocked, in a way, but I feel nothing for him. I wish him well, but I don't want to be with him. Honestly, Brenda – more than anything, I feel relieved.'

'So what happens next?' Brenda said. 'Are you going to stay here?'

Alice nodded. 'I've got a few more days in the room, so I might as well. It could be fun.'

'And after that?'

'I don't know. I had this whole life charted out for me – finish up the lease on the house in Nottingham, move in with Ned, get a job in journalism. Now it's all gone. I can do whatever I want.'

'What do you want to do?'

'Maybe travel a bit,' Alice said. 'Go around Europe. But other than that, I have no idea. And it feels *great*.'

Thursday, 22 July 2021

Alice

'CRUCIFIX' KILLER HAS A SIGNATURE
By Alice Sark

In a shocking development, reports have emerged which confirm that the murders of Jane Kirkpatrick, Amy Martin and Stan Davidson were committed by the same person.

Someone familiar with the investigation revealed to this correspondent that the crime scenes all share a chilling similarity. The arms of the victims were folded across their chests and a crucifix had been inserted into their right hands.

Detective Inspector Jane Wynne confirmed that the reports are true. 'We are disappointed that these details leaked, but can confirm that they are accurate.' When asked whether the police believed that this meant they were dealing with a serial killer, she added, 'Yes, it would seem to indicate that, and we are proceeding – indeed have been proceeding – on that basis.'

She did not answer further questions and would not comment on the significance of the folded arms or crucifix. While their meaning remains unclear, one thing is certain: there is a serial killer of the most depraved and twisted kind at work in this town.

Alice sat at the corner table of Gerrard's, a café in Stockton Heath village. She often went to work in cafés – there were four or five in different parts of the town that didn't mind customers sitting for a few hours on one cup of coffee and a cake. At first she'd found the ebb and flow of the customers distracting, but now she was used to it. In any case, it was better than being at home. Even if Martha or Tom's mum was there looking after Jo, she couldn't settle into her work.

She looked at the clock in the corner of her laptop. It was a few minutes past 1 p.m. She checked her inbox. There were forty-four new emails since she'd arrived, bought a coffee and found a seat.

The story had posted at eight that morning, and she had received the first message from a national newspaper just after ten.

Hi there, my name's Tony Walker, with the Daily Herald. We read your story with interest – you have great sources! – and would like to know whether you have any more details or angles on the 'Crucifix Killer'? (Awesome name by the way – did you come up with it?) We'd love to have you send them over if you do – we'd pay, of course – do you have an agent? – or if you prefer you could write the story for us? Whatever works, Alice – let me know, OK?

By midday she had similar emails from almost all the other national papers. They would send their own reporters to cover the story, but she had what they all wanted: an inside track. Serial killers were always hot copy – they were endlessly fascinating – and to be the closest journalist to a major investigation was a once-in-a-lifetime opportunity.

The kind of opportunity which could make her into a major name.

She was going to need more, though, for that to happen. She was going to need fresh information, more details about what the Crucifix Killer did.

She needed to speak to Nadia, but it would have to wait. It was 1.30. Martha was leaving at two.

Alice left some change on the table as a tip and packed up her laptop.

Tom

He was utterly wrecked. Not physically – physically he was unchanged – but psychologically. He couldn't focus on the simplest task. He could hardly think in a straight line. He understood now why driving tired could be as dangerous as driving drunk; your mental processing speed was a fraction of what it normally was. It felt as though there was a screen between him and the world.

He was sleeping from about 1 a.m. to 5 a.m. It was good sleep when he got it – he was out as soon as he closed his eyes, and it was the sleep of the dead – but nowhere near enough, and right now all he wanted to do was sleep. All he wanted to do was close his eyes and let himself slide into blissful unconsciousness.

But he couldn't. He couldn't fall asleep at his desk, so instead he stared at his computer screen, his eyes dry and blinking, trying to force his mind to do anything other than count as the seconds ticked by at the speed of something very, very slow. He couldn't really think of what it would be.

'Still not sleeping?'

Scott Daniels perched on the edge of his desk.

'Is it that obvious?'

'You look like you're just a shell, mate. The lights are on, but nobody's home.'

He shrugged. 'I might as well not be here. I can't do *anything*.'

Scott was the only person at work he would have admitted that to. He was his best – really his only – work friend. There were other colleagues who he liked and admired and enjoyed working with, but Scott was the only one with whom he felt he had a relationship outside of the office.

They had started on the same graduate training scheme, which involved about twenty newly qualified engineers being thrown into a rotational programme at the end of which some would leap into fast-track careers heading straight for the top, and others would start their more modest ascent of the corporate ladder.

Tom and Scott were in the second category, and happy to be there. The others all seemed to be – or to think they were – in the first category. The problem was there were only so many seats on the fast track, and so the corporately generated bonhomie and team spirit was exactly that – corporately generated.

Which meant totally and utterly false.

After they all fledged from the scheme they disappeared to various parts of the company, and much as he liked working with most of them, he did not feel they had his best interests at heart.

Scott was different.

As part of the programme they had gone for a weekend bonding retreat in Galway. On the Friday they arrived everyone had drunk masses of Guinness and Beamish and Murphy's and Baileys and whatever else was put in front of them. When they were all about ready to pass out, a message went around that they were to assemble in the hotel ballroom at 1 a.m.

84

They arrived to find three managers, plus May, the woman who ran the graduate training programme.

There'll be a treasure hunt tomorrow, May said. *7 a.m. sharp, in this room.*

Someone ventured the question of what she meant by 'treasure hunt'.

You'll have a map, a list of addresses, and a list of questions. You have to go to the addresses and answer the questions. So, one might be 'A famous person lived here. Who was it?' You go there, read the blue plaque, answer the question.

Jesus wept, Scott said. *We're a team. OK?*

May looked around the room.

It's just for fun, she said. *But there will be prizes.*

Prizes, it turned out, was the magic word for this group. Tom and Scott arrived at 6.59 a.m. in the ballroom – which, given the magnitude of his hangover, Tom thought was pretty respectable – but they were the last to get there, and by a lot.

They were also the only pair dressed in jeans and sweaters. The rest were in their running gear.

Well hello, Scott said. *It's like a pre-marathon race meeting.*

The maps and other paperwork were distributed and they were told to line up by the ballroom door. Then, with her hand in the air, May opened the door.

Ready, Steady – Go!

The graduate trainees set off at a run. Bewildered, Tom jogged after them. When he was outside, he realized Scott was not there and turned to look for his partner.

Scott was standing by the hotel door, lighting a cigarette.

Come on, Tom said. *We're going to be last. And it seems it matters.*

First, Scott said. *It doesn't matter. And second, we won't be last. We'll win. But let me explain how over a fry-up. There's a greasy spoon up the way.*

His plan was simple: a leisurely and restorative breakfast, then a taxi ride around Galway to the addresses on the list to find the answers. It was a good idea, and led to a pleasant morning. When they had completed the treasure hunt, Scott directed the taxi driver to drop them off around the corner from the hotel, and they walked into the ballroom, first to return.

A few minutes later the next two arrived, sweating and panting hard. Their eyes opened wide when they saw Tom and Scott.

Did you – did you do it? one of them asked.

Tom nodded and showed them the paper with the answers.

But you're hardly out of breath?

Scott winked. *Work smart, not hard*, he said.

They knew, of course, that Tom and Scott had cheated, but did not dare accuse them. That would have been being sore losers.

So had he left the company – or more likely, given how useful he was at the moment, been fired – he would not have kept in touch with any of the others. Scott, though, he would have seen again.

'How much sleep are you getting?' Scott said.

'Couple of hours here, couple there,' Tom said. 'It's brutal. I feel like I'm the walking dead. Had I known it would have been like this before I'm not sure I'd have gone through with it.'

'Could you have a chat to Karen?' Scott said. 'She's after having a baby and I'm trying to stave her off. But if you explained what your nights look like we may get away with a bit of a delay.'

'She could talk to Alice, too. She's not getting much more sleep.'

'I'll get her to call you.' He stood up. 'How about a beer after work? You look like you could do with one.'

'I'm not sure. I have to get home.'

'We could leave here early? Get you back on time.'

'It sounds good, I have to admit,' Tom said. 'But I don't think I can.'

'Come on,' Scott said. 'Just the one.'

It *did* sound good.

'OK,' he said. 'Just the one.'

Alice

Martha was sitting on the couch, her hand gently rocking Joanna's basket. When Alice walked in she made a shushing motion.

'Asleep,' she whispered, and nodded at the basket.

'How was she?' Alice said.

'Fine. She's a very sweet girl. She likes to be held.'

'She is,' Alice said. 'I missed her.'

Martha gave a small nod.

'I feel I have to mention something to you.' She sat upright, her smile suddenly forced. 'Tom brought up some bruises on Joanna's arm.'

'Yes,' Alice said. 'He told me he'd talked to you.'

'I have to tell you I felt a little bit' – she paused – 'put out after my conversation with Tom. I know he was only doing what he had to do as a father, but the idea that either of you would think I could do something like that – well, it upset me. I've got over it, but I wanted you to know.'

Alice held her gaze. 'I understand. But you can see where we'd be coming from?'

'Yes. But you can see where I'd be coming from, too.' She shook her head. 'It wasn't me. And if you can't be sure of that, I'll leave. For my own peace of mind, but also for yours. How can you be comfortable leaving me with Jo if you can't trust me?'

'It doesn't have to come to that,' Alice said.

'I hope not. Is there anyone else it could be?'

'Not really.' Alice paused. 'Me, Tom. His parents, and you. And then there's Roland.'

'His brother?'

'Yes.'

'He mentioned him. I didn't know he had a brother until then.'

'He reappeared recently. He was something of a pariah in the family. It goes back a long way, but he was a heroin addict. He's living with Tom's parents.'

'A heroin addict?'

'He's clean now.'

'Recently?'

'Quite.'

'Has he been left in charge of Jo?'

There was a heavy silence. 'No. At least not on his own.'

'But he's there when she stays with her grandparents?'

'He is.'

Martha's mouth pursed in something like distaste, and she stood up. 'It's two o'clock,' she said. 'I have to leave. And Alice – you have a heroin addict in her life, and you question me about the bruises?'

'We have to explore every avenue, Martha. It's nothing personal.'

'I hope we can keep it that way.'

Alice walked her to the door, then picked up her phone and called Nadia.

'Hi,' she said. 'I had a lot of interest in the story, from all the major papers. I gave them what I had – what was in the story I posted, really, but with some quotes from me.'

'That's good news,' Nadia said.

'I was wondering if there's more,' Alice said. 'Some other details?'

'Like what?' Nadia said.

'Theories on why the killer targets men as well as women? Don't they normally stick to one or the other?'

'Normally, yes. But not always.'

'Any thoughts on why this one's different?'

'Possibly,' Nadia said. 'But I can't talk right now. Could I call you later?'

'Five more minutes?'

'Really. I have to go. I'm free at 5.30? Call me if you can.'

'OK. Talk then. Thanks.'

She hung up. Possibly, Nadia had said. It sounded like she had more to share.

Tom

They met at their local, the London Bridge, and the quick pint turned into a quick two pints, or, in Tom's case, a pint and a half.

Scott went to the toilet when they were making their way through the second beer and Tom felt his eyes start to close. When Scott returned, he realized he could hardly focus.

'I think I'm going to fall asleep,' he muttered. 'My eyelids feel like someone's pulling them down.'

He let his head fall to his chest and closed his eyes. It was bizarre how blissful it was to simply have his eyes closed.

He forced them open. Sleeping in the pub was not a look he wanted.

'Man, it really is bad,' Scott said. He took out his phone. 'Close your eyes and let your head drop again. Let me take a snap to show Karen. I'll tell her she could end up married to a man who looks like this.'

'She's already married to one,' Tom said. 'After you've had a few pints.'

'Not too tired to be funny,' Scott said. 'Funny-ish, at any rate.'

'It was a good one for me,' Tom said.

'I wouldn't go that far.'

Tom pushed his drink across the table. 'You have that. I'm going to have to go.'

'Finish your pint? What do you think this is? 2019? No one wants a pint of coronavirus, mate.'

'No,' Tom said. 'I guess not.' His brain was shutting down and he was starting to worry about the drive home, even though it was no more than three minutes. 'Got to go. See you tomorrow. And thanks for getting me out. I might not be much fun, but I needed this.'

'Any time,' Scott said. 'And I hope you get some kip.'

Alice

Where the hell was Tom? It was 5.45 and he wasn't home. She bounced Jo in one arm, and called him again.

It rang through to voicemail.

This was totally unfair. He was supposed to be home by now, and she had made plans to call Nadia. It wasn't like it was just another call; it was important. It was her career.

And he hadn't bothered to phone home and tell her, let alone answer her fucking calls.

She put Jo in her basket. Maybe she would settle so she could speak to Nadia.

Her daughter held her breath for a second, then opened her mouth and started to wail. She couldn't have a conversation with that in the background; apart from anything else, Nadia would tell her to look after Jo.

She was starting to feel like screaming when she heard a key in the lock, and the swish of the front door opening. She stood up and walked into the hall.

Tom was closing the door. 'Sorry I'm a bit late,' he said. 'I went to the London Bridge with—'

'You did *what*?' Alice said. 'You went to the *pub*?'

'With Scott. For one pint.'

'You didn't think to tell me?'

'I didn't think it was a big deal.'

'Well it is. I'm supposed to be speaking to Nadia. She had something to tell me about the killings.'

'I'm sorry. I didn't know.'

'You didn't bother to find out.'

'Why didn't you call? I would have left.'

'I did. You didn't answer.'

He clapped his hand to his forehead. It was almost comical. 'Shit. I left my phone in the car.'

'Great. Well done, Tom.'

'And it's still there. I had to park two streets away. I'm sorry, Alice.'

'Never mind.' She grabbed her keys and phone. 'Your turn.'

Tom

He dipped his hand in the bath. It was cooler than he would normally have had it, but he was going to share it with Jo. Instead of bathing her and putting her to bed, then going down to eat dinner, he was going to take a bath with his daughter, put her down, and go straight to sleep himself.

No dinner, no TV, no work, no doom-scrolling his phone.

All he wanted – the only thing he could think about – was closing his eyes and going to sleep. Whatever else he had learned, he knew this: early-evening beers were only going to have one effect on him, and that was to make him even more tired.

He took off his clothes and picked Jo up, then sat in the bath, holding her upright in the space between his legs. She grabbed a fistful of water and watched it trickle out of her fingers, then laughed and did it again.

He scooped up some water and ran it over her back, gently massaging her shoulders. He took some more and cleaned her head, feeling the soft hair and smooth skin.

'You're beautiful,' he said, and touched her nose with the tip of his forefinger. 'You're my beautiful girl and I love you.'

She grabbed his finger and squeezed and he shook her hand about. She freed it, and with both arms, started splashing as hard as she could. Droplets flew around, landing on his face and running down his cheeks. She giggled, and he laughed with her.

After a while she stopped and he lifted her onto his chest. She lay with her head sideways, and his eyes started to close.

He let them shut for a blissful second, then forced them open. It was hard to keep them that way and they flickered shut. He felt himself slip towards sleep.

Just a minute, he thought. *I'll close them for two minutes. I won't go to sleep, but a few minutes can't hurt . . .*

Alice

'Sorry I'm late,' Alice said. 'Tom was at the pub.'

'He was?' Nadia said. 'Good for him!'

'He should have been back on time, though.'

'No problem. We're working late these days.'

'So,' Alice said. 'You mentioned there might be an update?'

'Not really,' Nadia said.

'Do you have any leads? Any suspects?'

'I can't say, Alice, you know that.'

'I know, but if you did have one – well, if the killer saw it in the news they might start to get worried. Slip up somehow, or even stop.'

'There's not much,' Nadia said. 'That's all I can tell you.'

'Can I quote that?'

'Not unless you want my boss to kick me down to playground duty,' Nadia said.

Upstairs she heard the sound of splashing and laughter. It must be bath time.

'Who's your boss?' Alice said.

'Detective Inspector Jane Wynne.'

Alice remembered her from the press conference. She was quiet and unassuming, but her eyes were quick and intelligent.

'Can I talk to her?'

'I don't know. I can ask.'

'That would be great,' Alice said. 'So what's the reason for the call? I don't need much – something about a new lead, or an avenue of enquiry. But something.'

'There's the question of the victims being men and women,' Nadia said.

'What does that mean?'

'We're not sure. But it could mean something. A different kind of killer, maybe. Some are motivated by sex or revenge or hatred of prostitutes, but this one – well, maybe they just like killing.'

'Which would make them hard to catch,' Alice said. 'Because there's no pattern. And if everyone's a potential victim then it's all the more terrifying.'

'That's the thinking,' Nadia said. 'How's everything else?'

'It's' – she paused – 'OK.'

'Only OK?'

'Things have been a bit strained with Tom.'

'That's normal enough. You've both been under a lot of stress.'

'I know. But he seems more than stressed. He's been erratic. Snappy.'

'I'm sure you'll get through it.'

'I think so. But it's tough. He's in the bath with Jo now.'

'OK. Well, I'll get back to you about DI Wynne.'

She ended the call and Alice put her phone down. Another evening of a rushed dinner and a broken night's sleep lay ahead of her. There wasn't even any food in the fridge, unless Tom had brought some back.

'Tom,' she called, quietly. There was no answer. She didn't want to shout; all was silent upstairs and she didn't want to disturb the peace. It was better to go up to talk to him.

He was not in Jo's room, or their bedroom, but she hadn't heard him come downstairs, so they were up there somewhere.

Which only left the bathroom, but the splashing sounds had all gone quiet.

She pictured him when he came in from the pub, bleary-eyed and exhausted. She pictured him, lying in the warm bath, his eyes slowly closing . . .

Tom

He was woken by a scream, then a shout of *Jo!* and the sensation of water lapping over his chest. He opened his eyes. Alice was standing over him, Jo naked and wet in her arms.

'Tom!' she shouted. 'What the hell are you doing?'

It took him a few seconds to wake up and remember where he was, and then he realized what he had done.

He'd fallen asleep in the bath. He'd thought he could just close his eyes for a moment, that he'd have a quick rest and then put Jo to bed, before calling it a night himself.

But he hadn't woken up. He'd lain there, fast asleep, with his daughter on his chest, unable to sit up or extricate herself if her mouth and nose slipped below the surface.

'Oh God,' he said. 'Oh God. Jo? Is she OK?'

Alice held her to her chest. 'She's fine.' She closed her eyes. 'But she was nearly under water, Tom. She'd slipped down your shoulder and the corner of her mouth was in the bath. 'She could have' – she held her hand to her mouth – 'I don't even want to say it.'

'I'm sorry, Alice,' he said. 'I'm so sorry. I didn't mean to go to sleep. I was tired and—'

She shook her head. 'No, Tom. Now's not the time. But this is not the kind of thing that can happen. You fell asleep in the bath with our baby. Do you not understand *anything* about being a parent?'

He didn't reply. There was no point. There was nothing he could say that would make any difference.

Alice walked out of the bathroom and he sank into the water. It was cold now, and an image came to him of him asleep, his head lolling against the side of the bath, with Jo face down beside him.

His eyes flew open and his skin crawled in horror. For a moment he considered lying down in the bath and letting himself slip under the surface, letting the water fill his mouth and nose and lungs. At least it meant he would not have to have that image intrude on his thoughts again.

What kind of a father was he? The kind who had a beer too many – and clearly even one was too many at the moment – and put his kid at risk? No, he was not. That was Roland, and he was not Roland.

And yet, here he was. An inch or two different and he would be a cautionary tale – *There was this dad who was super tired and he went for a drink after work and when he got home he had a bath with his baby . . .*

He shuddered again at the thought of what could have happened. It was almost as though, for an instant, it *had* happened, and he had a fleeting experience of what it would have felt like: a visceral, whole-body experience of intense pain.

It would pass, he knew, this feeling. But the lesson would be learned.

He climbed out of the bath and grabbed a towel. Alice was in Jo's room, bent over her crib, soothing her to sleep.

'I'm sorry,' he said. 'I really am.'

She glanced up, her eyes hard. 'Good.'

'I think I'm going to go to bed. When she wakes, I'll get up with her. OK?'

Alice barely acknowledged him. 'Have a good sleep.'

Alice

Kay was probably her closest friend. They had met at the swimming pool when she first moved here. Alice was halfway through her swim when Kay appeared at the end of her lane and asked if she could share it.

Sure, Alice said.

Left or right?

I don't mind, Alice said. *If you have a preference, go ahead.*

I prefer the right, Kay said.

Why, Alice didn't know, because it didn't seem to make any difference, because whatever Kay lacked in technique – and she lacked more or less everything – she made up for in enthusiasm. It was like swimming next to a slow-moving whirlpool, the swirling currents constantly buffeting her.

At some point, they found themselves at the same end.

You're really good, Kay said.

Not really. I used to swim a bit.

Better than me. Honestly, tell me what you think?

Of what?

Of my swimming.

There are some positive aspects, Alice said. *You move a lot of water around.*

Is that good?

Yeah – you just want to move it all in the same direction. Ideally behind you.

What do I do?

You move quite a bit of it in quite a few directions.

Damn, Kay said. *Is that why I'm so slow, even though I'm trying my hardest?*

I think it could be part of the explanation.

They had seen each other a few more times in the pool, then Kay had suggested meeting for a drink. She was bright-eyed and fun-loving and the most opinionated person Alice had ever known. She had an opinion on every topic and an answer for every question, and never failed to offer detailed advice.

She called her and held the phone to her ear.

'Hey,' Kay said. 'How's it going?'

'Good,' Alice said. 'Kind of.'

'Only kind of? Still not getting any sleep?'

'Barely a wink. And I think it's getting to Tom.'

'No doubt it is. Tough times.'

'It's more than that, and I'm worried, Kay.'

'Oh?' Kay said. 'In what way?'

'He's moody. And a bit withdrawn.'

Kay laughed. 'If a man being moody and withdrawn was something to worry about we'd all be in a state of constant anxiety.'

'It's not only that. He's been snapping at me.'

'He's tired,' Kay said. 'It's a stressful time.'

'That's what I thought,' Alice said. 'But I'm worried it runs deeper. I'm worried he's depressed.'

There was a moment of silence.

'Did something happen?' Kay said. 'Did he do something to you?'

'No,' Alice said. 'Not to me. Not to anyone. At least, I don't think so.'

103

'I don't like that "I don't think so",' Kay said. 'What's going on, Alice?'

'Jo had a bruise,' she said. 'On her arm. The doctor saw it and I could tell she was concerned. It's not the kind of thing that could appear from nowhere.'

'You think it was Tom?'

'There's only so many people it could be. Tom's mum, Martha. Tom's brother Roland. I didn't include Tom on the list initially—'

'Initially?' Kay said.

'Until just now.'

'Why just now?'

Alice took a deep breath. 'You have to keep this to your-self, Kay.'

'Of course.'

'You have to promise.'

'Cross my heart and hope to die.'

'He had a bath with Jo earlier. I was on the phone but I could hear them splashing around. After a while I realized everything was quiet, so went up to check, and he was asleep in the bath. Jo was on his chest, but she'd slipped down and her face was near the water.'

'Oh God!' Kay said. 'Is she OK?'

'Yes. But she might not have been.'

'That's pretty bad,' Kay said. 'But it sounds like he made a mistake. That's all.'

'That's what worries me,' Alice said. 'With the way he's been recently – the way he seems to hate me and resent Jo – I got the impression – just an idea, really – that it may have been deliberate.'

'Deliberate?'

'It's hard to even say it. But it was almost as if – as if he wanted to – that he was planning to drown them both.'

'No,' Kay said. 'Not Tom.'

'I know. It sounds crazy. I don't like to think it, let alone say it. But I can't ignore what happened, Kay.'

'Listen,' Kay said. 'I'm sure this is a temporary phase he's going through, because of the stress you're both under. You mustn't overreact. Have you talked to anyone else about it?'

'No, only you.'

'You could talk to a professional.'

'What if they did something?'

'Like what?'

'Took Jo away?'

'No,' Kay said. 'That won't happen.'

'This is such a mess,' Alice said. 'I don't know what to do.'

'Don't panic,' Kay said. 'That's the main thing. And nothing bad has happened yet.'

'Yet,' Alice said. 'But it wasn't far off tonight. How can I leave her with him after that?'

PART TWO

The Baby

You hate this thing. It is shocking to you how much.

How much you want to dismember it. Take it to pieces and break it forever. You cannot help but see it as an automaton. A clockwork device designed to irritate you. It has no soul. No inner life. No value.

But you cannot do that. However pleasurable it would be, it would bring more problems. So you must content yourself with pinches and prods with a sharp finger.

You have rarely hated anything as much. Your parents, maybe. Your interfering parents, always trying to save you from yourself.

It wasn't the interference you hated. It was the idea that they thought you needed saving.

Saving from what? A future in which you became like them? Tiny little people living tiny little lives like everyone else?

No – you have seen more. You have tasted what life can be, and you cannot – will not – be denied it.

You look at the baby. It smiles.

You laugh.

That will not work on you.

You grab its fat little thigh. It will not be smiling for much longer.

Carrie Sanchez

She'd heard about the serial killer, of course she had, and her mum would give her so much shit if she knew she was walking home alone, but what were the odds she'd be attacked really? Not very high, but just in case, she walked quickly and stuck to well-lit streets, even if it made the walk that bit longer.

And the alternative would have been to stay with Mike, which she was *not* going to do. She was sick of him, sick of his stupid jokes about her appearance – about her weight, specifically – and sick of him shrugging her off when she asked him to stop.

Don't be so sensitive, he'd said, when they got back to his flat from the pub, *it was a joke.*

I'm not being sensitive! she shouted. *It hurts my feelings!*

Exactly my point. You're letting your feelings get hurt over nothing. That's the definition of over-sensitive. You should be more like me. Have no *feelings.*

She knew he had feelings, everyone did, but sometimes she wondered. He could be so *mean*. Even if it was a joke, it was still unpleasant to be the person everyone was laughing at.

110

The first few times he'd mentioned her weight – comments like *Good job I like something to hold on to in bed* or *Just like me to end up with a salad dodger for a girlfriend* – she'd wondered whether she *was* being over-sensitive, but after tonight she knew she wasn't.

They'd moved in together a month before, and earlier at the pub, Carol, the fiancée of his best friend, Paul, had asked how it was going.

Lovely, Carrie had replied, and smiled at Mike. *We're like an old married couple!*

Yeah, Mike said. *It's great. Only thing is Carrie's eaten all my pies. I had a year's worth of Fray Bentos in, and she's scoffed the lot.*

His friends – the male ones – laughed, of course they did, while their girlfriends gave her little looks of sympathy. She'd felt herself blush, and headed for the loos. As she left the table, she heard Mike tut, and say *Bloody hell, there she goes. Can't take a joke.*

Well, it wasn't a joke, and she wasn't taking it any more.

You do have feelings, and you hurt mine. Anyway, this isn't about me or my feelings, it's about what you did. There's a name for it, Mike.

Yeah, he said. *Joking.*

No, she replied. *Fat-shaming.*

He burst into a fit of laughter.

Give over, he said. *Fat-shaming. What a load of bollocks. It's not*, she said. *It's real. And it's what you're doing.*

He shrugged. *If you say so. And you are a bit porky, Carrie. But like I said. I'm a fan of the larger lady.*

That was when she left. She could have called a cab but she didn't want to stay there a second longer. She didn't care about serial killers. It wouldn't happen to her.

And if it did it would serve him right.

She turned into her parents' street and relaxed. They lived

at the end in a large house. All the houses on the street were set back from the road at the end of long driveways. She walked past Neil and Shannon's place – they had moved in a few years back and she had babysat their kids – and then Mr Morrison's, a widower she had known all her life.

There was one more before her parents'. It had been bought by a lawyer from London a month or so ago, but she and her family were yet to move in. It was an island of darkness in the light.

She hurried past the driveway. As she did, she glanced up at the house.

There was a car parked a yard inside the drive. It was dark-coloured and the lights were off, but she knew instantly that it shouldn't have been there.

And nor should the hooded figure who stepped into the street from the shadows where the driveway ended.

She opened her mouth to scream, but never got the chance.

Sunday, 15 August 2021

Alice

'CRUCIFIX' KILLER MURDERS AGAIN
By Alice Sark

The Crucifix Killer has struck again.

Police confirmed that the body of a woman, 21, was found early on Saturday morning, in the driveway of a house in Grappenhall. The victim's identity has not been revealed.

DI Jane Wynne – who is leading the investigation – confirmed that this was the latest victim of the serial killer who has been operating recently in the Warrington area.

'I can confirm that this is consistent with the prior three murders,' she said. 'The killer folded the victim's arms and left a crucifix on their person.'

Fear was palpable on the streets of the town this morning. 'This has to end, and soon,' Andrea Jones, of Dallam, said. 'This person needs to be caught and stopped.'

It seems unlikely that they will be so obliging.

'These cases typically only end when the killer is brought to justice,' Professor Bob Collins, a noted criminal psychologist, said. 'Their motives for killing are highly personal and so a cessation is unlikely.'

The professor indicated that it is even more unlikely in this case, given the signature folded arms and crucifix found at the crime scenes.

'Many serial killers have a ritual element to their crimes,' he said. 'With the "Crucifix" Killer this is clearly present. My estimation is that there is a religious motivation for these murders – the crucifix is obviously a religious symbol, but I believe the folded arms are no less religious in origin. Arms folded over the chest indicate that the victim is at peace – and the killer may believe they are bringing peace to the people they are terrorizing.'

It's possible that this may explain one unusual aspect of the case – the mixed genders of the victims. If the killer believes they are leaving their victims at peace, then they could as well attack a man as a woman.

What is clear is that this killer is evil and degraded. Whatever significance they think their crimes have, however grandiose they think they are, they are nothing more than a common criminal – and they will be caught.

Tuesday, 17 August 2021

Tom

Tom folded the clingfilm around his half-eaten sandwich and put it back in his bag. Before the pandemic he had eaten at the company canteen most days – there was a well-stocked salad bar that was subsidized by the company to encourage healthy eating. It was cheap and good for you, and very popular.

Not any more. Buffet-style dining, with the shared utensils and multiple customers all hovering over the same food was now a thing of the past. Maybe it would return at some point, but for the moment it was another victim of the pandemic. Tom, like most of his colleagues, ate lunch at his desk.

A few rows down, Scott Daniels stood up and looked around. He raised his hand in a wave and walked over. He had a black eye.

'Been fighting?' Tom said.

'Five-a-side footie,' Scott said. 'We played some Mancs and you know what they're like. It got a bit tasty.'

'Really?'

'Nah. I fell over and banged into my goalie's elbow, but scrapping with Mancs sounds better.'

'I'd stick to that story if I was you.'

'Anyway – we're playing tonight and we're one short. Fancy a game?'

'Have you seen me play football?' Tom said. 'You'd be better off with four men.'

'You can just stand there and get in the way,' Scott said. 'And we'll be having some beers after, if you're in the mood.'

'Now you're talking,' Tom said. 'That I can take part in. But let me check with Alice. I don't want to leave her in the lurch.'

'Baby still not sleeping well?'

'Not really.' Tom shrugged. 'But we're getting used to it.'

He was still only getting four or so hours' sleep a night, but he had found ways to work with it. Two days a week he worked from home, so could have the odd nap. It was another pandemic effect – everyone had switched to working from home and it had been fine, so it was hard for the company to say people couldn't do it now. On the other days, he had found that a twenty-minute nap in the car was enough to take the edge off.

His phone started to ring. Scott glanced at it.

'It's Alice. She must be listening in somehow.'

'Who knows?' Tom said, and lifted his phone to his ear.

'Tom.' Alice sounded breathless. 'Are you free?'

'Not really. I'm at the office.'

'I need you to come home. Now.'

He sat up. 'Why? What's wrong?'

'I'll tell you when you get here.'

'Is it Jo?'

Scott frowned. *Everything OK?* he mouthed.

'No. But you need to get back, as soon as you can.'

'OK. I'll leave now.'

He put his phone in his pocket and closed his laptop. 'Gotta go.'

'You're white as a sheet,' Scott said. 'What's going on?'

'She didn't say,' Tom replied. 'But it can't be anything good.'

116

Alice

The letter had arrived with the morning post. She had noticed it as the address appeared as though it had been printed on a home printer. There was no branding, and there was a stamp affixed to the corner. It was that rarest of things these days: a private, personal letter.

It lay on the coffee table, face down, the words printed on the same home printer. She flipped it over and read it again.

Dear Ms Sark

Your news article caught my eye.

It is not the first time you have come to my attention. It was you – or some unusually creative police officer – who gave me the name 'the Crucifix Killer'.

It is a tawdry name, lacking in imagination. But I understand it's the best you can do, and I forgive you.

I find myself less forgiving when it comes to your choice of vocabulary. 'Evil', 'degraded': I am afraid you are mistaken. I am neither of those things and it is bordering on insulting that you choose to brand me as such.

But they are not the most annoying aspect of your

report. It is your last statement that makes me – I must confess – positively angry. 'However grandiose they think they are, they are nothing more than a common criminal – and they will be caught.'

This is mistaken and insulting: I am far, far more than a common criminal.

And I will not be caught. The police can no more catch me than a fly can catch the spider in whose web it is caught. The spider is a different order of being. It is the predator: the fly is the prey.

That is how I stand in relation to the hearty boys and girls in blue.

Remember this, Alice. Remember this when you write your drivel. And remember that beautiful daughter of yours.

Joanna. A lovely name, for a lovely girl. It would be a shame for her to be caught in a spider's web . . .

I have something else: a message for your friend on the force, the delightful Nadia: She and her colleagues will hear from me soon. My work needs further elaboration.

And – just so you know I am who I say I am, ask your friend on the force where the girl's house keys were. I left them in an unusual place.

I trust you are well.
Yours faithfully
The 'Crucifix' Killer

She took a photo of the letter, then typed a message to Nadia.

This came in the post. I guess it's going to be of interest to you guys

She sent it and sipped her tea. Seconds later the front door opened. Tom had made it home quickly. She'd not been expecting him for another five minutes or so. It wasn't much, but still.

'Tom?' she called. 'Is that you?'

Tom

The house was quiet, so his first thought was that there was something wrong with Jo.

Something seriously wrong, something so wrong she wasn't even crying. If she had been, at least he would have known she was alive.

It made sense. What else would have made Alice ask him to come home immediately? And of course she wouldn't have told him what it was or he wouldn't have been able to think straight to drive. She wanted him back before she gave him the bad news.

Then he heard her voice.

'Tom? Is that you?'

He hurried down the hall into the living room. She was sitting on the couch, looking up at him. Jo was swaddled in her Moses basket, eyes closed. He stared at her, looking to see if her chest was rising and falling.

It was. He felt dizzy with relief.

'So,' he said. 'What's going on? Is Jo OK?'

'She's fine.'

'Then what is it?'

Alice pointed to the coffee table. There was a piece of A4 paper on it, next to an envelope.

'That came in the post this morning.'

'Who's it from?'

And why, he thought, *did I need to come back from the office? How urgent could a letter be?*

'Take a look,' she said.

He picked it up and started to read. And he understood why she had called him home.

Alice

Tom put the letter back on the table. His face was drained of blood, his eyes wide. He sat on the couch.

'What the fuck?' he said, after a long pause. 'I mean – what the fuck?'

'I know,' Alice said.

'Is it real?'

'Yes,' Alice said. 'It's real. At least I assume it is. I'll have to ask Nadia about the keys.'

'So you think it's him? The Crucifix Killer?'

Alice nodded. 'It has to be.'

'And he knows about you,' Tom said. 'And Joanna. And where we live. This is not good, Alice!'

'I know.' She caught his eye. 'I'm scared.'

'Have you called the police?'

'I texted Nadia a photo.'

'You need to stop writing about this guy,' Tom said. 'It's not safe.'

'I can't. This is my story. And I can't be intimidated out of writing about it. I'm a journalist, Tom.'

'You're a mum.'

'Let's see what the police say,' she said. 'We don't have to decide now.'

'I've already decided.'

'It's not your decision, though, is it?'

Her phone rang. It was Nadia.

'Hi,' she said. 'Did you get my message?'

'Yes,' Nadia said.

'What do you think?'

'I think you need to stay where you are. I'm on my way over with Detective Inspector Wynne.'

'How long?' Alice said.

'Ten minutes,' Nadia replied. 'Sit tight.'

Alice opened the front door. Nadia was standing behind a short-haired woman wearing a badly fitting suit. She had a slightly disconcerting gaze; it was as though she was studying you, taking in every detail and weighing it to see what she could learn.

'I'm Detective Inspector Jane Wynne,' she said. 'I believe you know DS Alexander?'

'Come in,' Alice said. 'We can go through to the living room. Nadia – DS Alexander – knows the way.'

They followed Nadia down the hall. In the living room, Alice indicated to DI Wynne to take a seat. She perched on the armchair. Nadia remained standing by the door.

'I believe you received a letter?' Wynne said.

'It's there,' Alice said, and pointed to the table.

'I'll grab it,' Nadia said, and snapped on a pair of gloves. She picked it up and read it. Wynne put her own gloves on and, when Nadia was finished, held out a hand.

She scanned the letter.

'Who else has handled it?' she said.

'Only me and Tom.'

'Tom?' Wynne said.

'My husband. He's upstairs putting our daughter down.'

'No one else?'

'The post office, I suppose.'

'They would only have touched the envelope,' Nadia said. 'We'll need to take your and Tom's fingerprints to eliminate them from the letter.'

'And then you'll be able to get the prints of whoever wrote it?' Alice asked.

'If they're there,' Wynne said. 'I'd be surprised if they were so careless. But we'll look. Talk me through what happened, if you would, Ms Sark.'

'Not much,' Alice said. 'The post arrived and I saw the envelope. It didn't look like junk mail, so I opened it.'

'So it came with the post?' Nadia said. 'Not hand delivered?'

'Yes,' Alice said. She pointed to the envelope. 'It's been franked, so it went through the postal service.'

Nadia nodded. 'The article it refers to – that was published on Sunday, if I remember correctly?'

'Yes,' Alice said.

'So the letter was posted Monday and arrived today,' Nadia said.

'Or Sunday,' Wynne said. 'And picked up Monday.'

'And it's definitely the killer,' Alice said. 'There's the comment about the keys. Where were they?'

Nadia glanced at Wynne. 'In her mouth,' she said. 'They were stuffed in her mouth.'

'So it's the killer, all right,' Wynne said. 'No one else could have known that.'

There were footsteps on the stairs and the door opened.

'Hi Nadia,' Tom said, and then turned to DI Wynne and introduced himself. 'I'm Tom Sark.'

'Detective Inspector Jane Wynne. Pleased to meet you. You were out when this arrived?'

'I was at work. Alice called me to come home.'

Wynne took an evidence bag from her pocket and slid the letter inside. 'Do you mind if I take this?'

It wasn't really a question. Alice shrugged.

'Why do you think he wrote to Alice?' Tom said. 'Why pick her?'

'Because she called him the Crucifix Killer,' Wynne said. 'So the killer – we can't assume it's a man yet – knows she's in touch with us. She was the one who broke the story.'

'And now this psychopath has her in his sights?' Tom's lips were white, pressed together in fury.

'I don't think she is in their sights,' Wynne said.

'You don't think?' Tom said. 'What *do* you think?'

'I think this is a way to open a channel of communication. It can happen in these cases. Serial killers sometimes want to be close to the investigation. It's a game to them.'

'That's wonderful. But now she's – we're – in danger,' Tom said.

DI Wynne nodded. 'That's a possibility. And we will of course understand if your wife chooses not to publish any more on this case.'

Alice glared at Tom. 'I didn't say that,' she said.

'If it is an attempt to communicate' – Wynne held up the bag – 'then they will want a reply.'

'There's no return address,' Tom said. 'So how would Alice – assuming she wanted to – reply?'

'Through the press,' Nadia said. 'Through another story. But it's too risky. We can't ask you to do that.'

'You can't ask me,' Alice said. 'But if I wanted to, I could?'

'No way,' Tom said. 'Not happening.'

'Tom,' Alice said. 'Would you mind not speaking for me?' She stood up and walked to the window. 'I could, if I wanted?'

'That would be your choice,' Wynne said. 'But there would be risks.'

'How big?'

Wynne tilted her head to one side. 'Hard to say. The threats could be no more than a way to establish dominance. To come here and hurt you in cold blood would be unusual. Serial killers have rituals which are as important as the murders themselves. But there are no guarantees, Ms Sark.' She leaned forward. 'Let me be clear. You are free to act as you wish, but I cannot recommend – let alone ask – that you do so.'

'If I did,' Alice said, softly. 'Could you offer any protection?'

'We can have a patrol car pass by frequently,' Wynne said. 'And put an alert on your address, so if you make a call we'll have officers here in minutes. But we will do that anyway, on the strength of this letter.'

'OK,' Alice said. 'I'll think about it. There's one other thing. What about the message at the end?'

'The "they'll hear from me soon"?' Nadia said.

'Right,' Alice replied. 'And that their work needs further elaboration.'

'That's a threat I *am* worried about,' Wynne said. 'It means they're getting ready to kill again. And we need to warn people. DS Alexander – we need to get this in the public domain.'

'A press conference?' Nadia said.

'Yes. As soon as we can.'

Tom

Tom watched the police officers leave. He couldn't quite believe what had just happened. He had a hollow pit in his stomach, along with a feeling he didn't recognize.

It took him a moment to realize what it was.

It was fear.

'Alice,' Tom said. 'This can't be only your decision.'

'It isn't,' she said. 'We're talking about it.'

'Yes, but I'm saying don't do it and you're doing it.'

Alice was still standing by the window. She leaned against the frame. 'DI Wynne said she thinks it could be safe.'

'They advised you not to!' Tom said.

'They said I could.'

'But why would you?'

'It's a big story.'

'And you're at the centre of it and you get a scoop,' Tom said. 'Then afterwards you tell the real story.'

'Right,' Alice said.

'And our safety is less important than this story?'

'No,' Alice said. 'Of course not. But I don't know that our safety is compromised.'

'Of course it is.'

'We don't know that.'

'We don't? We do know this guy's crazy, and that he knows our address and all about us. Isn't that enough?'

'Wynne thought we're – I'm – not the target. There's a ritual. And even if I am, the police will be nearby.'

Tom knew his wife. She had a quiet determination that bordered on stubbornness.

Crossed the border, if truth be told. She could be stubborn to the point of intransigence. She tried not to be – she recognized it as an unpleasant characteristic – but she couldn't help it. In their first house they had argued about the colour they were going to paint the second bedroom. Alice had chosen the colour of all the other rooms, and so he decided to make a final stand about the last room to be painted.

She had refused to compromise, and in the end he had accused her of being stubborn. She had paused, then said, *OK, have your colour.*

He had painted the room, and then, the following Sunday come back from the pub to find it painted the colour she had wanted all along.

And she had that look about her now.

'There's nothing I can say to stop this, is there?' Tom said.

'No,' Alice replied. 'Not really.'

'Jesus,' Tom said. 'How did they get our address? And Joanna's name?'

'An address is easy to get,' Alice said. 'And they could have found out about Jo from your Facebook. That's why I don't have it. People post way too much personal information on there. Middle names, birthdays, kids' birthdays, favourite teachers, holiday dates and destinations. All that stuff used to be secret.'

'I'll close mine down.'

Alice looked at her watch. 'I have to go. The press conference is starting. Will you be OK with Jo?'

Tom closed his laptop. 'I'll be fine. And Alice – be careful, OK?'

'I will,' she said. 'Don't worry.'

Ambleside, 2013

Alice

Ned had left before breakfast, but he did not make it far before he contacted her.

> It's not too late. I'm at Oxenholme and can get a train back

It was at Oxenholme that the local train changed to the mainline, and he clearly saw it as the last chance to salvage their holiday.

Alice read the message and slipped the phone back into her pocket. If he asked she could say she had missed it.

'Was that Ned?' Brenda said. They were sitting on the bank of a river – the Rothay, a plaque said – their feet in the water.

'Yep,' Alice said. The sun was already high and hot and she reached down to cup some water in her hands to splash on her face. Despite the sun the water was cold; she had swum in the lake two days earlier and it had taken her breath away. 'He's offering me one more chance.'

'You interested?'

'I don't think so,' Alice said. 'It's weird, but it's like I'd known for a while that it was over, but I hadn't realized it. Once I saw it, it was obvious, and I went from feeling like I was in a relationship that was a bit wonky, to being totally sure it was finished. And now I just feel relief. I feel *light*.'

Her phone buzzed again and she took it from her pocket.

'Let's try again,' she read. 'What we have is too precious to throw away like this.'

She shook her head.

'I don't recognize those feelings, Brenda. I see that message and I disagree. Whatever we had died long ago. Things were good – great, even – at the start, but it's not been working for a while. And worse, it's not recoverable. We're not right for each other.'

'I doubt Ned agrees,' Brenda said.

'I know. But he's going to have to.'

Another message flashed on the screen.

Why are you ignoring me? What have I done to deserve this?

'He's persistent, I'll give him that,' Brenda said. She lit a cigarette. 'And a bit of a baby.'

'He's not all bad,' Alice said. 'He's a nice guy, really.' She typed a reply.

I'm not ignoring you. I'm out walking.

I don't have to leave. I could come back

I don't think that's a good idea

Alice, I love you, and I know you love me. I'm sorry for

131

being like I was but let's move on. I promise it won't happen again

This was the moment when, for Ned, this would turn from a bump in the road to the end of their relationship.

I'm sorry Ned, but it's over

She re-read the words, then hit send, and put her phone face down on the grass.

'Well,' she said. 'I feel like a right bitch now.'

'What did you say?'

'Not to come back. That we're done.'

'Congratulations,' Brenda said. 'That takes guts. But it's better to be honest. And now you've got three more nights out with me!'

'I was thinking about that,' Alice said. 'And I've got a spare bed in my room now. You could move in?'

Brenda grinned. 'Why not? Travel in style for a change. We can split it.'

Alice shook her head. 'That's OK. I was paying for it anyway. Just buy me a drink.'

'You sure?'

'Sure.'

She grabbed her phone. There were two more messages from Ned, as well as a missed call. She ignored them and pressed the camera icon, then held it up and leaned towards Brenda.

'Say cheese,' she said, and took the photo.

Alice lay on the bed, a bottle of beer between her thighs. She and Brenda had stopped in a small supermarket on the way home from a swim in Rydal Water and picked up some drinks and hotdogs to, as Brenda put it, 'pre-game it', before they went out.

They had heated up the hotdogs in the youth hostel kitchen and headed up to the room to get ready; Brenda was in the shower.

Alice sipped her beer, aware that she was smiling. A lazy day mooching about in the sun, then a purposeless dip in a lake, with cheap hot dogs for dinner and beer in the room: Ned would never have agreed to spend a day doing that.

It would have been a waste. The beers would have to be some kind of special Lakeland ale, dinner had to be an event, the day had to be spent wisely.

And there was a place for Ned's approach. She appreciated his interest in going places and seeing things and making sure nothing was wasted, but what he didn't see was that relaxing and doing nothing wasn't necessarily a waste.

It was *fun*. And that was enough.

She sat up and reached into her rucksack for her phone. She had heard it buzzing in there all day but had ignored it. She felt bad for Ned, but she couldn't answer all his calls and reply to all his messages. It would set a precedent she couldn't live up to.

She felt a mixture of sympathy and annoyance when she saw the missed calls – nine of them – and the multitude of messages. He needed to back off. She dismissed them and opened Facebook.

Nellie had posted a photo of her and Mads in front of the Sydney Opera House.

Tourist photo cliché, but it really is amazing!

God, she wished she'd gone with them. She couldn't blame Ned – in the end she was her own person and so she should have gone, but that didn't stop her resenting him for making it so difficult. In many ways that had been the beginning of the end. Looking back, the signs were there, but that was when she first started to really feel trapped.

She opened a message thread to Nellie.

133

Hi! Glad you're having a good time. Me and Ned broke up (don't worry, I'm not sad – I know, weird, right??? I'll tell all later.) so I'm in Ambleside alone. With new friends, actually. One Aussie called Brenda. Photo attached. Have a great trip and safe travels. Tell Mads hi. Love you both. Axxx

She attached the photo of her and Brenda by the river. It was a lovely photo: the trees were a deep green, sunlight sparkled off the river, she was smiling – she looked a little tired, but happy.

It was a new her. Her first day post-Ned. It was worth recording.

She finished her beer and got up to grab another. They were on the floor next to the bunk bed where Brenda was going to sleep. Alice bent down and picked one up, then reached for the bottle opener.

It was on the bed, next to a bottle cap, and Brenda's keys to the room.

They were in a clear plastic pouch, with her name on it.

Brenda Yates.

Alice opened the beer and sat on the bed. She typed Brenda's name into Facebook. A list of profiles came up, so she filtered on location.

Perth, Australia.

Alice scrolled back a few posts. She was interested to see Brenda back home – who her friends were, what she did, what her house was like. There was a photo of her with three other women, all about the same age. They were sitting around a pub table, plastic cups of beer stacked on it.

She pinched the screen to zoom in on Brenda.

It wasn't her.

It wasn't the same woman. She looked like Brenda – same

134

long blonde hair, same tan – but it wasn't her. They were similar – could have been sisters – but it was clearly not the Brenda who was in the shower.

It was a different Brenda Yates. It happened quite a lot – when you had the entire population of a city to choose from, it wasn't a surprise to find two people with the same name.

The shower stopped and she heard Brenda moving about in the bathroom. Would it be weird to show her the other Brenda's profile? She might think Alice was stalking her. But then again, people searched for other people on Facebook all the time.

Still, it was a bit creepy. And it was no more than an odd coincidence. Alice remembered what her maths teacher, Mrs Noble, had once explained to the class – coincidences should be expected. If you baked a cake, the raisins weren't evenly distributed in the cake. They clustered – and events did the same. You could never know *what* the coincidence would be, but you should expect coincidences to happen.

And that was what was going on here. It was a coincidence that there were two people called Brenda Yates from Perth, and there was no point making Brenda think she was stalking her by showing the Facebook page to her.

But she could ask some questions. She was going to be a journalist after all. Asking questions was in her nature.

Brenda came out of the bathroom in jeans and a tank top. She was lean and muscular; there was a sense of hidden strength in the way she moved.

'Beer?' Alice said.

Brenda turned to her; her expression was flat and emotionless, and, for a moment, there was an odd look in her eyes. Contempt, almost.

'Shit, yeah,' Brenda said, and smiled. 'Sounds perfect.'

135

'Are you on Facebook?' Alice said. 'I was looking at my friends. The ones in Australia.'

'Where are they?'

'Sydney. They took a photo at the Opera House.'

'Of course they did.' Brenda opened a beer and took a swig. 'And no, I'm not on Facebook. Can't stand it.'

'Really? It's a great way to keep in touch.'

'Too public for me,' Brenda said. 'I don't want the world knowing where I am and what I'm doing.'

'You can change the settings so only your friends can see what you post. Or your family. Your parents would be interested.'

'You've not met my parents.'

Alice hesitated. She did not like to interfere in other people's lives; her mum had had a friend, Pru, who gave unsolicited advice on everything from politics to choice of car to home decoration. Her technique was to introduce a subject and then link it to the topic she wished to give advice on – *I was reading an interior design article yesterday and thought of your living room. You could put the couch by the window and paint the walls purple* – and then from then on you were fighting a tide of well-meaning but unwelcome advice.

After Pru had been at the house, Alice's mum used to sit at the dinner table and go through all the advice she'd been given; any time anyone else did it, it was called 'doing a Pru', and Alice had decided never to do a Pru.

But sometimes you needed to, and maybe it was OK, if you trod carefully.

'I don't want to poke my nose in where it's not wanted,' she said. 'So take this as me offering a different perspective – but I'd give anything to see my parents again. Whatever's between you, it might be worth putting it in the past.'

Brenda closed her eyes. 'I'm sorry. That was insensitive. And you're not poking your nose in. But really – you don't know my parents. They're not like yours. I'm better off on my own.'

'OK,' Alice said. 'We should get going. The others'll be in the pub already.'

They walked along the road towards the youth hostel. The night was warm and soft in the moonlight.

Hendrik and Clara were ahead of her; Brenda and Lizzie were a few steps behind them, the smoke from their cigarettes drifting back to her and Donny.

'So,' he said. 'Hendrik and I leave tomorrow.'

'Where are you going?'

'Back to Rotterdam. We came to Hull on the boat and visited Durham and Northumberland and Newcastle.' He raised an eyebrow. 'Newcastle is famous in Holland for nights out and now I know why.'

'You had fun?'

'Maybe not the right word. We had an *experience*.'

'I bet you were popular with the Geordie girls.'

He wagged his head from side to side. 'It was a bit' – he paused, searching for the right word – 'intimidating.'

Alice laughed. 'I can imagine.'

They were approaching a path that led to a park by the lake. Donny pointed to it.

'Shall we walk to the water?'

She hesitated, then shrugged. 'Why not? It's your last night.'

The path led between two old stone walls and emerged onto another road. They crossed it and walked through a gate and into the park. There was a rocky outcrop by the edge of the lake and they headed towards it.

Donny sat down, took his flip-flops off and put his feet in the water.

'Sorry,' he said. 'I am polluting your clean English lake with my feet.'

137

'I think it'll be OK.' She sat next to him. 'I might do the same.'

'But your feet are not smelly like mine.'

'You don't know that.'

He nodded. 'True. But I am guessing.'

'As it happens I have very smelly feet. Quick, hold your nose, I'm taking off my shoes.' He laughed and pinched his nose while she slipped off her shoes and dangled her feet in the lake. 'There you go. Safe now.'

He peered into the water. 'Hmm,' he said. 'Maybe you're right. I see a dead fish.'

'Told you.'

'Well. The world is full of surprises,' he said. 'Who would think such a beautiful person could smell so bad she kills fish?'

'All part of life's rich tapestry.'

He shifted so they were a little closer, his hip touching hers, and put his arm around her shoulder. She leaned against him. It felt odd to be touching someone other than Ned, but it was strangely comfortable.

'I like you, Donny,' she said. 'It's a shame you're leaving tomorrow.'

'Yes,' he said. 'But always we will have this memory.'

He tilted his head to face her. She looked into his eyes and was struck by how blue they were, and how they were not Ned's eyes, which was weird, it really was, and then they were kissing.

The kiss lasted a long time. How long she didn't know, but kissing time was not like normal time. Sixty seconds of normal time was nothing; think of all the minutes that slipped by unnoticed, waiting for an appointment or idly surfing the web or passing the time of day with someone. But sixty seconds of kissing time was at once an eternity and gone in an instant.

'Wow,' she said. 'That was unexpected.'

'But nice, I hope.'

'Very nice.'

And then they were kissing again.

They parted at the bottom of the stairs. She wasn't ready for anything more than a kiss; Donny didn't suggest anything more.

'Goodnight,' he said. 'Perhaps we will see each other some time.'

'Maybe I'll come to Holland,' she said, although she knew that, even if she did, she would not seek Donny out. The kiss belonged to this night, and it fit perfectly. She wanted to preserve the memory as it was.

'You are welcome anytime,' he said. 'Good luck, Alice.'

Wednesday, 18 August 2021

Alice

'CRUCIFIX' KILLER COULD STRIKE AGAIN
By Alice Sark

The police confirmed in a press conference yesterday that they believe the Crucifix Killer is still a threat and may strike again soon.

Detective Inspector Jane Wynne urged the public to take precautions and avoid being out alone late at night, particularly in remote locations. 'We understand that life goes on, but there is a dangerous predator out there and, until they are caught, we would advise members of the public to be careful.'

When asked whether the fact the police were saying this now meant they had some indication the killer may strike again soon, DI Wynne clarified that there were no specific reasons. She added that 'in our experience, the gap between crimes often shortens, and we are concerned that is also true in this case.'

Speculation continues about the significance of the

folded arms and the crucifix. At the press conference, Professor Bob Collins, a noted criminal psychologist, said that, in addition to any religious significance, it indicated a narcissistic personality type.

'These symbols often suggest that the criminal has a grandiose self-image, typical of someone with Narcissistic Personality Disorder. It is important we remember that this is a disorder: at root they are no different to anyone else suffering from a mental illness.'

Whatever the truth, we can conclude that behind these delusions of grandeur, the Crucifix Killer is no more than a low criminal.

Tom

'Twenty Marlboro Lights,' Tom said. The cashier in the petrol station reached for the cigarettes and handed them over.

'Any petrol?' he said.

'No. Just the smokes. Oh, and a lighter, if you've got one.'

The man took a plastic lighter from a box by the till and scanned it, then handed it and the Marlboro Lights to Tom.

Tom headed for his car and drove off the forecourt. There was a reservoir nearby with a path around the edge. He pulled up, climbed out of the car, and set off around the water.

There was a bench on the far side. He sat down and unwrapped the cellophane from the packet. He hadn't smoked since before Joanna was born, but in the office he had been overwhelmed by a craving for a cigarette.

There was no doubt it was triggered by the stress. They were in danger, he was sure of it. He didn't care what anyone said about rituals and communication games, or what normally happened in cases like this. There was no normal. They were way outside of the normal. Nothing applied.

Other than the fact that a serial killer had sent a letter to his wife about an article she had written.

A letter that had come to their house.

So they *were* in danger. All it took was for someone capable of crimes of this magnitude to know you existed for you to be in danger. For them to be interested in you, however tangentially, was, as far as he was concerned, about as bad as it got.

And he blamed Alice for choosing to do it. She could have walked away, but the story was more important to her. To him it was hard to believe that anything could be more important than the safety of her family, but it seemed it was, and he hated that.

He understood why, he saw the appeal of the story, but he hated it.

His phone rang. It was Scott.

'Hi,' he said.

'Busy?' Scott said. 'Where are you?'

'At the reservoir.'

'At the what?'

'The reservoir.'

'What are you doing there?'

'Having a smoke.'

'Mate,' Scott said. 'Are you OK?'

'A bit preoccupied, actually.'

'Is that all?'

'Yes and no. You free tonight? I could do with a beer.'

Scott paused. 'Sounds good. I have to drop something off at home after work. Six p.m. at the London Bridge?'

'Six is perfect.'

'See you then. And enjoy the ciggies.'

Tom ended the call and sent a message to Alice.

Home a bit late. Going to the pub after work. Does that work?

143

She replied immediately.

> I arranged to meet Kay this evening. Could you go
> tomorrow?

She'd arranged to see Kay? Then why hadn't she told him?
He dialled her number.

'Hi,' she said. 'Did you get my message? Sorry about that.'

'Why didn't you mention it?' he said. 'I made a plan with
Scott.'

'I was going to.'

'Great. That's really helpful.'

'Tom,' she said. 'I made a plan to see a friend.'

'When?'

'Tonight.'

'Not when are you going to see her, when did you make
the plan?'

'Kay called this morning.'

'And you didn't think to tell me?'

'I haven't seen you!'

'You could have called! Or sent a message!' He took a
deep breath to try to fight the mounting anger. 'Then I
wouldn't have made plans.'

'I'm sorry. I didn't know I had to inform you of every
movement I make.'

'You may not have noticed, Alice, but we share a life. We
have a child. It's not about informing me of what you're
doing for the hell of it – it's about managing our shared
responsibilities.'

'I think you need to calm down,' Alice said. 'This is a bit
of an overreaction.'

'Is it? Or is it a perfectly natural reaction to someone who
does whatever the fuck she likes, despite the consequences

for her family? Provoke a serial killer to help her journalistic career? Why not?'

'Is that what this is about? Because we discussed this, and agreed the risk is minimal.'

'According to the police, who want you to do it. Hardly impartial advisers, are they?'

'We can talk about this later,' Alice said. 'You go out tonight and I'll see you when you get back.'

'So you're cancelling Kay?'

'No. Don't worry about it.'

'What about Jo? What will we do with her?'

'She's at home with Martha now. Maybe Martha can stay later.'

'Where are you?'

'I'm working in Sliders.'

'Sliders?'

'The café in Penketh. I often come here. Anyway, I can ask Martha if she's free this evening.'

'And if she isn't?'

Alice paused. 'I'll drop her off with your mum. It'll be fine. I'll let you know what I arrange.' She ended the call abruptly.

He wanted to hurl his phone into the water, but he stopped himself. It would be satisfying, but he'd regret it when he had to foot the bill for a new one.

He closed his eyes, his heart racing. For the first time in their marriage he wondered whether he'd be better off without Alice, whether they simply weren't compatible.

No. It was just the stress.

But it was not a happy thought.

The Baby

It is such a strange thing. Most of the time it is just there, something to be dealt with, but when you stop and look at it, you see how odd it is.

It is hard to believe it is human. It does not think or speak or feel like a human. It does not have plans. It does not have any sense of who it is.

It merely has a sensation – hunger, or cold – and it cries so that someone alleviates it. Like a drunk or an addict, it has only needs.

You understand all about needs.

That is not what it is to be human.

That is what it is to be an animal.

And animals can be eaten or harnessed or exterminated if it is to a superior being's benefit.

Humans can too, as far as you are concerned, but you know many others disagree. But animals? Yes, there are those who wish to protect them, but the majority of people eat their morning bacon without giving a second thought to the pig who died to provide it.

It is a failure of logic, as far as you are concerned: that bacon could come from another animal – a dog, or cat – and they would be up in arms. But what's the difference?

146

It could come from another human.

Why are people so squeamish about that? It is just meat. If you can eat a pig you can eat a human. You would, without a second thought.

You have often thought you would like to feed people human flesh, then tell them afterwards – days later, so they could not vomit it up – what they had eaten.

That is for another day.

Now you have to deal with this baby.

It is worse than an animal. It cannot move or feed itself or do anything animals can do from the day they are born.

Does it even feel pain, really? People ask the same of animals. Of fish.

They do feel pain. You know this from personal experience. If you burn a dog with a cigarette butt there is no doubt it feels pain.

And it learns. It learns to avoid cigarette butts.

Could a baby learn the same?

You circle its thigh with your thumb and forefinger. It's flesh is soft and fat.

You squeeze. It does not react.

You squeeze a bit harder. Your pulse is racing. Its face screws up.

You squeeze a bit harder. This will leave a mark, but that's OK.

It starts to cry. It feels pain, that is clear.

And it is very satisfying to witness.

Alice

They had arranged to meet in the Red Lion; Tom would be in the London Bridge and Alice didn't want to run into him. She was a few minutes late – Martha wasn't free so she had dashed to Tom's parents' to leave Jo with them and Roland – and when she arrived Kay was already sitting at a table in the corner, two glasses of white wine in front of her.

'Got you a drink,' Kay said. 'Save you going to the bar.'

'Thanks.' She raised her glass and they clinked them together. 'Cheers.'

'How's Jo?' Kay said. 'And Tom?'

'They're fine.'

'You still worried about him?'

'A bit.' She sipped her drink. 'Quite a bit, actually.'

'Tell me more.'

'I worry he's not coping well. We had a blow-out row earlier.'

'What about?'

'Me coming out tonight.'

'I didn't think he was the possessive type?'

'He's not. It's more that I didn't tell him we'd arranged it.'

'We only decided on it this morning. There wasn't much time to tell him.'

'I know,' Alice said. 'But he didn't think that. He had his own plans. Anyway, I dropped off Jo at his mum's place, so we can both go out.'

'Sounds like a normal married couple's argument to me,' Kay said. 'Having a baby's stressful.'

'It's more than that,' Alice said. 'That's what bothers me. It's like he's fighting to keep it together. I'm worried he'll crack. And I'm worried what he might do when he does.'

Tom

Was he being unreasonable?

It was hard to know. He had no experience of figuring out what the right approach was when your wife was contacted by a serial killer and you were seriously sleep deprived and wondering whether the cause of your sleep deprivation – your beautiful baby daughter – was safe.

He had overreacted to her going out, that was for sure, but it hadn't only been about that. It was her decision to keep writing about the Crucifix Killer. She was so sure that the cops were right and they were safe that she was prepared to take the risk, but how *could* she be so sure? He suspected that the real reason was that she *wanted* it to be true, so she didn't have to stop.

Which wouldn't help him sleep any easier.

He turned into his parents' drive and pulled up. He'd only had one beer with Scott, but he felt like he could fall asleep at any moment.

He rang the doorbell, and his mum opened the door. She put a finger to her lips.

'She's sleeping. And so's your dad. Come in. I'll make you some tea?'

'Not at night, Mum. It keeps me awake.'

'Not me, it doesn't. I can't sleep without tea.'

'You can't wake up without it, either.'

'True,' she said. 'It works both ways.'

'It doesn't, Mum.'

'I think it does.'

'Science would disagree,' he said.

'I don't doubt it would,' she said. 'But it works for me. How are you?'

'Tired.'

'Have you been drinking? You smell of beer.'

'Just one, Mum.'

She looked at him through narrowed eyes. 'I hope so, if you're driving my granddaughter home.'

'She's my daughter as well,' Tom said. 'I'm hardly going to put her in harm's way.'

Unlike my wife, he thought. He wanted to tell his mum what was going on, but he did not want to worry her.

'All right. I'll go and get her. She's upstairs with Roland.'

He nearly shouted at her. She was with Roland? But he didn't need any more friction in his life, and he had agreed to give Roland a second chance.

He waited by the front door. A few minutes later, Roland came downstairs. He was holding Joanna in his arms.

'I'm getting better at this,' he said. 'I'm not scared I'll drop her any more.'

'You want to put her in the car seat?' Tom said. 'I'll open it up.'

He walked outside and opened the back door then stepped aside. Roland leaned down and placed Joanna in the car seat. Her eyes flickered open for a moment, then she settled back to sleep.

'What do I do now?' Roland said.

'Put those straps over her arms, then plug them into that clasp.'

151

Roland picked up one of the straps and pulled it over Joanna's shoulder. 'I don't think that's right,' he said.

'You have to put her elbow through.'

Roland tugged her arm, trying to put it through the strap. Joanna twisted away and he tried to hold her down in the seat. Her face screwed up and she started to cry.

'Roland!' Tom said. 'You have to be gentle! You can't twist her into the seat!'

Roland backed away, his hands up. 'I'm sorry. I'm new to this.'

Tom pushed past him and buckled Jo in. 'Forget it. I'll see you later.'

He climbed into the driver's seat and put the key in the ignition. Roland walked into the house, his head bowed.

'Fuck it,' Tom said. 'The sooner this day is over, the better.'

Alice was at home when he returned. She was watching a wildlife documentary, a mug of herbal tea in her hand.

He sat next to her. Jo was asleep and he rested her on his chest.

The tension was thick. He glanced at her, but her eyes were fixed on the screen.

'OK,' he said. 'Let's talk. Me first. I'm sorry. I was tired and grumpy, and I shouldn't have snapped.'

She muted the TV.

'Thank you,' she said. 'I'm sorry too. How was the pub?'

'You know. Fine. Kay OK?' It was a joke he made every time he asked about Kay. Alice rolled her eyes.

'She's good.'

'I saw Mum. And Roland. He nearly dislocated Jo's arm putting her in the car seat.'

Alice sat up in alarm. 'Really? What happened?'

'It was an accident. He doesn't know what he's doing.

152

But it made me think. What if he had a similar accident, when Jo was at Mum and Dad's?'

Alice nodded. 'It's not impossible.'

'No. That's what worries me.'

'You think he bruised her?'

'Not deliberately. I think he may have tried to pick her up and nearly dropped her and then held her too tightly.'

Alice pursed her lips. 'You need to talk to him.'

'He'll think I'm accusing him.'

'You'll have to be sensitive.'

'Great. My strong point.'

Alice sipped her tea. 'Since we're on the topic of Roland, why don't you finish the story? You never told me the end.'

'OK,' Tom said. 'Strap yourself in.'

Summer, 2012

Tom

I'd found the watch he'd asked for – a rectangular gold thing he'd somehow ended up with – and so a week after the gig – if you could call it that – I was standing in a dimly lit corridor outside the door to his flat. No one had answered my knock; then again it was before midday and even I was not naïve enough to think they'd all be up at the crack of dawn. Early to bed, early to rise, makes a man healthy, wealthy and wise: true as they may be, these were not words that my brother lived his life by.

I tried the handle; the door opened. The air inside was stale and had a rank smell, like body odour but more acrid. It smelled unhealthy and I wanted to get out of there. There was a half-open door to the left through which I could see a messy kitchen table. Ahead was one door; to the right was another.

Two rooms, four people, I thought. Don't want to get the wrong one.

'Hello?' I said. 'Hello?'

A minute later I heard a cough from the door to my right.

'Who is it?'

It was Roland's voice. Thank God he was there. I could give him the watch and get out of there. The smell, the darkness, the whole atmosphere of the place put me on edge. Without thinking, I opened the bedroom door.

'It's me,' I said.

Roland was lying on a bare mattress in the corner of the room. On the floor at the foot of the mattress was an empty bottle of Vladivar vodka and an ashtray stuffed with cigarette butts. The table by the bed was covered with foil squares, blackened where they'd been burned.

Roland was naked, and he was not alone. There was a girl lying next to him, asleep, her head resting on her outstretched arm. She too was naked.

'Fuck!' Roland said. 'Get the fuck out of here!'

He grabbed a sheet which was crumpled against the wall and threw it over the girl, covering her head as well as her body.

It was too late. I may only have had a couple of seconds to look at her, but that was enough for me to see that it was my – our – cousin. Roland was in bed with Chrissy.

I stood outside the room, my heart pounding.

Oh. My. God.

The door opened and Roland stepped out. He had put on a pair of jeans. His eyes were red.

'Kitchen,' he said. He sat at the table. 'Put the kettle on, would you? Tea's in the cupboard. There's no milk.'

I filled the kettle and put it on the hob. There was a mug in the sink. It was from New York, and was stained brown with tannin. I dropped in a teabag and waited for the kettle to boil.

'Jesus,' he said. 'You didn't see that, all right?'

See what, exactly? That Chrissy was using heroin as well? That her and Roland were sleeping together? Were they

155

sleeping together, in the sense of having sex, or were they just sleeping in the same bed? Was she taking heroin? I didn't really know.

'Don't tell anyone.' He held my gaze. 'Promise?'

I wish I'd made a different decision; things might have worked out better then, but I didn't. I should have, but I didn't. I have three excuses. One, he was my brother. Two, I didn't really know what I'd seen, so what would I tell someone – someone being my parents? Three, what the fuck was I supposed to do?

'I promise,' I said.

'You probably shouldn't come round here again.'

I nodded and handed him his tea.

'Thanks,' he said. 'See you round.'

'Yeah. See you.' I walked towards the door.

'Hey,' he said. 'Have you got the watch?'

The watch. Of course. I put it on the table.

'Nice one,' he said.

They were the last words he said to me for more than five years.

Families are places of half-hidden secrets. People would prefer to keep them fully hidden, but when you live in such close proximity they spill out, in overheard conversations or muttered asides. That meant that I never really knew what was going on with Roland and Chrissy, but I heard enough to piece it together. He had introduced her to heroin (Mo's version: got her hooked on that shit), she had left school (Mo, again: thrown away her education because of that bastard) and was living in his flat and working a series of low-paid jobs (Mo: working her fingers raw to support that useless piece of trash). I also knew that Dad had fallen out with his only sister about it all. She blamed him. I suppose we all need someone to blame.

I had a secret of my own, though, or at least I thought I

did. They knew about the heroin and the jobs and the shared flat. What they didn't know about was the shared bed. How could I be sure they didn't, in this world of half-truths? Because I was there when they found out.

One day – about a year since I'd last seen Roland – I went round to see Dad. He was in the garden, and there was a woman there with him.

It was my Aunt Mo.

'Arthur!' Mo was a woman who could work up to quite a pitch from an apparently calm start. The fact she was already shouting was not a good sign. 'We need to talk.'

'Do you want some tea?' Dad said.

'No, I bloody don't.'

'Is everything OK, Mo?'

There was a long pause. When she spoke she was screaming. 'That bloody son of yours! He's —' Her words were choked off by a sob.

'He's what?'

'She's pregnant, Arthur.' She must have sat down; the garden chair scraped on the patio. 'Your son – Roland—'

'It's not him, is it?'

'Aye.'

'How do you know?'

'She told me. She says they're in love.'

'Good God. She's his cousin!'

'What are we going to do?'

'I don't know,' Mo said. 'I have no bloody idea.'

In the end, most stories are quite simple, when you look at them from a distance. They tried to get her to have an abortion; she refused. In the end it didn't matter; she had a miscarriage anyway. Heroin use and pregnancy don't mix that well. I talked to Mum about it: *It's a mercy*, she said. *Poor girl, but it's a mercy.* They tried to get her off drugs – I think they'd given up on Roland – but they failed. She was on a slippery slope, and she stayed on it. I doubt the miscarriage helped; junkies tend to find it harder to kick the habit when they need what it offers more than ever.

And that was it, really. Chrissy died a year or so later. Overdosed. Another statistic; another life thrown away.

Dad saw Roland one more time, Mum told me later. The evening he heard Chrissy had died he went out. When he came back his right hand was wrapped in a piece of cloth. I went home the next day and his knuckles were red and swollen.

Mo never spoke to Dad again. Like I said, we need someone to blame, and she blamed him. We went to Mo's funeral, a few years later. It was the only time I'd ever seen Dad cry.

Wednesday, 18 August 2021

Tom

Telling the story had brought it all back, but in telling Alice what had happened, he had remembered something else.

He had remembered the feeling that everything he had thought his life was made of, everything he had thought his family was, was falling apart around him. On the Sunday evening after Chrissy's funeral he had sat in his flat getting ready to go to work the following Monday, and he had realized that his colleagues would see this bright, professional, committed person and have no idea what was happening in his life.

His wayward but charming brother was a wreck, his dad and his aunt were no longer speaking, his mum was withdrawn and nervy, and his cousin – brilliant, beautiful Chrissy, who had had the whole word at her feet – was dead.

It was not a feeling he ever intended to experience again.

'So,' he said. 'That's why I'm a bit tentative about allowing Roland back into my life.'

'I can see that,' Alice said. 'And why you might think he could have hurt Joanna, accidentally or otherwise.'

'But if Dad wants it' – he shrugged – 'I suppose I can go along with it.'

'You don't have to.'

'I don't want to. I lost my faith in' – he searched for the right word – 'stability, I guess. I'd always thought that things moved along slowly, bits and bobs changed here and there, but for the most part they stayed the same. But the whole episode taught me that life is fragile. You think you have all these structures around you – relationships, jobs, institutions, even your own beliefs and principles – but they can all vanish in an instant.' He took her hand in his. 'But you'd know all about that.'

She frowned at him. 'What do you mean?'

'Your parents. The car crash.'

'Oh,' she said. 'Right. I guess I never thought of it in those terms. It was just something that happened.'

'Did you ever see a therapist about it?'

She nodded. 'A bit, early on. It was helpful, kind of. Did you?'

'No. No one ever offered it. It was swept under the carpet.'

'Until now.'

'Yeah,' he said. 'Until now.'

Joanna lay in the crook of his arm, her eyes wide open. It was dark outside, the warm summer air drifting in through an open window. He heard a group of people walking past the house, laughing and joking on their way back from the pub.

He moved into the living room, away from the noise.

'Come on,' he muttered. 'Come on, baby girl. Go to sleep.' He rocked her gently. She smiled and made a gurgling sound. It was adorable, but it was not what he was hoping for. She didn't look like she had any interest in sleeping.

Which was unfortunate. His mind was fogged; it was an

odd sensation, almost like his thoughts were heavy and slow moving.

'Well,' he said. 'You're a night owl, that's for sure. I suppose I'm going to have to be one as well for a while. The only problem is that my job takes place in the day and I'm too tired to do it.' He kissed her warm forehead. 'But it'll pass. One day I might even miss this.'

'You might,' Alice said, from behind him. 'But then again, you might not.'

She came up and put her arms around his waist. She yawned into his neck. 'Nearly 1 a.m.,' she said. 'My turn.'

'Did you sleep?' Tom asked.

'Out like a light at nine,' she said. 'So nearly four hours.'

'I'll set the alarm for five,' Tom said. 'See you then.'

'OK.' Alice squeezed him tighter. 'Let's not argue, all right?'

'Sounds good to me. I'm sorry about getting mad at you.'

'Don't be. It's a difficult time.' She kissed him and let go. 'I'm going to the loo. Then you can go up.'

He waited for her on the couch, then handed Joanna to her and went upstairs. He lay on his bed, feeling the warmth where Alice's body had been. He had just enough time to think *I'm going to be asleep in seconds,* and then he was asleep.

Mike Andrew

He didn't know much, but he knew he was in love. He'd met Diane at a pub in town a few weeks back and he'd realized immediately she was different. When he'd told Trent the next day Trent had laughed, and said, *yeah, different because she's interested in you, that's all*, and he had wondered if that was true. Maybe we told ourselves that the person we were with was special, the one for us, because otherwise we'd have to accept they were the same as anyone else, except you simply happened to have met them in a pub.

Either way, he didn't care. Diane was *fantastic*. And she was posh, at least by his standards. She lived with her dad and his girlfriend in Stockton Heath in a detached house, which was twice the size of the place he and his two brothers shared with their mum across the swing bridge in Latchford.

He hadn't taken her home yet. He wanted to make sure she'd really fallen for him before she met his family.

He'd been to her house, but only when her dad was out. Like tonight – except her dad had come home.

Shit, she said. They were on her bed and his T-shirt was on the floor. *You have to go. Out the window.*

Why? I could meet your old man.

162

You don't want to. Not if he's had a drink. Out.
Diane? You home?

Her dad's voice had a harsh, strained tone to it. Mike grabbed his T-shirt and wriggled it on. The kitchen roof was below her window and he could climb onto it, then scramble down somehow.

OK, he said. *Call me.* He kissed her. *Love you.*
Love you too.

He could have floated down to earth on those words. She had said she loved him!

She loved him!

He wanted to run into the house and hug her dad, but no. That was not a good idea. Once he was down he scuttled to the back of the garden and let himself out of the back gate, then headed for home.

He glanced at his phone. It was 2 a.m. He strolled along the middle of the road, grinning from ear to ear. She loved him. She fucking *loved* him.

It was the best night ever. At the bottom of the road he turned left and headed for Lumb Brook, where it headed under the aqueduct. It was dark, and for a moment he thought about the serial killer, but he shook off his anxiety. Nothing could ruin a night like tonight.

There was a car parked to his left. It was a strange place to leave a car; there wasn't much around, but he carried on and walked under the bridge.

The air was cooler there, damp from the canal running overhead. He sped up, just a touch.

And then he heard it. A scuff in the darkness, like a shoe scraping on the ground.

Thursday, 19 August 2021

Alice

Alice fastened the tabs to close the nappy and poppered Joanna's onesie shut. She picked her up and walked into the kitchen. Tom was stacking the dishwasher, a piece of toast dangling from his mouth. He looked exhausted, his eyes red and sunken. At five that morning his alarm had gone off, but he had slept through it, so she had gone into their room to wake him.

She felt bad, but she needed a few hours' sleep before the day started.

'Have a good day at work,' she said. 'Manjit invited us over for a drink this evening.'

'Perfect. It's only next door, so we can take Jo.'

'I'll let her know.'

'Great. See you later. You have plans for today?'

'None yet. Maybe get some work done when Little Miss Cranky allows it.'

He picked up his car keys and kissed her, the kiss dry and perfunctory. In her back pocket, her phone started to ring.

Her arms were full so she nodded over her head. 'See who that is, would you?'

He pulled her phone out and showed her the screen.

'It's Nadia.' She handed Jo to him. 'I'd better take it. Can you hold her?'

'Hey,' Nadia said. 'Can you talk?'

'Sure. Something to share?'

'Oh yes,' Nadia said. 'There's something to share, all right.'

'What is it?' She held up a finger to Tom, as if to say *Give me a minute*. 'Is it the killer?'

'It is.' Nadia paused. 'There's been another one.'

'Another murder?'

'Not a murder,' Nadia said. 'An attempt. But the victim got away.'

'Who was it?'

'A seventeen-year-old boy, walking back to his dad's house in Grappenhall just after 2 a.m. He'd been at his girlfriend's place and her dad came home unexpectedly. He wouldn't have been best pleased to find him there – he doesn't think much of him, apparently – so he scarpered.'

'Where do they live?'

'Lyons Lane. He was walking through Lumb Brook when it happened.'

'How did he get away?'

Tom raised an eyebrow, then looked at his watch.

Alice shrugged, and mouthed *Sorry*.

'The assailant was hiding under the aqueduct – the one the Bridgewater Canal runs over.'

'I know it,' Alice said. 'I know it well.'

'They had a large hammer – maybe a mallet or a smallish sledgehammer, and they jumped him, but he managed to duck out of the way.'

'My God. Is he OK?' Alice said.

'More or less,' Nadia replied. 'He took the blow on his upper arm and it broke the bone. It would have caved his skull in if it had hit. Then he ran.'

'Name?'

'Mike Andrew.'

'Seventeen, you said?'

'That's right.'

Alice grabbed a pen and paper and made some notes. 'What did the attacker do after he ran?'

'They ran, too. He heard a car start up a few seconds later.'

'Did he see it?'

'No. He had run up to the canal towpath heading towards Stockton Heath.' Nadia paused. 'There is one thing, though.'

'Which is?'

'His heard his attacker speak. When they missed, they swore, and he thinks they had an Australian accent.'

'Male?'

'He thinks. So it's possible the killer is an Australian male.'

'There can't be too many of them around,' Alice said.

'Exactly. Anyway, there's going to be a press conference at eleven, when we'll release some of the details I just gave you.'

'Can I put a story out before?'

'No,' Nadia said.

'Then why are you telling me now?' Alice said.

'You can write your story now,' Nadia replied. 'And then as soon as we're done you can release it. You'll be first. And go heavy on the cowardly attack from behind, ambush, et cetera.'

'Got it,' Alice said. 'See you at eleven.'

Alice put the phone down.

'Tom,' she said. 'Is there any chance you can stay at home this morning?'

He didn't reply. He was sitting on the couch, examining Jo's leg.

'Did you see this?' he said.

'See what?'

'Jo's leg.'

'What about her leg?'

'There's a bruise on it. She's got *another* bruise.'

166

DI Wynne

Wynne looked up as the door opened. DS Alexander walked into the incident room and leaned on a table. Behind it on the wall was a map of the area, with the locations of the murders marked on it with coloured pins.

The murders, and now the attempted murder.

'This changes things,' Wynne said. 'This guy's going to be feeling inadequate after botching this killing.'

'You think it'll provoke him?' Nadia said. 'Make him try again?'

'I think there's every possibility.'

Nadia nodded. 'So it's a he, now?'

'Not certain, but yes, it's a reasonable assumption.'

'And an Aussie?'

'I'm not sure about that,' Wynne said. She had been giving it a lot of thought. 'What did Mr Andrew say his attacker said, exactly? In fact, talk me through the whole thing, from when he realized someone was under the bridge.'

'He said he heard a noise – like the scraping of a foot as someone slipped – and then the guy jumped out and tried to hit him with the hammer. He was on edge because of the noise, so he managed to dodge it, at least enough so it only hit his arm. That's when he heard the attacker speak.'

'What did they say?'

'Just "fuck", when the hammer missed.'

'And he thought it was said in an Australian accent?' Wynne pursed her lips. 'Hard to tell from one word, especially a short one, said in exasperation.'

'If it had been "strewth", or something like that, it'd be easier to be sure.'

'Yes,' Wynne said. 'Then Mr Andrew ran?'

'He jumped into the road. The attacker swung at him again, but he ran up to the canal towpath.'

'And the guy didn't chase him?' Wynne said.

'No.'

'Curious. If the attacker thought he'd been heard speaking in an Australian accent, you'd think he wouldn't have wanted Mr Andrew to get away. It's a pretty clear piece of identifying information.'

'Which means he wasn't worried about it,' Nadia said. 'Because he didn't say it in an Australian accent.'

'Or it was deliberate,' Wynne said. 'To make us think the killer is Australian.'

'Or they *are* Australian and it's a double-bluff.'

'Or that,' Wynne said. 'So it's hard to be sure.'

'You could say the same for the gender,' Nadia said. 'Could be a woman speaking in a deep voice.'

'Could be. Which could be why the attacker didn't give chase – not much hope of catching a fit seventeen-year-old boy unless she's very quick.' Wynne stood up. 'On balance, though, I think we're looking for a male, maybe Australian.'

'Or a New Zealander,' Nadia said. 'They sound the same.'

Wynne raised an eyebrow. 'Don't say that to a New Zealander,' she said. 'They'll be mightily offended. It's a good point, though – if our assailant did have an accent, it might not be Australian. Could be London, or American. Hard to tell from one word.'

'So what do we do?'

'Take it at face value, for now,' Wynne said. 'And have a chat to any Australians or New Zealanders we can find.'

Tom

He had emailed his boss and asked her if he could work from home for a few weeks. He didn't specify exactly why – simply mentioned some troubles with his daughter, and that he needed to be with her until this was over.

There was one more loose end to tie up.

He opened his email and composed a message.

Martha,
I wanted to thank you for your help with Jo, but for the moment we won't be needing any assistance. I'll be working from home for a while, so between Alice and me we should be OK. Thank you once again, yours, Tom

Her reply was instant.

Tom
I understand. I hope this is nothing to do with the bruises. If so, I want to state once again that I had no part in them. I enjoyed working with you and spending time with your beautiful daughter, and wish you all the best in the future.
Martha

He didn't reply. What could he say? *No, it's nothing to do with the bruises?* That was a lie, and Martha would know it. *Yes, we think you hurt – or may have hurt – our daughter?* There was no need to say that. So he said nothing.

He sat on the couch, a mug of tea on the coffee table. Jo was asleep on his chest, the sound of daytime TV seeming not to bother her. He ran his finger over the bruise on her leg. It circled her thigh, a red ring with a darkening central band.

How the hell had it happened? It wasn't there yesterday morning, he was sure of that. Almost sure, anyway. It was impossible to be a hundred per cent certain, but he thought he – or Alice – would have noticed. Before she left for the press conference she said she had not seen it, and had no idea where it came from. So it had happened some time later that day, or evening.

Which meant there were a few options.

The first was Martha. Jo had been with her until Alice picked her up and took her to his mum's house. He imagined Jo crying uncontrollably and Martha trying to calm her, growing more and more agitated as she refused to settle, then squeezing her around the thigh.

And Jo screaming even louder.

No. He couldn't believe Martha would do that. He knew appearances could be deceptive, but it didn't fit with anything about her. She was experienced with kids, she was a mum: she wouldn't deliberately hurt a child.

And she would know that if she did it would be obvious. Whoever did this – presuming they knew they were doing it – would know it would leave a mark, and that he and Alice would see it.

So, for now, he would dismiss Martha. That left his mum, who had taken care of Jo before he picked her up, and Roland.

It could not be his mum.

So it was Roland. It had to be him. If he couldn't imagine Martha doing it, then there was no way he could picture his mum hurting her granddaughter. It went against everything he knew of her.

But Roland was different. He was not a bad person, all said. He was not malicious or spiteful or nasty.

But he was – could be – misguided. And he wasn't quite the same as other people. He didn't think the same way.

He could have been high. How did Tom know he was *really* clean? He didn't have a great track record, after all.

Tom could imagine him squeezing Jo's leg to see if it stopped her crying. He could imagine Roland not knowing it would leave a bruise. He could imagine Roland being drunk or high and not knowing what the hell he was doing. He could imagine that because he'd seen it.

And he'd seen Roland twist her arm to get her in the car seat.

He felt a cold dread well up in his stomach. If it was Roland he'd have to stop him seeing Jo, and that meant telling his parents what had happened, and that would break their hearts.

There had to be another explanation. What if there was nothing going on? What if Jo simply bruised easily? That was a thing, right?

Although normally that meant something bad was going on, medically, which was hardly any better.

He reached for his tea. He wished it was something a bit stronger. He was going to have to talk to Roland, and he was not looking forward to it. His brother was not the most stable person, and he couldn't be sure how he would react – it could be indignant anger, disappointed silence, maybe even a return to the drugs.

Whatever it was, though, Tom would have to deal with it. He had to keep his daughter safe. That came above everything else.

172

Alice

Detective Superintendent Marie Ryan coughed and the room fell silent. There were many more people here than for the last press conference – the room was nearly full – and there were tens of faces on the video call.

'Thank you for being here,' she said. 'We have an update on the Crucifix Killer case. Detective Inspector Wynne will give more details, but there's been another attack. This one was different, however. The attacker failed, and the victim escaped.'

A woman sitting a few rows in front of Alice put her hand up.

'Did they see the attacker? Any identification?'

'DI Wynne will address that,' Ryan said. She nodded at Wynne.

'Thank you, Detective Superintendent,' Wynne said. 'The attack took place just after 2 a.m. this morning. The victim, Mike Andrew, seventeen, of Latchford, was walking back to his home from his girlfriend's house. He was walking from Lyons Lane down through Lumb Brook when he was attacked.'

'Where did the attack take place?' a man called out.

'Under the Bridgewater Canal aqueduct,' Wynne said. 'The attacker was waiting there with a large hammer.'

'Any idea how they knew Mr Andrew was coming?' the man asked.

Wynne nodded. 'Mr Andrew reported that he was passed by a car. It's possible this was the attacker, and they stopped up ahead and waited for him.'

'Any details on the car?'

'Dark in colour,' Wynne said. 'But no identification of the make or model. Mr Andrew walked under the aqueduct and was assaulted. He dodged the blow and was able to run away. He suffered a broken arm, and the attacker fled the scene.'

'How is Mr Andrew now?' a woman asked.

'Stable,' Wynne said. 'He's fortunate he did not sustain the blow to his skull. It was a killing blow.'

'Does he remember anything else?'

'He does. The attacker swore, and Mr Andrew indicated that it sounded like a male voice with an Australian or New Zealand accent.'

'So you're looking for an Aussie or Kiwi man?' the woman said.

'That's one line of enquiry,' Wynne replied. 'Mr Andrew could be mistaken. It's hard to identify an accent from one or two words. But we are certainly looking into it.'

Alice raised her hand. 'Are you sure this is the Crucifix Killer? Without the presence of a crucifix, it's not certain, surely? It could be an unrelated assault. A mugging, perhaps.'

'I'll take this one,' DSI Ryan said. 'That's very true. And we've considered it as a possibility. But our conclusion is that this is the same perpetrator.'

'Any further details on why?' Alice said.

'There are other similarities,' Ryan replied. 'In the other three murders, we saw the use of a hammer to inflict fatal head injuries. This was an attempt to do the same.' She folded her arms and leaned forward. 'Let's all remember – crucifixes aside, these are brutal, callous murders, inflicted by a cowardly killer upon innocent members of society. There's nothing special or grand about what this criminal is doing, and they will be caught.'

Alice wrote down the final sentence. It was perfect to close her next story.

'CRUCIFIX' KILLER STRIKES: VICTIM ESCAPES
By Alice Sark

The Crucifix Killer selected another victim in the early hours of this morning, but this time they did not have it all their own way.

The victim, Mike Andrew, 17, was injured by a blow to the arm from a hammer, while walking under the Lumb Brook aqueduct. The blow was intended to strike his head – and would almost certainly have been fatal – but he had heard something as he approached the ambush and managed to avoid it.

Mr Andrew suffered a broken arm but is otherwise unharmed.

The police confirmed in a press conference that they believe this to be an attempted murder by the so-called Crucifix Killer. Despite the absence of the signature crucifix, the use of a hammer to inflict a fatal blow is consistent with the four prior murders.

They also confirmed that Mr Andrew had heard his attacker speak, and believed it to be a male voice, with an Australian accent.

176

If this is correct, it is potentially a valuable lead for the police.

Whatever the truth, the Crucifix Killer has slipped up and revealed what they truly are: a coward who hides in the shadows and attacks their victims from behind.

In the words of Detective Superintendent Marie Ryan. 'There's nothing special or grand about what this criminal is doing, and they will be caught.'

Friday, 20 August 2021

Tom

Tom opened his eyes. Alice was sitting on the bed, her hand on his shoulder.

'Tom,' she said. 'Wake up.'

'What?' he said. 'What is it?' It was dark in the bedroom, darker than normal when he woke up. He looked at the alarm. 3.45.

It wasn't time for him to wake up. He had another hour. More than an hour.

'Alice,' he said. 'I'm sleeping.'

'I was too,' she said. 'Jo's been asleep for a while, for a change. I was on the couch, but something woke me up. You need to come and see it.'

'Where is she now?'

'Downstairs. She's fine. Out like a light.'

He smiled. 'That I do need to see.'

Alice didn't smile back at him. 'This isn't a joke, Tom.'

Her tone was serious, and his adrenaline spiked, waking him up fully. He climbed out of bed and pulled on a T-shirt.

'OK,' he said. 'I'm coming.'

He followed her downstairs and into the living room. Jo was asleep in her basket. There was a dent in the pillow on the couch where Alice had been lying.

'What?' he said. 'I don't see anything.'

'On the table.'

There was an envelope lying on it, the address printed on a home printer. There was no stamp.

'Holy shit,' he said. 'When did that arrive?'

'Just now,' she said. 'I was sleeping and I was woken by the letter box snapping shut. I got up to take a look and this was there.'

'Have you read it?'

She shook her head. 'I don't want to touch it. It'll mess up the forensics. He was *here*, Tom. At our house, in the middle of the night.'

He glanced at Joanna. The serial killer who, one night ago, had tried to kill someone with a hammer, who already had at least four victims, had been at their house, twenty minutes ago.

Tom paused to consider what this meant. It was not only a letter. It was a signal: *I'm getting closer.*

He could have killed them all in their sleep.

'This is crazy,' he said. 'Have you called the police? He could be out there right now. We need the cops here.'

'I'll do it now.' Alice was pale, her expression serious. 'And when they get here we can find out what it says.'

DI Wynne

Wynne was woken by her phone ringing. She looked at her alarm clock and sat up. It was just past four in the morning, and nothing good came from phone calls at that time.

Her sense of foreboding only increased when she saw it was Alice Sark. She had no reason to call Wynne that wasn't related to the killings, at least not at this hour of the morning.

She answered the call.

'Wynne.'

'This is Alice Sark.'

'Has something happened, Ms Sark?'

'Sorry to call so early. I tried Nadia, but she didn't pick up.'

'Not a problem. What is it?'

'Another letter,' Alice Sark said.

Wynne paused. It didn't make sense. 'The post doesn't come until later,' she said.

'It was hand delivered.'

Wynne tensed. 'Hand delivered?'

'Yes. He – or she – was here. At the house.'

'Are your doors and windows secured?' Wynne said.

'I think so.'

'Make sure they are. I'll have an officer there in minutes, and I'll be there as soon as I can. OK?'

'OK,' Alice Sark said. 'Thank you.'

Wynne hung up and called DS Alexander. On the second attempt she picked up. A male voice muttered something in the background and DS Alexander shushed him.

'What is it?' she said, her voice sleepy.

'It's Ms Sark. There's another letter. Hand delivered. I'm going over there now. You don't have to come.'

'I will. Of course.'

'I'll pick you up.'

DS Alexander was outside her house ten minutes later, a mug of coffee in her hand. She climbed into the passenger seat.

'Hand delivered,' she said. 'That's a step up. And quite a risk, with patrol cars going past every ten minutes.'

Wynne nodded. 'It is. It's the killer saying they're in charge, and that ten minutes is enough. They can get to her if they want to.'

'She may need to stop writing about the murders. Take herself out of the firing line.'

Wynne looked up at DS Alexander. 'It may be too late for that.'

Tom

Tom stood behind Wynne, reading the letter over her shoulder. Alice was next to him.

G'day, Alice!

That's what they say Down Under, isn't it? It should be easy for the super-sleuths on the force to find me now. Can't be too many Australian males in the area, after all. I might have to disappear for a while, or DI Wynne will be slapping the cuffs on me!

Or maybe your friend DS Alexander. Nadia. Nice girl. She shouldn't be mixed up in all this.

And neither should you, for two reasons.

First, you don't understand what you are messing with. You don't want to irritate me. You don't know what I'll do.

I don't know what I'll do.

Second – and more importantly – it won't work. I know what the police are getting you to do. Call me a coward, a common criminal, make me angry. Make me slip up, reveal myself.

I am not so foolish, my little lady.

So here's my suggestion: you stop all this. You go back to your husband (an engineer! How charming!) and daughter and forget all about me.

Then I'll forget all about you.

But if you don't – well, I might remember you. You might pop into my mind at just *the wrong time.*

Wrong for you. Right for me: I'll enjoy what I do to you.

But very wrong for you.

G'day!

PS – an Australian male! You lot really are quite something

The letter was unsigned. Tom turned to face his wife, his eyes fixed on hers.

'Alice,' he said. 'This has to stop.'

Ambleside, July 2013

Alice

Brenda handed Alice a plate of scrambled eggs on toast then sat at the table.

'There you go,' she said. 'Soak up some of the hangover.'

'I feel like shit,' Alice said. 'Not enough sleep.'

'Why did you get up so early?'

'I woke up and couldn't go back to sleep,' Alice said. 'So I decided, fuck it, I'll get up.'

'And you got me up too.'

'I didn't mean to!' Alice laughed. 'And if you'd been in the dormitories you'd have been woken up in any case.'

'Fair,' Brenda said. 'What time did you get back in the end?'

'I dunno. Two? Donny and I hung out by the lake for a while.'

'Hung out? Is that a polite English way of saying you did the dirty?'

'No!' Alice felt her cheeks flush. 'A kiss! That was all.'

'He's a nice bloke,' Brenda said. 'Hendrik too.'

'Shame they left,' Alice said. 'Lizzie and Clara went home this morning too.'

'Only us left now,' Brenda said. 'You leave tomorrow?'

'Yeah. I booked a train ticket for the evening. Originally Ned and I were going to spend the day here and then head back to Nottingham.'

'I'm going to Liverpool to meet my friends. I'll head out the same time as you. Anyway, since we're up we might as well do something. Want to go hiking? I can't come all this way and not see the famous mountains of the Lake District.'

'I'd love to,' Alice said. She cut a piece off her slice of toast and lifted it to her mouth. 'Let's ask at reception where we should go.'

The woman at reception smiled. She was a few years older than Alice and had close-cropped red hair and a nose stud. Her name badge read *Sharon*.

'You want something tough?' Sharon said. 'You guys look in pretty good shape.'

'Not *too* tough,' Alice said.

'Well, I'll give you my two favourite walks in Lakeland, and you can decide.'

'Sounds good,' Brenda said. 'Shoot.'

'The first is a cliché,' Sharon said. 'But like a lot of clichés there's a reason they're popular. In this case it's because the walk is spectacular.' She looked out of the window. 'Especially on a day like this.'

'What is it?' Alice said.

'Striding Edge to Helvellyn,' Sharon said.

'That was one my boyfriend – ex, actually – wanted to do,' Alice said.

'He has good taste. Striding Edge is amazing – it's incredibly narrow, with sheer drops, hundreds of feet down, on either side. Then you get to the summit itself.'

'Sounds like the real deal,' Brenda said. 'Is it safe?'

'Someone dies up there every summer,' she said. 'But today's nice and dry. You'll be fine. And it's worth it.'

'What's the other walk?' Alice said.

'It's very different, but just as spectacular. You start at the north-east end of Wast Water and walk around the lake. There's a path up a small fell called Illgill Head which has great views of the lake. It's Lakeland's deepest lake, and the most dramatic, if you ask me. The mountains that surround it are some of the highest in the Lakes, and they drop down – on one side at least – in a sheer slope.'

'I like the sound of them both,' Alice said. 'It's hard to choose.'

'Then let's do both,' Brenda said. 'We can hike Striding Edge today and then go to the other one tomorrow before we leave.'

Sharon pulled a map from a rack behind the counter. 'That's what I'd do,' she said. 'Let me show you the routes.'

They left Patterdale – the start point for Helvellyn – late morning, and headed up a lush green valley, past farm buildings and along a shallow, crystal-clear stream. Sharon had given them an Ordnance Survey map with the route marked in pencil; Alice stopped to look at it.

'I think we head to the right here,' she said. A narrow path snaked up towards a lowering mountain. 'That's where we're going.'

It looked innocuous enough, but it steepened quickly and her thighs started to burn with each step. After a while they came to a stile over a stone wall; Alice climbed over, then paused on the other side.

'Let's take a break,' she said. 'This is tough.'

Alice was breathing heavily, sweat running from her forehead. She was surprised to see Brenda was hardly out of breath. She was fit, lean and muscular, but Alice had not thought she was as strong as this.

They sat against the wall; the stones were warm against their backs. To the left was the valley they had come from;

ahead was a narrow, razor-edged ridge that led to the summit of Helvellyn itself.

'She didn't lie,' Alice said. 'This *is* spectacular.'

'Yeah,' Brenda said. She seemed strangely unmoved. 'It's lovely. Want to keep going?'

Alice swigged some water and got to her feet.

'Let's do it,' she said.

Alice had never been anywhere like Striding Edge. It seemed to stretch on for ever, a narrow ribbon of rock suspended between mountain tops. In parts she felt secure; in other parts the path was only a few feet wide and she was painfully aware of the vertiginous drops on either side. To the right there was a kind of bowl with a small lake – Red Tarn, the map said – visible far below. That side was incredibly steep, but at least you could see where it led. The left dropped into nothingness.

'One slip could be fatal,' she said. 'You'd never be able to stop yourself sliding down.'

'I know,' Brenda said. 'If I ever have a husband I want to get rid of, I'm bringing him here. A little shove in the back when he's not expecting it, and it'll be Goodbye, Mr Chips.'

'Brenda!' Alice said. 'That's awful! I can't believe that's what this majestic scene inspired you to think.'

'I'm a practical type,' Brenda said. 'That's all. And you have to admit, it is an obvious thought.'

Alice didn't think it was that obvious; it was natural to imagine herself falling down, but not her pushing someone who she didn't like off the ridge. However annoying Ned – or anyone – was, she wouldn't push them off a mountain.

She wouldn't be looking for any way to kill anyone.

But whatever. It was probably just Brenda's Aussie sense of humour.

'Maybe,' she said. 'Remind me never to get on the wrong side of you, though.'

'You don't need to worry about that,' Brenda said. 'You'll never be on my bad side.'

They carried on. There was a steep scree slope leading to the summit. It was going to be a tough few minutes, but the rewards would be worth it.

The climb was worth it, and then some. The summit was broad and unexpectedly flat. A woman who was there with her teenage son told them an aeroplane had landed on it some years back. They talked about routes down and she pointed them in the direction of Swirral Edge. It was, if anything, even steeper and more unnerving than Striding Edge, and Alice was quite relieved when they were be back on surer ground.

She was even more glad when they arrived back in Patterdale, and found their way to the White Lion pub.

She sat at a table, her legs aching. Brenda came back from the bar with two pints of dark beer.

'Warm beer,' she said. 'Not sure I could ever get used to it, but when in Rome.'

'Thanks.' Alice took a sip. It was delicious and well-earned. 'What time's the bus?' she said.

'About an hour,' Brenda replied. 'Time to finish these and then we can head back. Then we have to decide what to do tonight.'

Alice took a long drink of the beer. 'Honestly, I think I'll grab something to eat and then crash. I'm exhausted after staying up late, and now this.'

'It's the last night,' Brenda said. 'We have to do something.'

'Let's see how we feel,' Alice said.

'What will you do after you get home?' Brenda asked.

'The lease runs out in three weeks,' Alice said. 'I would have gone to live with Ned, but now I'll have to think of something else.'

'You could travel.'

'Maybe. I'm not sure I want to go alone, though. And Nellie and Mads will have done their travelling.'

'You'd be fine on your own. You'd meet people. Like I have.'

'I know. I'm just not sure it's for me. What will you do?'

'Hang around with my friends for a while. Perhaps head over to Europe.'

'We're *in* Europe!'

'You know what I mean. Paris, Berlin, that kind of thing.'

'And then back to Perth?'

Brenda shook her head. 'No way. I'm never going back there.'

'Why?' Alice said. 'What's so bad there, if you don't mind me asking.'

'Don't mind at all. It's my parents. We don't get along.'

'Any reason in particular?' Alice said.

'Every reason you can think of,' Brenda said. 'And a few more you can't. Let's leave it at that.'

'So where will you go?'

'Melbourne, probably. Got some mates there. I can crash with them, find a job. See what happens.'

'Well,' Alice said. 'You're braver than I am. I need a plan. I can't go with the flow like that. I envy you.'

'Thanks,' Brenda said. 'But you shouldn't envy me. My life's a fucking mess.'

'That why you're here?' Alice said. 'You're running away from something?'

'I sure as shit am,' Brenda replied. 'But then we're all running from something, aren't we?'

Friday, 20 August 2021

Alice

'CRUCIFIX' KILLER MAKES CONTACT: LETTERS
SENT
By Alice Sark

In a shocking development, the Crucifix Killer has made contact with the police – and with me. I have received two letters, both sent to my home.

Why the killer chose me, I have no idea, but choose me they did. The first came a few weeks ago. The second arrived today. Of course, the letters are now in the possession of the police as they could contain vital evidence.

Although the content cannot be revealed, the police confirmed they think the letters are genuine as the author includes details only someone who was present at the crime scenes could be aware of.

It is a chilling development, and shows how confident the killer is that they will not be caught. Tina Rhodes, Professor of Criminal Psychology at Liverpool University, said this is not uncommon in these kind of cases.

'Serial killers often want public attention for their crimes. They suffer from low self-esteem and start killing precisely to bolster their self-image. The crimes themselves become insufficient, and they need to insert themselves into the investigation or control the narrative. One way they do that is by feeding details to the press.'

It seems the killer wants to prove their superiority to those investigating them – and I can confirm that this is the tone of their letters – but it bears repeating: they are a low, common criminal, and they will be caught.

She had written the story first thing and it was on the website by breakfast time.

The first phone call had come an hour later. The *Daily Herald* wanted a feature by the end of the day. They wanted to run it under the headline *Brave Journalist Risks All for Justice – My Experience with the Crucifix Killer*, and they needed it soon.

'So can you do it?' Sid Jones – the editor of the *Herald* – asked.

Sid Jones had emailed, asking for her phone number, then called to pitch the article to her.

Him, pitching to her.

'I can,' she said. 'I'll send it over later.'

'Email it to me direct,' he said. 'I'll be waiting for it. This is the perfect story. The killer was at your house. Once they're caught, there's a best-selling book in this. I know some agents. I can put you in touch, if you'd like?'

'That would be amazing.' She realized she was grinning. 'Thank you.'

'No problem. And send that story asap.'

He ended the call and she got to her feet and walked into the kitchen.

191

'Tom,' she said. 'That was Sid Jones. The editor of the *Daily Herald*.'

He was sitting at the table, a jar of baby food in one hand and green spoon in the other. Jo had orange food smeared around her mouth.

'Really?' He did not smile. 'What did he – or she – want?'

'A story. On the letters.'

He closed his eyes and shook his head slowly. 'I thought we agreed this has to stop.'

'It's the *Herald*,' Alice said. 'It's a national newspaper.'

'And this is our family.'

'He said he'll put me in touch with an agent. About a book.'

'Hopefully you're alive to write it.' He lifted the spoon to Jo's mouth and she ate some more of the orange food. A small globule rolled down her chin.

'Tom. We talked about this. We're not in any danger. I told him no photos of me. Nothing personal at all.'

'A serial killer puts a letter through your door in the middle of the night, and we're not in any danger?' He gave a sardonic laugh. 'What would be danger, in your world?'

'It's not that simple, Tom, and you know it. The letters are a way of getting involved in the investigation. This guy doesn't want to harm me. Serial killers have a specific way of getting their kicks. We're safe, Tom.'

'I don't agree.' He fed the last of the jar to Jo, and put the lid back on. 'But nothing I can say will change your mind. I'm taking Jo for a walk.'

'I'm taking her to the doctor at ten,' Alice said. 'Can you be back by then?'

He nodded.

'See you later. Good luck writing your story.'

Tom

He pushed the stroller through the gates and into the park. Two teenage girls and their boyfriends were in the playground, sitting on the swings and talking. As he approached they stood up and started walking towards him. The girls stopped as they passed him and smiled at Joanna.

'She's gorgeous,' one of them said. 'How old is she?'

'Thank you,' Tom said. 'She's five months.'

'What's her name?' the other said.

'Joanna.'

'That's me aunt's name,' the girl said. 'Aunty Joanna. I like that name.'

'Don't get any ideas,' one of the boys said. 'I'm too young for kids.'

The girl blushed. 'Fuck off, Matty!' she said, then clapped her hand to her mouth. 'Sorry. I didn't mean to swear.'

'It's OK,' Tom said. 'She doesn't understand yet.'

The teenagers headed out of the park and he pushed Joanna over to a bench. He unclipped her and took her out of the stroller and held her on his lap.

'Feel that,' he said. 'Sunshine on your face.'

His phone buzzed. It was a message from Alice.

I know you're worried, but this is a fantastic opportunity.
I can't turn it down

He'd made his position clear. He didn't want to ruin this morning sunshine going over it again. A minute later his phone buzzed again.

I have to go for it. I hope you understand

He typed a reply.

Then go for it. But don't expect me to be happy about it

I don't. But I have to do what I have to do

I get it. But don't be surprised if I do what I need to do.

What's that supposed to mean?

Nothing. Just that I'll take care of myself and my daughter if I have to

He switched off his phone. What had he meant by that message? That he'd leave her if he had to? He was surprised he'd sent it, but it was true. He would take care of Jo.

He had enough to think about without adding an argument with Alice to the list. He was concerned about the bruises, mainly. They'd made an appointment to discuss any possible medical causes. So hopefully they'd be able to rule those out.

Which would leave him one step closer to knowing what was going on.

Alice

She read over the article for a second time. It was good – full of dramatic details about the letter box banging and waking her, how she glanced at her daughter as she left the room, how shocked she was as she and her husband realized the Crucifix Killer had been at their door, the torturous discussion about the safety of their daughter as they decided she had to continue to cover the story.

She hit send, then picked up her phone and called Kay.

'Hi,' Kay said. 'You're the woman of the hour. I read about the letter. That's fucked up.'

'I know,' Alice said. 'But that's not why I'm calling. I need to talk.'

'That's *not* why you're calling? What kind of a life do you have? What else is going on?'

'It's Tom.'

'Oh?'

'I'm worried about him.'

Kay paused. 'Has something else happened? After the bath?'

'Not exactly.' She opened up her messages on her phone. 'Hang on. I'll send you an exchange we had earlier. Let me know when you've read it. The background is that I got some interest from the national papers and was saying I have to keep on with the story about the Crucifix Killer.'

She sent a screenshot of their recent texts.

'What do you make of it?' Alice said.

'I don't know,' Kay replied. 'It could just be him saying he'll look after Jo.'

'You don't think it's a threat?'

'I suppose you could see it like that. Maybe he's saying he'll take her somewhere safe.'

'Or worse,' Alice said.

'What are you saying, Alice?' Kay said. 'Spell it out. Because now I'm worried too.'

Alice took a deep breath. 'You can't tell anyone,' she said. 'If it gets back to Tom, he'll kill me. But I'm worried he's becoming depressed. Suicidal, even. And I'm scared what he might do to Jo.'

'This is pretty serious stuff,' Kay said. 'I mean, really, really serious. What makes you think it?'

'Jo had a bruise on her arm. Then there was the bath—'

'He fell asleep, Alice. That's hardly a sign of suicidal intentions.'

'I know. But I got the impression it was more than that. And now there's another bruise. We're taking her to the doctor to see if there's a medical problem, but – well, it's obvious someone did it, Kay. Someone squeezed her.'

'It might not have been Tom.'

'Then who? His mum? Martha? They wouldn't. He thinks it could be his brother, but he's not with her enough.'

'It could be his mum or Martha,' Kay said. 'Just as much as it could be him.'

'It's him that's under stress,' Alice said. 'It's him that isn't sleeping. It's him who's lost it with me a few times recently. And it's him who sent a text message that looks like a threat of some kind.'

'Fuck,' Kay said. 'You'd know better than me, mate. So what do you do?'

'I don't know. That's the problem. I have no idea what to do, but I'm worried, Kay. I'm really worried.'

Alice met Tom and Joanna at the doctor's surgery. Tom held Joanna on his lap as they waited for their appointment. His face was obscured by the mask over his mouth and nose, but she could see from the blank expression in his eyes that he had not got over their argument.

The receptionist tapped on the plexiglass screen and smiled at them.

'Through the door, down the corridor, second left,' she said. 'Dr Quinn's ready for you.'

Dr Quinn was sitting next to her desk looking at her computer.

'Hello,' she said, turning to them. 'How are you all?'

'We're good,' Tom said. 'Thank you. And you?'

'I'm excellent. Thanks for asking.' She turned to Alice. 'Is this about Joanna? I believe you wanted to see me about another bruise?'

'Yes,' Alice said. 'On her thigh.'

'Could I see?'

Tom took off Jo's baby pants and held her up. Dr Quinn took her thigh between her thumb and forefinger and examined it. The bruise had darkened into a purple ring.

'That's very odd,' she said. She looked serious, worried even. 'Is there anything – anything at all – you can think of that might have caused it?'

'No,' Tom said.

Alice shook her head.

'The one on her arm could have been someone grabbing her,' Dr Quinn said. 'But I doubt that in this case.'

'Is there anything that could cause her to bruise easily?' Tom said. 'An underlying medical problem?'

'There certainly are some things,' Dr Quinn said. 'Some of them can cause spontaneous bruising, but I haven't seen them present like this. Normally there would be bruises in more than one location. Then there are conditions that can make the body more susceptible to bruising.' She turned first to Alice, then to Tom. 'But there still needs to be a cause for the bruise in those cases.'

'You mean someone still has to do something to her?' Tom said.

'Yes,' Dr Quinn replied. 'I mean exactly that.'

'This is crazy,' Tom said. 'No one would hurt Jo, not deliberately. There has to be another explanation.'

Alice caught his eye. 'I hope so,' she said. 'I really do.'

Tom

Tom sat on the couch in his parents' living room, holding Joanna on his knee. His dad was in the armchair opposite him. He was wearing a tweed cap to hide his head, but it did nothing to disguise the missing eyebrows, or the hollow cheeks.

It was still shocking for Tom to see him like this. His dad had always been big: in character and stature. Some of Tom's earliest memories were of watching him play rugby at the local club. There were bigger men, but his dad had a kind of raw power that sent him barrelling through opposition players as though they weren't there. He was the same in work: he had started as a bricklayer, and slowly built up his own small construction company, but, even when he was the boss, he took pride in working harder than all the people he employed.

The only person who works harder than me's your mam, he once said. *And she's doing the most important job too.*

It wasn't just rugby and work. His dad ate more and drank more than the other dads too. For every memory Tom had of him playing rugby, he had ten of him standing by the bar in the clubhouse, the pint of beer in his hands rarely full for long. He was a fun, happy drinker, the person everyone wanted to talk to in the pub.

And now he was vanishing in front of Tom's eyes, being eaten from the inside by the cancer that had grown in his stomach. The treatment would slow the inevitable, but that was all it would do. And in the meantime, his father slipped away by degrees.

'Son,' his dad said. 'Don't look at me like that.'

'I'm not looking at you like anything.'

'You are. You're looking at me like you pity me. Fear, disgust, I can take. But don't pity me, son.'

Tom felt tears spring to his eyes. 'I'm sorry, Dad. It's—'

'It's just it's hard to watch someone go through this, especially your dad. But trust me, I'm OK. It bloody hurts, I won't lie, but I've had a good life Tom. I've no regrets.'

He lifted a mug of tea and took a swig.

'No regrets?' Tom said.

'Maybe one. I wish we'd been able to help Roland.'

'Why couldn't you?' Tom said. 'I've thought about it often. Whether I could have done anything to stop him going off the rails.'

'You couldn't,' his dad said. 'And neither could we. We tried, believe me, but he had to walk his own path. We all have to walk our own path.' He paused. 'People are who they are, Tom. It's hard to watch your own child make the choices Roland made, but at the end of the day they were his choices to make. We treated him the same as we treated you, but you're different people.'

'At least he's better now,' Tom said.

'Better? He's not better. He's clinging on, trying to get through the days. He's hurting, Tom. I don't know why, but he's hurting. For most people life's a mixture of good and bad. If you're lucky you get more of the former than the latter. For Roland, life's a series of problems and worries. So don't pity me. Save it for that brother of yours.'

'I will.'

'And how are you doing?' His dad fixed him with his dark brown eyes. Despite his illness, his gaze was still sharp and penetrating. 'You seem a bit down.'

Tom did not want to burden his dad with any other concerns. 'I'm OK, Dad. Tired. Still not sleeping much.'

'And Alice? How's she?'

'She's tied up in this serial killer story.'

'I'll bet she is.'

'I wish she'd stop. The letters have come to our *house*. It's frightening.'

His dad nodded slowly. 'It would be.'

'What would you do, if it was Mum?'

His dad puffed out his cheeks. 'I'd have told her to go for it. This is the story of her life. It could make her career.' He paused. 'But more than that, this is what she *chose*. This is her passion. You can't ask her to turn an opportunity like this down. Sorry, son. But that's what I think. You have to be bold. You only live once.'

'So you'd be OK with it?'

'I would. I'd add some locks to my doors and windows, make sure the cops were nearby, and tell my wife to do what she needed to do.'

It was not what he had been expecting to hear, but it was strangely welcome.

'Thanks, Dad.'

'No problem. Anyway, I'm getting tired. I'm going to have a nap. But before I do, how about a cuddle with my grand-daughter?'

Roland was in the garden with his mum. His forearms were lined with scars.

'How's Dad?' he said.

'Gone to sleep.'

'He's tired these days,' his mum said. Every time she talked

201

about her husband, Tom was acutely aware of how much she was going to miss him. They'd been married for nearly forty years. He'd been a constant fixture in her life; Tom couldn't fathom how she would be able to adjust when he was gone.

'He gave me some good advice, though. About Alice and the letters.'

'I bet I can imagine what it was,' his mum said.

'What do you think he said?' Roland asked.

'I think he said she should go for it and you should support her.'

Tom nodded. 'In a nutshell.'

'It's good advice, and it's very your dad,' she said. 'But let me give you some advice too. You need to be comfortable with the decision you and Alice make, Tom. That's as important as blind devotion to your wife.'

'I know,' Tom said. 'And I think I am. I think there's a way for us both to get what we need. We can find ways to feel safe, which is all I really want. And it's been coming between us, which is no good.'

'You're a good husband,' his mum said. 'Have you told her?'

'Not yet. I'll do it later.'

'When you do, can you ask her what she wants for her birthday? It's coming up,' his mum said.

'When is it?' Roland said.

'Just under two weeks,' Tom said. 'I need to get her something myself.'

'If you're having a hard time, get her something to remind her of your relationship,' his mum said. 'Something about you two and Joanna.'

'Like what?' Tom said.

'I don't know. Think about it.' His mum sipped from a large glass of water. 'A photo book. I made your dad one, once. Photos of him and me and you two. From all the phases of his life.'

'Did he like it?' Tom asked.

'You know your dad. He didn't say much, but he kept it, all these years. I found him looking at it once, tears in his eyes. I'd forgotten he could cry.'

'I could do that for Alice,' Tom said. 'But she doesn't have many photos from her childhood.'

'Why not?' Roland said.

'When her parents died and she sold the house, they got lost,' Tom said. 'We talked about it once. A lot of her parents' stuff – furniture, that kind of thing – was given away or sold. She had nowhere to put it. The photos disappeared in the shuffle.'

'See if you can get any,' his mum said. 'Ask her friends if they have any.'

'She's not really in touch with her childhood friends,' Tom said.

'Tom! Get creative! Find them on Facebook and ask them. Do you know their names?'

'I know one, Nellie Clarke.'

'Then contact her. Say it's a surprise. She'll be glad to help, I'm sure.'

'You know,' Tom said. 'That's not a bad idea.'

'Don't sound so surprised,' his mum said. 'I'm not a total idiot.'

'I know, Mum. I have to go soon, but there was one thing I wanted to talk to you about.'

'Oh?'

'It's Joanna. She's had' – he hesitated – he wanted to bring this up without it sounding accusatory – 'she's had a couple of bruises.'

'Bruises? Where?'

He touched his upper arm. 'There. And a new one on her thigh.' He pulled down her pants. 'Look.'

203

His mum came over and examined Joanna's leg. 'Gosh,' she said. 'That's quite bad. How did it happen?'

'We don't know,' Tom said. 'We're trying to figure it out. Maybe she was falling and someone grabbed her' – he glanced at Roland – 'which would be fine. We'd like to find out.'

'Well, I have no clue,' his mum said.

'The thing is,' Tom continued. 'We noticed both bruises after she was with Martha—'

'Martha wouldn't hurt her,' his mum said. 'And she'd say if an accident happened.'

'I know. The other place she's been is – here.'

His mum frowned. 'It's not me, love,' she said.

'That's not what he's insinuating,' Roland said. He stood up slowly. 'He's saying it's me.'

'No,' Tom said. 'You're putting—'

'That's OK. I'm used to it.' Roland gave a sardonic shake of his head. 'Something goes missing, the junkie stole it. I'm late somewhere – I must be back on the drugs. A baby gets hurt, the smack head did it. Don't worry.'

'Roland,' Tom said. 'Let—'

Roland held up his hands, palms facing Tom.

'Forget it. Like I said, I'm used to it. Almost everyone assumes the worst of me. ' He gave a slow shake of his head. 'I hoped my own brother was different, but I guess not. I'm going for a walk. I'll see you later.'

'No you won't,' Tom said, a fierce anger gripping him. 'You'll wait there. And you'll cut out the self-pity. The reason people assume the worst, Roland, is because for most of the last decade it's been a safe bet that whatever you did wasn't helping. Remember Chrissy?'

'Tom,' his mum said. 'Please.'

'He needs to hear it. Or I need to say it. Either way, he's going to stop the self-pity. Yes, he deserves – barely – a second chance, but not a free pass. And not the right to play the victim.'

Roland nodded slowly. 'Fair enough,' he said. 'I can see why you think it was me. But – this time, Tom – it wasn't.'

Tom and his mum were silent as Roland stalked out of the back gate.

'Well,' his mum said. 'That went well.'

Tom turned to her. 'You know what? I think it did.'

Saturday, 21 August 2021

Alice

PUBLIC ANXIETY HIGH AS 'CRUCIFIX' KILLER REMAINS AT LARGE
By Alice Sark

With two days now passed since the Crucifix Killer's most recent appearance, the general public remains tense and anxious about where and when the next attack could occur.

Blame for the failure to apprehend the killer is being attached to the police. 'It's about time the police did something,' Marjorie Davies, a long-time resident of Stockton Heath, said. 'They have a lot of information now – they need to catch this monster before there are any more victims. People are scared. They need to act.'

That is easier said than done. Police sources indicated that the line of enquiry related to this being an Australian male has not turned up any credible suspects. It is still considered a possibility, but their attention is moving to other avenues.

In the meantime, the public wonders when the next attack will come. Tina Rhodes, Professor of Criminal Psychology at Liverpool University, said it could be soon.

'It's an unpleasant subject to address, but having failed to kill his last victim, it is possible, indeed likely, that the Crucifix Killer will act again in the near future. This kind of personality type often needs a "fix", which they get from their horrendous crimes. Having missed the last fix, the need to kill again may sharpen.'

It is a troubling thought, but the facts are clear: we must remain vigilant until the streets are rid of this scourge.

Tom

He sat by the bay window at the front of the house, the early morning sun already warm on his face. Next to him, Joanna slept. Alice was in bed; he'd woken early so she could have a lie-in.

He opened Facebook and searched for Nellie Clarke, then composed a message.

> Hi. You don't know me but I'm Alice Barnes's – now Sark's – husband. It's her birthday coming up and I was thinking of making her a photo album – old school, I know, but it's nice to have a physical object these days. I have loads of photos of us before we had our daughter (and even more since – she's more photographed than a pop star!) but I've got hardly any from before we met. She lost them all at some point, which is the reason I'm getting in touch – I hope it's no trouble, but I was wondering whether you have any photos of her you could scan and send? I can get them printed my end. If you can help, would you also mind asking Madeline? Thanks, and sorry to be a pain! Tom

He hit send, then lay back and closed his eyes.

He was woken by Joanna crying. He took her from her basket and held her to his chest. She started to settle, and he reached for his phone.

He'd noticed recently that checking his phone had become a kind of reflex action. Get out of the shower: quick check of the phone. Break in conversation: quick check of the phone. Jo settles: quick check of the phone. It had really hit him when he got in a lift at work with a group – a small group, as people still didn't like enclosed spaces – and all of them immediately checked their phones, him included. He'd only checked it seconds before, but still, there he was, glued to the screen to see if any emails or messages or notifications had popped up.

He had one now, from Facebook Messenger. It was Nellie.

Hi Tom. I see you're on the early shift. Me too! What a sweet idea! I'd love to help. I'll have to have a dig around though, so give me a while. I'll let Mads know. I talk to her from time to time. And tell Alice to get in touch! It's been too long. In fact, I'm going to send her a message. But I'll wait until after her birthday so I don't ruin the surprise! Nellie xxx

Excellent. Alice would love to see the photos. He was interested too. Her past was a bit of mystery to him, so finding out some more about it would be welcome.

Joanna started to cry again. He smiled at her. She had her hungry face on.

Time to eat.

Alice

Tom was feeding Jo at the table. He got a lot of pleasure from feeding her, moving the spoon like an aeroplane and landing it in her mouth.

Or near her mouth. Whenever he fed her half the food ended up on her face, with the other half on the table. It was cute, in a way, but it was also irritating. It didn't need to be so messy or such a production. For her part, Alice found it a bit tedious – just another task to get done – and thought Tom's approach a touch infantile.

'Morning,' she said. They had not spoken much the night before and she was expecting an awkward tension between them. Instead, he smiled warmly.

'Morning. Sleep well?'

'As well as ever.'

'Let me feed Jo and I'll make you some breakfast.'

She sat on the chair next to him. 'You're in a good mood.'

'I had a chat to my dad yesterday. About you keeping on with the Crucifix Killer stories.'

'What did he say?'

Tom spooned the last of the baby food into Joanna's mouth, then started to wipe up the mess. 'He said it's a great opportunity for you – too good to turn down – and I should get behind you.'

'Really?' Alice said. 'I've always liked your dad.'

'He suggested finding a way to make it work for both of us. Maybe adding some extra locks to the doors and windows, and make sure the police are close at hand in case anything happens.'

'So are you saying you're OK with it?'

Tom nodded. 'That's what I'm saying. We'll find a way to make it work. After breakfast I'll go and buy some bolts.'

'The detective, Wynne, is coming over to talk about the letter. She's coming with Nadia.'

'Do they need me here?'

'I don't think so,' Alice said. 'We should be OK.'

'Then I'll let you handle it.' He stood up and took Jo's bowl to the sink. 'Maybe you can ask them for some extra protection. An officer nearby, that kind of thing.'

'I'll mention it,' Alice said.

'What do you want for breakfast? I've got grapefruit, then maybe some eggs?'

'I'll stick to grapefruit,' Alice said. 'You don't have to do all this. It's sweet, but it's not necessary.'

'Maybe not,' he said. 'But I'm quite hungry, so if I'm poaching some eggs for me, it's easy enough to add a couple for you?'

'OK,' she said. 'And thanks, Tom. Not just for breakfast. For everything.'

DI Wynne

Wynne stood by the window. DS Alexander was sitting on the couch. Alice Sark sat at the other end. Wynne was not sure she liked the fact that DS Alexander and Ms Sark were friends, but it was perhaps inevitable in a small town that a police officer would know a lot of people of their own age.

She held a copy of the letter. The original was with the forensics team, but they had not discovered anything of value. Whoever had handled it had done so carefully. They had left no trace.

It had been printed on a Canon printer, with standard ink. If they could find the printer there might be some way to link it to the letter, but that meant having a suspect whose printer they could examine.

She held the letter up.

'What did you make of it, Ms Sark?'

'That they were trying to make light of the Australian accent, which maybe meant it was real.'

'The thought crossed my mind,' Wynne said. 'Anything else?'

'I don't know,' Alice replied. 'I don't have much experience of this kind of thing. Is there something I should be noticing?'

'I'm not sure, exactly.' Wynne glanced at the letter. 'But there's something not quite right about the letter.'

'Like what?' Alice said.

'The tone, maybe,' Wynne said. 'The threats to you – and to DS Alexander.' She read from the letter. '"First, you don't understand what you are messing with. You don't want to irritate me. You don't know what I'll do. I don't know what I'll do."' She shook her head. 'It doesn't ring true. And then there's the suggestion that the killer knows the details of your life because they know your husband is an engineer. It all feels – unnecessary.'

'In what way?' Alice said.

'Well,' DS Alexander said, 'the killer chose to write to you so they could establish a channel of communication between them and us. Why now threaten you? They'll simply need another channel.'

'There's too much focus on you,' Wynne said. 'These people are all about their own ego, about how they're outwitting the authorities. This letter is about *your* role in this. It doesn't ring true,' she repeated.

'Maybe not,' Alice said. 'But it's still pretty damn frightening.'

'Are you scared?' DS Alexander said.

'I think we're OK,' Alice said. 'But it's unnerving, for sure. Tom's gone to get some additional locks.'

'In my view you're quite safe,' Wynne said. 'I don't think the killer is interested in you. Which is why I don't fully understand these letters. But we can provide some protection, if you'd like?'

'That's OK,' Alice said. 'As long as your officers know to prioritize a call to this address, I think that's enough.'

'Me too,' Wynne said. 'I must say, you're very calm, Ms Sark.'

Alice shrugged. 'I believe what you say about me not being

a target. It *feels* that way.' She shifted on the couch. 'Do you have any leads?'

'We're pursuing a number of lines of enquiry,' Wynne said.

'That's the on-the-record statement,' Alice said. 'I get that. But what does it mean?'

Wynne folded the letter and put it in her pocket. What it meant was that the investigation was going nowhere. They had no leads, no suspects, nothing. She had meant what she said about considering that the letter was mocking the idea it was someone with an Australian accent because it really *was* an Australian, but it hadn't helped. They had interviewed all the Australian males – and females – they could find, and all of them had alibis of some type or other.

And, other than that, they had nothing. It was frustrating, and she was starting to worry they were going to see more murders before they caught the perpetrator.

But she did not want that showing up in Alice Sark's news stories.

'It means,' Wynne said, 'that we are pursuing a number of lines of enquiry.'

Tom

He had sliding bolts for the top and bottom of the front door and back door. It would still be possible to break in, but would take a lot of effort and a pretty big axe, which would make a lot of noise. A stealthy entrance would be impossible.

He also had bolts for the interior doors downstairs, so when they were upstairs they could lock those doors as well. Given the fact that one or other of them was awake most of the night he was confident that – in their house at least – they'd be safe.

He stood on a chair and drilled a couple of holes in the front door frame, then reached down for the bolt.

'Handy man,' Alice said. 'Did you get what you wanted?'

He had a couple of screws in his mouth. 'Uh-huh.' He pointed at the bolt and gestured for her to pass it to him.

'This?' She lifted up the bolt and he held out his hand for it. He fixed the top screw, then the bottom one.

'Thanks,' he said. 'There's a couple for the back door too. It should be enough.'

'I'd think so,' Alice said.

'What did the cops have to say?'

'More of the same,' Alice said. 'Wynne thinks the letters are unusual.'

'She's not wrong.'

'Unusual even for a serial killer,' Alice said.

'Why so?'

'Because they're focused on me and not on the killer. She finds that strange.'

Tom drilled another set of holes. 'The whole fucking thing is strange.'

'That's what I said. She also thinks the killer's not interested in hurting me – or us.'

He gestured at the bolts. 'So all this is a waste of time?'

'No. Not if it makes you – us – feel better.'

'Did you ask about more protection from the police.'

'We talked about it. They'll make sure there are officers in the vicinity, and they know to get her immediately.'

'Is that enough?' Tom said. He stepped off the chair. 'Couldn't we have someone here?'

'I don't think we need it.'

'I do.'

He studied his wife. He'd known she was stubborn, but this was different. He was beginning to wonder whether she was the person he thought she was.

Perhaps, he thought, she was beginning to wonder the same.

'Tom,' she said. 'We'll be OK.'

Ambleside, July 2013

Alice

It was time to pack up and return to normal life.

Specifically, to Ned, and the inevitable fallout from what had happened. He would not give up on her easily, but he was going to have to.

Before that, though, she had to actually pack her rucksack, which was proving a lot more difficult than it should have. It was already full, but next to it were a pair of jeans, two T-shirts and a pair of sandals, all of which had fitted inside when she had packed to come here.

She had not bought anything else, so how did they not fit?

Brenda sat on the bunk bed and grinned.

'That always happens,' she said. 'Things expand.'

'Not to you,' Alice said. Her rucksack was packed; there was even a space at the top for the small day pack she used.

'Yeah, but I've got more experience than you, mate,' Brenda said. 'I'll let you in on the secret.' She reached into her pack and pulled out a shirt. 'Roll, don't fold. Then you can stuff them in. You also don't get creases. Try it.'

Alice studied her rucksack. She didn't want to unpack it and start again, but it seemed she had no choice. She needed everything in as they were going to have to carry their ruck-sacks on their walk. They had to check out of the hostel, and then go straight to the train.

'I'll give it a go,' she said.

'I'll grab some breakfast and bring it back,' Brenda said. 'We have to get moving if we're going to catch the bus we need.'

She left the room, and Alice emptied her rucksack. Her legs were stiff from the walk up Helvellyn the day before, and she stood up to stretch them out. Brenda's rucksack was on the bunk bed, so she bent over to have a look at the rolling technique.

The day pack was at the top, so she pulled it out. The flap at the top was unclipped, and it swung open as she set it down on the bed.

She did not intend to pry, but something caught her eye. There was an envelope – normal letter size – slit at the top.

It was stuffed with banknotes.

She looked closer.

They *were* banknotes, but not pounds. She reached in and put her finger between the envelope and the notes so she could see them better.

They were fifty-dollar Australian notes. There was a thick stack of them – maybe fifty, maybe a hundred.

And there were more – maybe another ten – unopened envelopes which presumably were full of bank notes too.

Why did Brenda have so much cash? All you needed these days was a bank card and access to an ATM. Maybe she had that too, and this was some kind of insurance policy, in case she lost her bank card. Or maybe she just preferred cash. But it was risky to carry this much. Now she knew why Brenda kept the day pack close, though.

There were other things in there. Her wallet, sunglasses. A passport.

Two passports.

Why did she have two passports? Maybe one belonged to her friend, and she had it for some reason. She realized she didn't know Brenda's last name. She reached for the passport.

And then she heard footsteps approaching the room, and the door opening.

She stepped back and looked into the rucksack.

'Checking out my stuff?' Brenda said. She was standing in the doorway, holding two bananas and a plate of toast.

Alice turned around, putting what she hoped was an easy smile on her lips.

'Just seeing how it's done. It's impressive you can travel for so long with so little.'

'It's easy enough.'

Brenda put the food down. She was suspicious, her expression hard. Alice turned to her bed and started to roll up her clothes. She picked up a pair of jeans and threw them to Brenda.

'Here,' she said. 'Give me a hand. We don't want to miss that bus.'

If Striding Edge was majestic and imposing, Wast Water was intimidating.

No less majestic, and no less imposing, but neither was the main feeling Alice got when she stood on the narrow shore, the black mirror of the lake stretching ahead of her, a sheer scree slope shooting up behind her.

The feeling she got was fear. This was an ancient place, unchanged and unchanging, totally indifferent to the humans who came and went.

One shore of the lake sloped up to a broad fell. The other was bordered by the scree slope behind her now. It was a solid wall of rock, and it towered menacingly over the lake and everything – her included – near it.

She shrugged her rucksack off and sat down. Brenda knelt by the water and put her hand in.

'Jeez,' she said. 'It's freezing. Even in the summer.'

'I don't think it gets that much sun,' Alice said. 'Didn't Sharon say it's the deepest lake, too?' She pictured a yawning chasm beneath the water, a crack in the surface of the world that went deep into the crust. How far down did it go? Hundreds of feet? Thousands? It felt like it could be anything, an endless depth.

Brenda splashed water on her face. 'Lunch?' she said. 'I made some sandwiches.'

'Sounds good.'

Brenda opened her rucksack and took out the day pack. She put it on the rocks beside her and opened the flap, then took out a plastic bag.

'Ham,' she said. 'That was all I had left.'

She took a sandwich from the bag and handed it to Alice. The sandwich was warm and a bit squashed, but Alice was hungry after the walk around the lake and her hunger made it taste good.

'Thanks,' she said. She took a bottle of water from her bag and took a swig. It too was warm, so she put it in the lake and held it down with a rock. 'You want some water?'

Brenda shook her head. 'I have some.' She opened the flap of her day pack again and took out a flask. Alice saw the envelopes. It really was a risk to carry that much money. She could drop the bag in the lake, or off a cliff, or someone could find out it was there and take it from her.

People had killed for less than that, after all.

'What will you do when you get to Liverpool?' Alice said.

'Go to the youth hostel,' Brenda said. 'My friends are there already.'

'What are their names?' Alice said.

'Nicky and Donna,' Brenda said.

'Have you known them long?'

'Yeah, we go way back. We met in high school.'

'I'd like to meet them,' Alice said.

'Maybe we can get together before we go back,' Brenda said. 'We could come to Nottingham. That'd be cool.'

'I need some way of getting in touch,' Alice said. 'You're not on Facebook, and you don't have a phone – maybe they're on Facebook? I could contact them.' She took out her phone. 'What are their surnames? I'll look them up.'

For a moment Brenda's expression froze, then she shook her head. 'They're not on it either. I can give you my email address.'

'Sure. What is it? I'll type it in now.'

Brenda gave her email address – her name followed by some numbers and a domain name. Alice typed it into the to: bar, then hit send.

'I've sent you an email,' she said. 'That way you'll have my email address too.'

'You did?' Brenda said. 'OK.'

Alice went back to her inbox. She had a few emails from Ned, and one from her landlord. Ned's could wait; the one from her landlord could be important.

She was about to open it when a new email appeared.

Undeliverable: email address does not exist.

'Hey,' she said. 'I think I got your address wrong. It bounced back.' She read the email address to Brenda, who frowned.

'That's it,' Brenda said. 'That's right.'

'I'll try again.'

The same thing happened. The email came back.

'Are you sure that's the correct address?' Alice said.

'Hundred per cent,' Brenda said. 'You know, I've been having some issues with my account. Maybe because it's in Australia. We can try again later. If it doesn't work, I'll give you Nicky and Donna's too.'

She took off her boots and socks. 'Anyway, how about a swim?'

* * *

221

Alice had intended to swim, but now she was here she was not so sure.

'I dunno,' she said. 'It's freezing!'

'We have to,' Brenda said. 'We can't come all this way and not go for a dip. And it's my last chance to swim in the Lakes.'

'OK,' Alice said. 'But one thing before we do. I wanted to show you something weird.'

There was something unusual about Brenda, something she couldn't put her finger on. When she had mentioned the names of her friends – Nicky and Donna – Alice had realized that she had not mentioned them before. She had hardly referred to them at all – just two friends she was travelling with.

Yet they went back together a long way. Was it weird that the places they'd been hadn't come up in conversation?

She wasn't sure. But she got the impression Brenda was hiding something, and she wanted to prod a little. Then there was the cash and the two passports. It was probably nothing, and she knew it was none of her business, but she'd probably never see Brenda again, so she might as well ask.

'Yeah?' Brenda said. 'What is it?'

She opened her Facebook app and searched for Brenda Yates. The lookalike profile came up.

'Take a look.'

Brenda took the phone. She stared at it for a while, scrolling down the screen.

'That *is* weird,' she said. 'Very fucking weird. She looks a lot like me.'

'And she's from Perth. And has the same name.'

'Yeah.' Brenda looked up at her and shook her head. 'I don't know what to say. Perth's a pretty big place – couple of million people – but still. I mean, I could imagine another Brenda Yates, but the same age, looking like my sister? That's crazy.'

'That's what I thought! And I wasn't stalking you. I searched for you on Facebook and this came up.'

Brenda waved her protest away. 'No worries. Everyone does it. I'm glad. I might look her up when I get home.'

'It's kind of unbelievable,' Alice said. 'I mean, it's really hard to believe it.'

'Don't think we have much choice,' Brenda said. 'Unless she and me are the same person and I'm bullshitting you. And it's pretty obvious we're not, when you look closer.'

She was right, but you had to look quite closely. They were really very similar. They could have passed for each other at a glance.

But they weren't the same person.

'I know,' Alice said. 'But it's really an amazing coincidence. Anyway. Time for that swim.'

Tuesday, 24 August 2021

The Baby

It is just a thing. And it cries. Every time you are with it, it cries.

Not in the way most people say. You've heard other people say they can't bear to hear a child cry because they worry what's wrong and want to help. That's an emotional response. A weak response. They think it is in distress and that bothers them. They say it is worse than any other noise for that reason.

That is not why it annoys you. It annoys you in the same way a dog barking annoys you.

It is something that must be dealt with. Removed from your environment.

There was once a dog, when you were a teenager. It was bought for you by your parents. They knew you had a problem – a problem that was growing ever greater – and they thought it would help you. Teach you about responsibility, about how to love something. About how to love yourself.

Fools.

The stupid thing was outside all the time, yapping away, so you got rid of it. You'd wanted to make it suffer first, but that would have been too obvious, so you settled on rat poison.

You blamed it on someone else. They suspected it was you, you could tell, but they wanted to believe you were innocent, so they did.

When they asked you about the dog, you shook your head and said No, I have no idea what happened, *but you gave them a little smile, and let them look for a moment into your eyes – not much, but enough to get a glimpse of the soulless, bottomless evil at the heart of you – and then said* It must have been someone else. Some kid, *and they nodded. What else could they do? To accept the truth of what you were would have destroyed them.*

But they were scared. More than scared. Terrified.

The baby is not scared, though. It does not know fear. Can it? You think not.

It will be interesting to find out though. It will be interesting to stare into its eyes in its last seconds and see whether it knows it is about to die.

You don't think it will, but you are looking forward to finding out.

Janice Kettering

She was in a pub car park, for God's sake. It couldn't happen here.

Yes, her car was the only one there, and yes, it was in the corner. But come on. Here?

She and Sanjay had shut the pub – the landlord was always too pissed by this time – and lingered downstairs for a quiet drink.

As well as a few other things. Sanjay lived with his girlfriend, so they couldn't go to his house, and he had to be home at a reasonable time, so they couldn't go to hers.

Which left the pub. They hadn't had sex in it yet, but it wouldn't be long. They'd done everything else, and they could hardly keep their hands off each other, so it was only a matter of time, and she couldn't wait.

She loved him, and he loved her. He had to extricate himself from his relationship, and then they could be together.

Except that would never happen.

Not now.

Because she was going to die. She was going to die in this shitty pub car park, still a virgin.

Sanjay couldn't help. He had walked home. He had kissed her at the pub door and headed off up the road to his girlfriend.

So she was alone, and she was going to die. She knew it the moment she hit the clicker on her key fob and the lights of her car flashed as it unlocked.

The batteries were old and the range was poor, so she was quite close to her car when they flashed, and illuminated the person standing there.

Who was just as close to her.

And who moved incredibly quickly, the hammer in their hand swinging viciously towards her head.

Tom

Tom sat by the window, Joanna asleep in his arms. It had been a rough night; Jo was awake for most of it, which meant either he or Alice was too. He had finally gone to bed around two in the morning, handing his daughter off to his wife, only to be woken before seven by Alice, holding a still crying baby.

That was their life now. Work, baby, sleep. They'd got married four years ago – although they'd met a few years before, after Alice moved to Stockton Heath. He'd admired her from a distance – she was tough and independent and seemed very self-contained. He hadn't thought she'd be interested in him, but over time they'd met at various parties and pubs, and one day she'd asked him out on a date.

Thankfully, Jo was finally sleeping. He took a series of deep breaths. Recently he'd started feeling as though his chest was constricted, his stomach tight. It was constant, and he'd mentioned it to Dr Quinn.

That's anxiety, she said. *It's when your body's stress response is constantly being triggered. It can go haywire, and so you're flooded with adrenaline. Adrenaline's great – it helps you focus and primes your muscles to deal with*

228

whatever threat has caused the body to produce it, but when you don't need it, it just makes you feel on edge and hyper-alert.

She had suggested deep breathing exercises – there were medications available, but she preferred to use those as a last resort. The exercises worked, to an extent, and he had started to do them whenever he felt the anxiety rising.

He did them now.

After a few minutes, he felt better. He stood up. He needed a cup of tea. Dr Quinn had also mentioned that caffeine could make things worse, but he was not ready to give up tea. Things weren't quite that bad, yet.

He set Joanna down in her basket and walked into the kitchen. Sunlight streamed in through the skylight, and he felt it lift his spirits. He filled the kettle and switched it on, then turned to the cupboard where they kept the teabags.

He froze.

There was a letter on the counter top.

It was like the others. There was no stamp. Just a name printed on a home printer.

Alice Sark

His chest tightened and he felt dizzy. He tried taking deep breaths again, but this time they had no effect.

This panic was not his body overreacting and running wild. This panic was fully justified.

Alice

Alice lay in bed upstairs and typed a message on her phone.

Are you awake?

Kay replied immediately.

Yes. Getting ready for work.

Can you talk?

Her phone rang seconds after she sent the question.

'Hi,' she said, keeping her voice to a whisper. 'Sorry to bother you so early.'

'What's the matter?' Kay said. 'Why are you being so quiet.'

'I don't want Tom to hear me. He thinks I'm asleep.'

'Is everything OK?'

Alice paused. 'I don't know.'

'What's happened?'

'He's – I think he's cracking up.'

'Alice,' Kay said. 'Are you safe?'

'I think so. For now.'

'OK. Why do you think he's cracking up?'

'Last night was rough,' Alice said. 'Jo was colicky and fussy and neither of us got much sleep. I grabbed some at around one, but I was woken up by Jo crying *really* loudly. I went downstairs and she was in her basket, screaming at the top of her lungs, and Tom was just sitting there, his hands over his ears, shaking his head and staring into space.'

'Jesus. Is Jo OK?'

'She is. He didn't know I'd seen him – and I didn't want to surprise him – so I crept back upstairs, then came down noisily. When I went into the living room he'd picked her up. She was still wailing, but at least he was trying to soothe her.'

'What did you do?'

'I asked him what was going on, and he said he'd tried everything but she wouldn't stop crying. I asked if he'd been holding her the whole time, and he nodded. He *lied* to me, Kay. And he looked *awful*. He had this crazy, desperate expression in his eyes. It was like looking at an animal.'

'Are you sure you're safe?'

'He was better this morning. But he's been suffering from anxiety, too. I'm really worried about him, Kay, and about how he's treating Jo. I feel almost like he hates her. Like he could *hurt* her.'

'I think you need to get out of there,' Kay said. 'You and Jo.'

'That might be the final straw for him,' Alice said. 'I love him, Kay. I can't abandon him. It might tip him over the edge.'

'Safety first,' Kay said. 'You know—'

She was interrupted by a loud shout from downstairs.

'Alice!' Tom shouted. 'Alice!'

'What the hell was that?' Kay said.

231

'It's Tom,' Alice said. 'He's shouting for me. Something's happened. I have to go.'

'I'm coming over,' Kay said. 'Right now.'

'That's not necessary,' Alice said. 'Really—'

'I don't care. I'm on my way.'

The phone went dead, and Alice swung her legs off the bed.

'Yes,' she said. 'What is it?'

'Come downstairs now!' Tom called. 'Now!'

Alice walked quickly downstairs.

'What is it?' she said. 'Why are you shouting?'

He held out the envelope. 'There's another letter,' he said. 'It just came. I looked outside but nobody's there.' He leaned against the wall, his breath short. 'He was *here*, Alice. He was in our house.'

'What do you mean?'

'The letter was on the kitchen counter.' He started shouting. 'It was *inside* our house, Alice. Inside!'

'Put it down,' she said. 'You shouldn't touch it.'

'I don't care,' he said. His face was red, his voice shaky and out of control. 'I don't care. I want to know what it says.'

He opened the envelope and took out a single sheet of A4 paper. He held it so they both could see it.

Alice!

Well, the time has come. I'm getting bored and I've never been good with boredom. You understand: you're a bit like me. You like the attention, don't you?

I have to say – I don't like it, Alice. I don't like that you're becoming the story. That article is all about you! All about the cat and mouse game you are playing with me.

I rather think it's the other way around, Alice. Without

me you're nothing! Another small town scribbler, no more, no less.

I have a plan for you, though. I'll let you know later what it is. I don't want anything to spoil today.

Today is my day.

I had to work a bit harder for this one. Look a bit further afield. People are nervous. Delicious, isn't it? The fear? You can taste it. All those people living in terror because of me. They're more likely to die in a car wreck than at my hands, but still they fear me.

Can you imagine how it feels to control the population of an entire town like that? To know that you are the chess master, moving the pieces as you see fit? No one has a clue who I am. I could vanish if I wanted, never to be caught.

Maybe I will. But not now. This is too much fun. It makes me feel so alive!

So yes, this one took extra work, but I found her. What was she doing out in the small hours? I'll never know. I'm sure she has a story, but it doesn't matter to me.

What matters is the expression in her eyes as she realized what was about to happen, the sensation of her skull as it splintered, the soft sigh as she slumped to the ground and breathed her last.

I stayed with her body for ten minutes, Alice. It was a risk, but it was worth it. I stayed there and admired what I had done.

But enough of that: like I said, I have plans for you. On my chess board you are a rook. An important piece. A powerful piece, in the right situations. But a piece that only knows how to move in straight lines.

And that will be your downfall, Alice

Yours, etc

'My God,' Tom said. 'I feel sick, Alice. This is so twisted.'

'I know,' Alice said. 'This is' – she paused, and held his gaze – 'this is pretty out there.'

Her phone was in her hand. It started to ring and she glanced at the screen.

'It's Nadia,' she said.

'Nadia,' Alice said. 'I think I know why you're calling. There's been another one.'

There was a long pause, then Detective Inspector Wynne's voice came on the phone. 'You're on speaker,' she said. 'How do you know that?'

'There's another letter, too. It came this morning. It was in the kitchen.'

'The kitchen?' Wynne said.

'Yes. And it's quite graphic.'

'How do you know?' Wynne said. 'Was it open?'

'No,' Tom shouted at the phone. 'We opened it. It was addressed to us.'

There was a pause. 'I understand, Mr Sark,' Wynne said. 'We need to see it. We'll come over now.'

'Who was the victim?' Alice said.

'Female, nineteen,' Wynne said. 'Janice Kettering. To be confirmed, but I'd say that's her. She'd been working at a pub, last to leave. Just unlucky. Anyway, sit tight. We're on our way.'

They arrived twenty minutes later. Alice handed Wynne the letter and watched as she read it.

'It's accurate,' she said. 'Ms Kettering died of a head wound.' She handed the letter to Nadia. 'There's a lot in that letter. The part about being bored, then the stuff about it being too much about you. I can see how that would be annoying. And then there's the mention of plans for you.' She held Alice's gaze. 'That has to be a concern.'

'It depends what the plans are,' Alice said. 'And I don't intend to be intimidated by a criminal like this.'

'Admirable,' Wynne said. 'But I think you need to be careful.' She leaned forwards. 'This was inside your house. That puts this whole situation on a different level.'

'Exactly,' Tom said. 'This has gone too far.'

'We can talk later,' Alice said.

'Nadia folded the letter and put it in an evidence bag. 'We'll need this,' she said. 'OK?'

'No problem,' Alice replied. 'I already took a photo.'

DI Wynne

Wynne drove, with DS Alexander in the passenger seat.

'What did you make of the letter?' she said.

'Twisted,' DS Alexander replied. 'Sick. All that stuff about the look in her eyes – it's disgusting.'

'Indeed it is,' Wynne said. 'But the letter seemed a bit forced to me. Like the emotions being described weren't genuine. I didn't get a sense of real relish.'

'The murder was real enough,' DS Alexander said.

There was something else, something Wynne's mind had snagged on but she couldn't quite bring into focus.

'Read the letter to me,' Wynne said. 'There was something that didn't seem right but I can't put my finger on it. Hearing it out loud might help.'

'OK,' DS Alexander said. She took the letter from the evidence bag in gloved hands and began to read. Wynne listened, waiting for something to catch her attention.

Nothing came. Nadia carried on reading. 'All those people living in terror because of me,' she said. 'They're more likely to die in a car wreck than—'

'Read that again,' Wynne said.

'They're more likely to die in a car wreck—'

'Would you say that?' Wynne said. 'A car wreck?'

DS Alexander paused. 'No,' she said. 'I'd say car crash.'

'Right,' Wynne said. 'Car wreck sounds American.' She raised an eyebrow. 'Or Australian.'

DS Alexander nodded slowly. 'You've got a point.'

'I need to make some phone calls,' Wynne said. 'To our Australian colleagues.'

Tom

Tom lay on the bed. His eyes were closed but he was far from asleep. He was concentrating on each breath, forcing his chest to expand and take in air, then slowly expelling it.

It wasn't easy. His chest was banded with iron and every instinct urged him to hyperventilate, but he had to fight the feeling. His heart was thumping in his chest, the surges of blood pounding in his ears. He was scared there was something wrong, that his heart was going to explode.

He told himself to calm down, that everything was going to be OK, that he could somehow secure the house even though whoever this was could apparently pick the locks he'd added with ease, that the police were nearby, but none it made any difference. His body was out of control, its mechanisms rebelling against him.

He opened his eyes and the room started to spin. He was overcome with nausea, and he curled himself into a ball.

'Tom.'

He squinted at the door. Alice was there, silhouetted against the light.

'Tom. Are you OK?'

'I feel like I'm having a heart attack.' It was an effort to get the words out. 'I can't think. I can't get my breath.'

She sat next to him and put her hand on his forehead. He shrugged it away. He didn't want to be touched. It was too much stimulation. What he needed was total calm, total stillness.

'What can I do?' she said. 'Can I help?'

'Nothing. I'll be OK. I need to be alone.'

'OK.' She stood up and he heard her leave the room. He let out a low groan. This was torture, and it felt like it would never end.

It had to. He couldn't bear much more.

Right now, he thought, *right this second, if I could press a button and end it all I would.*

He buried his face under a pillow, and sank into the darkness.

Alice

'Well,' Kay said. 'What happened? Where's Tom?'

'He's upstairs,' Alice said. 'He's having a hard time.'

'In what way?'

'He's been having panic attacks. This is a bad one.' She passed her phone to Kay. 'Read this.'

Kay scrolled down the letter. When she had finished reading it she looked up from the screen, her eyes wide.

'Holy shit,' she said. 'That is crazy.'

'I know,' Alice said. 'It arrived this morning. It was inside our house, in the kitchen.'

Kay's eyes widened. 'What did you say?' she said.

'I know. And there's been another murder. Nadia was here with the detective earlier.'

Kay shook her head. 'It's sick. All that stuff about her skull breaking – I mean, who the fuck does that kind of thing?'

'I don't know. I really don't.'

'And what do they mean, they have plans for you?'

'I don't know that, either.'

'So what are you going to do?'

Alice puffed out her cheeks. 'Write about it,' she said.

'Aren't you scared what might happen? They've been in your house, Alice.'

'I haven't been,' Alice said. 'Up until now.'

'Up until now?' Kay said. 'Are you safe, Alice?'

'I'm not sure,' Alice said. 'For the first time, I'm starting to wonder.'

Thursday, 26 August 2021

Alice

SICKENED BY GRUESOME LETTERS FROM CRUCIFIX KILLER, BUT JOURNALIST WON'T STOP
By Alice Sark

Like the rest of the public, I recently learned of the tragic, pointless death of Janice Kettering. Ms Kettering is the latest victim of the so-called Crucifix Killer – I use this name reluctantly as it feels wrong to dignify this second-rate excuse for a human being with any moniker that suggests they are anything other than a sick and twisted murderer – her body found early on Tuesday morning.

Unlike the rest of the public, however, I was expecting a new victim, as, after committing their latest crime, the killer had posted a letter through my door.

It is the latest in a series of such letters, but by far the most disturbing. In it, the Crucifix Killer talks of their boredom and the need to kill it inspires in them.

There is talk of the pleasure – they use the word delicious – they take in knowing a town – a country – is waiting in fear, anticipating their next move.

There is talk that they are a chess master, manipulating the police, their victims, the public – and me.

But worst of all, there are details of the crime itself. Of the look in Janice's eyes as she realizes what is about to happen, of the feeling of the hammer sinking into her skull, of watching her breathe her last.

It is the letter of an ill person. Of an evil person.

As I read it, on Tuesday morning, that is what I felt. The chilling presence of true evil.

The kind of evil that must be stamped out, so that Janice Kettering is the last person to encounter it.

It was the most read feature on the *Daily Herald*'s website. It had posted Tuesday evening and overnight Alice had had requests for pieces from India, Australia, Canada, the US, and South Korea. She agreed to them all; now she had only to write them.

And she had the spare time to do so. Tom had left, pale and tired, to take Jo to his parents' house.

She took out her laptop and started to type.

Tom

His dad winced in pain as Joanna squirmed in his lap, her elbow pressing against something broken inside him. His dad, hurt by a baby. Tom could hardly watch. He jumped to his feet to get Jo.

'I'll take her,' he said.

His dad frowned. 'Don't be soft, son. I'm fine.' He shifted her so her back was against his chest. 'Every second with her is precious.' He caught Tom's eye. 'Every *second* is precious, but you don't need to wait until you're dying to realize that.'

'I know.'

'How's Alice? I read that story in the *Herald*.'

'She's OK.'

'You don't like it, do you?'

'No,' Tom said. 'You should read the letter. It's sick.'

'Let's say she doesn't react. Hands the letter to the police and never mentions it to the press. What happens then?'

'We live a more peaceful life,' Tom said.

'Maybe. But that killer has chosen her,' his dad said. 'And that might not be what you – or Alice – would have wanted, but it's what's happened. She could ignore it, but there's no guarantee that puts a stop to it. Maybe they want her attention, so they start sending more letters. Or showing up at the house while you're at work.'

'So what do I do?'

'Support her. Same as last time.' His dad kissed Jo's forehead. 'And you keep her safe. Her and Joanna.' He held Jo up. 'You can take her now. Time for me to have a nap.'

Tom parked behind Alice's blue Astra and stepped onto the pavement. Jo was asleep in the car seat and he eased her out, being careful not to wake her up. The house was quiet; Alice's laptop was open on the dining-room table, but she was not there. He laid Jo in her basket in the living room and went into the kitchen.

There was still no sign of Alice. There was a mug on the counter top, a teabag in a freshly poured cup of tea. Wisps of steam came off it.

He went to the bottom of the stairs. 'Alice?' he called, softly.

There was no response. He started up the stairs, listening for any trace of her. At the top of the stairs he paused. The bathroom door was open, but the room was empty. He was about to call again, but he stopped himself. If she was sleeping – which was the most likely explanation – he didn't want to wake her.

He walked softly into the bedroom.

It was empty.

His chest tightened and he felt the first flutterings of panic. Her laptop was open and there was an un-drunk and un-milked mug of tea in the kitchen.

It looked like she had left in a hurry.

Or been removed in a hurry.

He took his phone from his jeans pocket and called her. It went straight to voicemail.

The panic solidified and he sat on the edge of the bed, his legs suddenly weak.

'Alice!' he shouted. 'Alice!'

He couldn't go out to search for Alice; he couldn't leave Joanna alone. And he'd tried calling her, but her phone was dead – or switched off by someone so she couldn't be traced.

He called Nadia.

'Hi, Tom. What's up?'

'It's Alice.'

'What about her?'

'She's missing.'

'What do you mean, missing?'

'I came home,' he said. His words were tumbling over each other, his voice breathless. 'I was at my parents' house with Jo, and when I got back she wasn't here. I tried to call, but it goes to voicemail.'

'There's probably a simple explanation. Maybe she just went for a walk?'

'There a cup of tea on the kitchen counter. The water's hot and there's a teabag in it. She wouldn't have done that if she was going for a walk.' He tried to calm himself. 'I think someone was here, Nadia. I think someone took her.'

'We can't jump to that conclusion, Tom.'

'Then where is she?' he said.

'Are there any signs of a struggle? A fight?'

'I didn't see any.'

'Have a look,' Nadia said. 'Start in the kitchen, by the tea.'

He went into the kitchen. There was nothing broken, no cupboard doors open, nothing on the floor.

'I don't see anything,' he said. 'But that doesn't—'

He heard the sound of the front door opening, then footsteps in the hall.

'Alice?' he shouted. 'Is that you?'

There was a click – heavy and foreboding as the front door closed.

'Is she back?' Nadia said.

'I don't know. Someone's here.'

'Tom. Be careful—'

He ran into the living room. He had to get to Joanna. He had to make sure she was safe. She was sleeping in her basket; he searched around for some kind of weapon. There was a poker by the fireplace. He snatched it up and hefted it in his hand. It was heavy, its solidity reassuring. He wouldn't hesitate to use it if he had to.

'Who's there?' he shouted, and walked into the hallway. 'Who is it?'

Alice was standing by the front door.

'*Alice*?' he said. 'Why didn't you answer?'

She held up a letter.

'There's another one,' she said.

She handed it to him. 'You read it.'

'When did it come?' he said.

'I saw it when I came back. I opened the door and it was on the mat.'

He took it from her. 'I've been home for ten minutes,' he said. 'There was nothing there when I arrived. We're being watched, Alice. Right now, probably.'

She shook her head. 'No. That's not possible.'

'Then how do you explain the timing?'

'It's a coincidence, Tom.'

'No,' he said. 'It isn't. Where were you?'

'I went for a walk.'

'I called. Your phone went to voicemail.'

'It's out of battery,' Alice said. 'I went for a walk.'

'I thought' – he shook his head – 'never mind. You want me to read this?'

She nodded, and he walked into the living room, opened the letter and sat down.

Alice!

I am afraid that you have pushed my patience too far. Don't say you weren't warned. I told you last time that this is not about YOU. It is about ME.

This is the last missive you will receive from me, but it is not the last time you will hear from me.

I cannot allow this to go unpunished, so we will meet face-to-face, Alice.

You are next.

When, where, how: these are details. What matters is only this: You are NEXT.

'What does it say?' Alice asked.

Ambleside, July 2013

Alice

Brenda took off her shirt. She was wearing shorts and a tank top; Alice noticed again how muscular her arms and shoulders were. She stepped into the lake until the water was up to her thighs.

'It's bloody cold,' she said. 'But it'll be OK once we're used to it. Come in!'

Alice laughed. 'I'm freezing just watching you. Maybe I'll give it a miss.'

'OK,' Brenda said. 'I'm going to take the plunge.' She turned and dived into the black water of the lake, disappearing from view for a few seconds. She surfaced a few yards away and swept her blonde hair back from her face.

'It's nice once you're in!' She duck-dived and began to swim with a smooth, powerful stroke. It wasn't long before she was twenty or thirty yards away. She turned and beckoned to Alice.

'Come on!'

Alice knelt by the water and put her hand in. It really *was* cold, but if Brenda could do it, she could too.

Although she didn't have to. She glanced at Brenda's bag. How much cash was in there? Was it safe to leave it unattended, even for a few minutes? If someone saw it they could empty it in seconds.

There was no one to see. It was only her and Brenda, who didn't know Alice knew she had the money. If she *had* known, she might not have left it with her. Alice could grab it and run off – although she was pretty sure Brenda would catch her quickly enough.

Or she could simply transfer the envelopes to her rucksack when Brenda wasn't looking. Not all of them – she'd miss them – but a few.

It was a good job she was not that kind of person. Brenda ought to be more careful.

She watched Brenda. She was swimming, head down, parallel to the shore. She was a good swimmer, but in a lake anything could happen. She could get a cramp, hit a rock, have a heart attack. Not likely, but possible. Then she would be gone, vanished into the depths of the lake.

And then what would Alice do? She couldn't rescue her. And who would know? There'd be no one other than Alice to report her missing. It would be up to her to call the authorities and hand over Brenda's belongings to them.

But Brenda would be fine. They'd have a swim in the lake and everything would be OK.

More than likely, anyway.

'Brenda!' she called. 'Hold on. I'm coming in!'

Alice tiptoed into the lake. It deepened quickly and she raised her arms as the water level rose to her waist. The rocks were slippery under her feet and she had to place them carefully.

Eventually, she could avoid it no longer. She took a deep breath and dived in.

The cold took her breath away, and she held her head out

250

of the water, hyperventilating. Eventually her body began to adjust and it started to feel comfortable, then exhilarating. She trod water, surprised at how steeply the lake bottom had shelved away.

She tilted her head back to look up at the scree slope, looming above the water's edge. Presumably the gradient continued like that under the surface. She had a sudden feeling that she was suspended above a chasm, and could fall into it at any second. All that was stopping her from sinking into it was this flimsy, cold water. It was easy to imagine yourself sinking, swirling down into the abyss.

Brenda called to her.

'It's warmer over here,' she said. 'Must be in the sun or something.'

Alice swam towards her, breaststroking to keep her head above the water.

'It doesn't feel much warmer,' she said.

'It's here, in this patch,' Brenda said. 'Maybe there's a thermal spring or something. You get that in lakes. Called a thermocline.'

She dived down, her feet kicking as she disappeared under the water. When she came up she was gasping. 'It's *much* colder even a few feet down,' she said. 'But this patch on the surface is nice.'

Alice swam closer until she was no more than an arm's length from Brenda. 'It doesn't seem warmer to me.'

'Maybe I'm just getting used to it,' Brenda said. She rolled onto her back and floated, her arms outspread. She was graceful in the water, like an otter.

'Isn't this *amazing*?' Brenda said. 'I'll remember this for ever. When we're done, can you take a photo of me? My phone's in my day pack.'

Alice looked at her, startled. She'd never suggested anyone looking in her day pack before; in fact she kept it close to

251

her at all times, the reason for which Alice now understood.
So why was she suggesting Alice look in her day pack now?
She must know she'd see the money.

Maybe she didn't care. If Alice asked her about it, she'd
say it was the way she preferred to manage her finances.

Or maybe she knew Alice had looked in her day pack and
was seeing how she'd react.

'OK,' Alice said. 'But we're not getting out for a while,
are we?'

'God no,' Brenda said. 'I love it here. And it's so peaceful.'
She turned a slow 360, scanning the area. 'There's not a soul
in sight.'

She was right, Alice thought. They were completely alone.

Anything could happen, and no one would ever know.

She found it an oddly thrilling feeling.

'Good idea, Brenda,' she said. 'Let's stay a while.'

Friday, 27 August 2021

Tom

He was not staying a day longer in this house. Whether Alice agreed or not, he and Joanna were leaving. A few years before, one of his colleagues had been held up at knifepoint when he was getting into his Audi A3, and the car had been stolen. He had been left by the side of the road with no transport home, but that wasn't his problem. His problem was that there was a printout of a holiday booking on the front seat, giving the details of when he and his girlfriend would be away, as well as their home address.

They'd gone to a hotel until they felt safe enough to return home, so that was what he and Alice would do. First a hotel and then a move to somewhere they couldn't be found until the killer was caught.

He told his boss most of what was happening, and she agreed he could work remotely for as long as it took.

Now he just had to talk it through with Alice.

'We have to go,' he said. 'When all this started we thought that there was no threat to you. The killer was using you to communicate with the police or the public or whatever fucked up reason they had, but they had their method of killing and they would stick to it, so you and me and Jo would be safe. But that's changed.'

She nodded, and sipped her coffee.

'It's personal now,' he said. 'There's a direct threat to you. You're next, Alice. That's what it said. It might be bluff, but we can't risk it. It's not safe.'

She nodded again, then spoke.

'I know,' she said, simply. 'I agree.'

He was taken aback. He had been expecting more resistance, arguments about how she couldn't walk away from this story, couldn't miss this opportunity. He had not anticipated this immediate agreement.

'OK,' he said. 'That's great.'

'So what's the plan?' she said. 'Where do we go?'

'A hotel,' he said. 'Then find a place and don't tell anyone the address.'

'Works for me.' She smiled. 'I can still write about the threat and what we're doing.'

'Alice,' he said. 'I'm not sure that's a great idea. It's better to get off the radar.'

'We'll be hidden away. It'll be fine. But we can discuss that later.' She finished her coffee and put the mug on the table. 'Where do you want to go? I can look for a rental place.'

'I don't really care. I just want to get away.'

'How about the Lake District?' she said.

'Fine by me.'

'Great,' Alice said. 'There's a place I know which has special memories for me. I'll see if there's somewhere there.'

'Where is it?' Tom asked.

'The deepest lake in the Lake District,' she said. 'Wast Water.'

Alice

She sat at a corner table, an espresso in front of her. The door opened and Nadia walked in. A few heads turned to look at her. Even in plain clothes in was obvious she was a cop; there was something about the confident way she moved, the way she looked around the café, taking everything in.

She saw Alice and raised a hand in greeting, then spoke to the barista and placed her order.

'So,' she said, when she got to the table. 'You wanted to talk?'

'Thanks for coming.'

'How are you? After the last letter?'

'I'm fine. The officer outside the house helps.' After she told Nadia and DI Wynne about the threat in the letter, they had sent two uniformed officers to look over the house. It was the only way Tom would stay another night.

'Good. They can stay as long as you need.'

'It might not be that long,' Alice said.

'Oh?' Nadia frowned. 'Why not?'

'We're going to stay in a hotel tonight, then head up to the Lake District. There's a house free which we're going to rent.'

'You got lucky.'

'I told the owner we'd take a month at peak rate. I think a few bookings might have been moved. Probably upset some people.'

'I think that's a good idea,' Nadia said. 'Get away for a while.'

'Do you think it'll work?' Alice said.

'What do you mean?'

'Could someone find out where we are?'

Nadia bobbed her head from side to side. 'I mean, in theory, yes. You'd leave a trace – credit card payment, or they could track your phone's location – but in practice, no. They'd need access to a lot of information that they would have no way of getting. Unless you told someone where you were and they somehow found out from them, I'd say you're pretty safe.' She sipped her drink, a herbal tea of some kind. 'I wouldn't tell many people, if any. Keep it to yourself and you should be fine.' She grinned. 'And it'll be fun! Some family time away from home. Change of scene.'

'Yeah,' Alice said. 'It should be. Although Tom's been' – she chose her words carefully – 'a bit erratic lately.'

Nadia leaned forward. 'You mentioned that a while back. Is it still happening?'

'Maybe he's tired. I don't want to talk behind his back. But – he's been angry and upset – partly reasonably, given all that's been going on. But part of it seems more than that. One night he was downstairs, his head in his hands, rocking back and forth while Jo screamed and screamed.'

'What did he say about it?'

'Nothing,' Alice said. 'He didn't know I saw him, and I didn't want to bring it up.'

Nadia raised an eyebrow. 'I think you might be better talking to him about it.'

'You're right,' Alice said. 'But – it's not easy.'

'Listen,' Nadia said. 'People can act strangely when they're under pressure. Often they get past it, but sometimes – well, I've seen it all in my job. If you think he's struggling – with anything – you need to talk to him and get him some help.'

'I don't think it's come to that, yet,' Alice said.

'I hope not,' Nadia replied. 'And if it has, I hope you don't find out when it's too late.'

Tom

Roland had a distant, glazed look in his eyes. Tom tensed. It was the way he had been when he was using.

He stood in the front hall and beckoned Tom inside. 'Dad's sleeping,' he said. 'Mum's gone for a walk.'

'And you're taking advantage of the free time?' Tom said. He had meant for it to sound jokey and light, a friendly reminder that he was watching his brother.

It did not come out like that. It sounded pointed and accusatory.

'What's that supposed to mean?' Roland said.

Tom closed his eyes. 'Maybe you fell off the wagon. You seem a bit stoned.'

'Well, I'm not,' Roland said. 'I'm sober. No booze, no junk, no weed. I don't expect you to believe me, but it's the truth. That's all that matters to me. Although I won't say I don't think about it, all the fucking time. That's the worst part, actually, Tom – not the craving, that I can deal with. It's that I'm constantly thinking about it. About how it would feel, about how it would make my anxiety go away. About how I could slip away into the bliss that I know is right there, right at my fingertips. I never stop thinking about it – and that

258

terrifies me. Is this what I've done to myself, Tom? Is this the rest of my life? Because if it is, I'm not sure I can stand it.'

'It'll get better,' Tom said. 'I'm sure it will. And I'm sorry. That was judgemental. But I'm having a pretty shit day of my own.'

'Care to elaborate?'

'The Crucifix Killer sent another note. This time telling Alice she's next.'

'My God,' Roland said. 'That is a bad day.'

'So we're going away for a while.'

'Away? Where away?'

'Tonight we'll be in a hotel, then we're going to a house in the Lake District Alice rented.'

'Is it that bad?' Roland said.

'Worse. She's the target now. And they've been at our house, posting letters through the door.' He shook his head. 'Even if it's not a real threat, I can't stay there. I can't sleep at night. This morning I looked like you. Maybe not that bad, actually.'

'You should be safe up there,' Roland said. 'Where is it?'

'We're keeping it secret.'

'Oh. I understand.'

'Although I was worried about Dad. If something happened and you needed to contact me it might be worth you having the address.'

'I could phone you.'

'Could be no reception. So just in case, I thought I'd give you the address.' It was a way of signalling to Roland that he was trying to trust him. A small step, and harmless enough, but something. He took out his phone. 'Alice emailed it to me. Here. I'll forward it on.'

'OK,' Roland said. 'Stay safe.'

'I will. And don't tell anyone where we are.'

'I won't,' Roland said. 'You can count on me.'

Saturday, 28 August 2021

Tom

They were staying in a hotel at Manchester airport. It felt safe, with all the security about. He, Alice and Jo were having breakfast. The breakfasts were his favourite thing about staying in a hotel – there were no more buffets, but you could still order eggs and fruit and bacon and porridge, and start the day properly.

His dad used to order kippers whenever they were on the menu, but Tom drew the line there.

He sipped his coffee. 'I didn't know you used to go up to the Lake District?'

Alice buttered a piece of toast. 'Yep. I went after university.'

'Camping?'

'Stayed in a youth hostel,' Alice said. She didn't elaborate. She had never talked much about her parents and childhood; he'd pressed once and she'd snapped at him that she preferred to leave some things in the past.

He could understand; some wounds were too raw to expose. He'd felt like that about Roland for years, but it was amazing how things could change if you gave them a chance. Maybe there was a lesson there for Alice.

'I'm glad we're going there,' he said. 'You can show me some of your childhood haunts.'

'Not really childhood. I was there with my boyfriend. Sure you want to hear what we got up to?'

'Maybe not,' he said. 'He was called Ned, right?'

'He was. We actually broke up while we were there.'

'Who dumped who?'

'I did the dumping,' Alice said. '*Please!*'

'You dumped your boyfriend on holiday?' Tom shook his head. 'That's a hell of a move, Alice.'

'It wasn't working,' she said. 'He had to go.'

'I guess I'll watch my step then,' he said.

'Yes,' she replied. 'I would, if I were you.'

Alice

The cottage she had found was a remote, converted farm-house, overlooking the lake. It had not been cheap, but money was not an issue. It was exactly what she wanted; she had been planning to browse for a suitable place to stay, a place which had the characteristics she needed, and then to find one which was so *perfect* – well, it had made this seem fated.

In the lounge there was a large picture window looking out over the lake. Opposite her the steep scree slope ran down to the black water. It was as still and deep and indif-ferent as she remembered.

She remembered this place. It hadn't changed at all.

Wast Water. It was not the kind of place that changed.

Tom appeared by her side, Jo in his arms.

'This place is amazing,' he said. 'It's like something out of *Lord of the Rings*. I half expect a Balrog to rise up from the water.'

'A what?'

'A Balrog. Although they may be fire demons, so perhaps it's unlikely there's one in the lake '

'What the bloody hell are you going on about?' she said.

'Never mind.' He smiled at her. 'I take it you didn't read *Lord of the Rings*, then?'

'No,' Alice said. 'Perhaps I can while we're here. I think we're going to have plenty of time.'

'I hope so,' he said. 'Maybe things will settle down.'

Tom

There was more or less no phone signal in the area, but the house had wireless. At least, it was supposed to, but it was hit and miss at best. Downstairs you were OK if you were in the kitchen or dining room; the living room seemed to depend on the time of day or alignment of the stars or some other arrangement, and upstairs was a dead zone. Tom had discovered that it also worked outside on the stone terrace that overlooked the lake, which was where he now sat.

He glanced over his shoulder. He did not want Alice to appear behind him and read the email he had just received.

Hi Tom

Hope you're well. Here are some photos of Alice from her university days. Some of them were prints that I scanned, but most were already digital so the quality is pretty good. I had quite a lot of fun looking through them – it brought back a lot of happy memories – so thanks for doing this!

They're quite self-explanatory and Alice will recognize all the people. I'll let her explain to you who they are.

If you need any more or have any questions, let me

know. Happy to help – and looking forward to getting back in touch with Alice after you give her the album!
    Nellie

He typed a reply.

Nellie,
    Thanks – this is fantastic, I really appreciate it. I'll take a look at them.
    One thing I wanted to let you know – we're away on a kind of extended holiday. It's pretty remote so I won't be able to get the photos printed. I was going to make an album online, but decided to do it by hand – tape them in and write my own captions – so am asking my brother, Roland, to get them all printed and then bring them to me in the next couple of days (her birthday is coming right up!)
    I'll forward these to him and copy you so you have his email address in case anything comes up.
    Thanks again!
    Tom

He sent the email then went back to the photos. There were nine attachments, and he opened the first one.

Three young women – Alice, Nellie and Mads, he assumed – looked at the camera, their faces slightly flushed. They were in a bar – probably on campus somewhere – and all three had cigarettes in their hands.

Which was odd. He had never known that Alice smoked. She had a bit of a thing about it, in fact – when he'd met her she wouldn't go anywhere near anyone who was smoking. He'd thought she was a bit obsessed with her physical fitness. She ran or did yoga or weights every day, and as often as she could she went swimming. He'd gone with her once; she was like a fish, scything through the pool.

She was a little less obsessed now, but still – smoking? He'd have to ask her about it when he gave her the album. Or maybe he shouldn't include this photo. She might not like it.

As a matter of fact, he wondered whether she would like the photo *regardless* of the cigarette. She was quite a bit different in it. Her face was fuller, and her arms – she was in a Nirvana T-shirt – were nowhere near as muscular as they were now.

In fact, it didn't really look like her at all.

The hair was the same, but young Alice had a wider smile and warmer, more expressive eyes.

He opened the next one.

It was a troupe of actors on a stage. It took a while for him to recognize Alice as she was dressed as a boy, a wool cap on her head. It was a pantomime; behind them on the stage was a Christmas tree.

She had never mentioned acting, either. He bent closer, zooming in on her face.

It was clearly the same person as in the other photo, but she bore no more than a passing resemblance to his wife. Had he not known better, he would almost have thought it was not the same person.

Well, people's appearances changed. They lost weight, gained weight. It wasn't that uncommon to hear someone say something along the lines of *she almost looks like a different person.*

His wife had changed a lot, probably after – and because of – her parents' death.

He just hoped Alice would be OK with being reminded of her former self.

Wast Water, July 2013

Alice

They swam lazy circles in the lake. Alice was aware that next to Brenda's sleek elegance, she was like a barrel bobbing about.

'This is magical,' Alice said. 'Makes me want to stay here for ever.'

'It really is,' Brenda said. 'Maybe we *could* stay here for ever.'

It was a bit of an odd thing to say. Alice looked at Brenda, and she was smiling, but the smile seemed forced.

Then the smile fell away, and with a sudden flick of her legs, Brenda lurched towards her. With her left arm she did a freestyle stroke; her right came out of the water, fingers spread wide. Too late, Alice understood what she was doing. Too late, she realized that the hand was aimed at her head. It was like in school swimming lessons when someone ducked you for a joke.

Except this was not a joke.

And this was not a swimming pool.

Brenda's hand slapped against her head and pressed down

with a shocking and intolerable force. Alice kicked her legs hard and circled her hands, trying to counter the pressure from Brenda's hand.

'Brenda,' she gasped. 'Stop. Please. What are you doing?'

Brenda stared at her. Her eyes were hard and expressionless. And empty.

There was not a flicker of recognition in them. It was as though she was looking at someone she had never met before.

They were the eyes of an animal.

Alice struggled, but it was pointless. Brenda was too strong, and, inch by inch, she sank under the surface. As her mouth and nose dipped under the water she twisted and took a final deep breath, and then she was surrounded by cold, cold water, with only that final breath in her lungs.

She reached above her head and grabbed Brenda's hand. It meant she was no longer able to fight the downward pressure, but that didn't matter; it was making no difference anyway. If she could move Brenda's hand then she could get away.

Brenda would chase her down, though. She was a much better swimmer than her. But so what. She could deal with that when – if – it happened.

It had been only seconds, but her lungs were already burning, her heart pounding in her chest. She had only moments to get away

She thought of her friends, Nellie, Mads. Of Ned. Of them all at her funeral, in tears.

She had to survive.

But Brenda's hand was impossible to move. Part of the problem was that Alice was still struggling upwards, which was forcing her into Brenda's grasp. It seemed crazy, but she needed to go *down*.

She stopped kicking and paddled down with her hands.

It worked; she felt the pressure from Brenda's hand vanish,

and she kicked away on her back. She needed to get to the surface, and quickly.

Her head broke into the sunlight. She gasped in lungfuls of air, water streaming down her face, then something hit her head. It was a foot, crashing into her chin. Brenda was on her back, lashing out with her feet.

There was another blow and pain exploded in her jaw. She tried to swim away, but Brenda, a much better swimmer, came after her.

A hand gripped her bicep.

Another hand clamped down on her head, and pushed.

Her vision narrowed, the edges darkened, and her lungs felt like they were going to burst.

As her oxygen-starved brain began to shut down, she had time for one final thought.

Why? Why is she doing this?

Brenda

Brenda felt calm, and good. She felt at peace.

The last few weeks had been hell. It had been hard to keep herself together. She had felt unmoored.

Moving from place to place, no idea what came next, just knowing she could not stay still, could not risk being caught. It had made her want to kill.

That was all she could think: *I have to kill. It will make me feel in control, and then I can focus on other things.*

Make a plan.

And then she had met Alice. No parents to look for her. Her boyfriend dismissed. Her friends abroad.

She was the perfect victim. All Brenda needed was an opportunity. A swim in a deep lake.

But, as she planned it – and her hunger grew and became harder to hide – she saw that Alice was more than merely a way to ease her need.

More than just a victim.

She was the answer to *everything*. All Brenda's problems would be removed at one stroke.

She left the body in shallow water, taking care to make sure no one was around. Then she took her large rucksack – she had no need for it or its contents any more, not now she had Alice's – and carried it into the lake. She opened the flap and stuffed in some large rocks, then turned the body on its front and twisted the arms through the straps.

Then she clipped the waist strap around Alice's hips and dragged her out into the middle of the lake.

It was a struggle to move the body and the rucksack – the weight of the rocks and rucksack dragged it down, which was exactly the point – but fortunately the lake deepened steeply so she didn't have to go more than thirty or forty yards.

Still, when she got to the spot she wanted, she was panting, and it was a relief to let go and watch the body sink into the darkness.

She lay on her back and stared up at the blue sky. It was cloudless and she felt a sensation of perfect peace.

Beneath her, the body of Alice Barnes drifted to its final resting place.

PART THREE

Saturday, 28 August 2021

Tom

He sent the email, then forwarded the original to Roland.

Hey – look at these photos! Alice has changed a lot. I'm going to ask for a couple more – will copy you. Then can you get them printed and we can meet up? Thanks, Tom

He was interrupted by Alice.

'Tom,' she said. 'Let's go. I'm ready.'

She was standing by the back door, Jo perched in a back-pack. In her hand she had a small rucksack.

'Is that new?' he said. 'I haven't seen it before.'

'No,' she said. 'I've had it years. I forgot about it. The last time I used it was when I was here, and so I dug it out.'

'Give me a minute. I have to send an email.'

She walked outside and stood looking at the lake. He opened his laptop and started to type.

Nellie

    Thanks once again for the photos. It's coming together well! One more question – do you have anything from the post-university years? I don't have any from before I met her.

    If so, could you send them to me and Roland (on copy)?

    Best

    Tom

As he hit send, an email notification popped up. It was from Roland.

Wow – she is really different. Like another person. Will watch out for the email. All OK? We're fine. Will keep you posted if anything changes with Dad. You can always get back if necessary, right? R

Tom typed a quick reply.

Yes, I can. And keep me posted. My phone will be on but reception is patchy so keep trying.

'Tom,' Alice said. 'Can that wait? Let's go. I want to see the lake up close. It has a lot of memories for me.'

He closed his laptop. Alice had a strange, faraway look in her eyes. This place was obviously special to her for reasons he didn't understand. He could ask her more about it later.

    'Coming,' he said.

Alice

She was surprised how many memories the walk by the lake had evoked. It was all so clear to her: she could almost take herself back to the day she had been here. It was as though no time had passed at all.

Tom had his arm around her shoulder, Jo in a papoose on his front.

She almost flinched away from him. When she'd met him she'd barely noticed him; he was one of those people who blended into the background. He held nothing of interest to her. He was simple; he lived in the moment and took everything and everyone at face value. Everybody liked him; there was nothing to dislike.

Which was why she had eventually seen he was perfect for her. He'd bumble around, smiling at everyone, trusting them all, trusting *her*. Whatever she wanted from him, he'd provide. Whatever she told him, he'd believe.

And he had. The overnight trips for work, when she had fed her hunger? He had never questioned them. Not once.

She had done whatever she liked, and to the world she was just another person, married and happy. He was the perfect disguise.

And then the baby came.

She had had no idea how fucking *disruptive* it would be. She'd thought things would be like before, but with a baby in the house. The reality was awful. It needed her constantly. The demands were endless. It was degrading. Humiliating.

Tom's mum had said, early on, *You have no idea how hard it will be, but it's worth it. You love them so much.*

Not her. She hated the damn thing. All she had felt was how hard it was.

And worse, Tom had changed. He saw the baby as a shared project. Gone were the days of her swanning off hunting some fictitious story.

And so her hunger grew. The need to kill became so sharp she could no longer ignore it. But how could she satiate it? When?

At night, was the answer. Jo would only sleep in the car: well, so be it. She'd take advantage of those night-time drives to find her prey.

Now, though, the cops were too close. She'd made a mistake with the letters, but she hadn't been able to resist doing it. It was a display of her superiority, but it had cost her the freedom to move.

'Brings back memories, huh?' Tom said.

'Kind of.'

'Sad ones? Anything to share? Are you nostalgic for something?'

Tom – foolish, foolish Tom – had asked her if she was feeling nostalgic. He had given her his stupid little grin and asked if she was feeling sad, and if she wanted to share anything.

'Not now,' she replied. 'Maybe later.'

She had, for a second, contemplated telling him the truth.

I don't feel any nostalgia. I don't feel any sadness. I don't feel anything.

Ever.

At least, not the way you do.

278

I feel the emptiness that can only be filled by one thing.
I feel that all the time, growing and growing until it cannot
be contained.

But other than that, I do not have feelings. I don't know
what they are. Love? Pity? Compassion? Fear? These are
meaningless words. Empty sounds.

But it is too soon to tell him that. Not much too soon.
But still too soon.

There were still some pieces that had to be arranged
before that.

Although the wait must come to an end shortly.

The need, the void, the *hunger*, demanded it.

They arrived back at the house, Joanna still asleep.

'I'll put her down,' Tom said. 'Maybe she'll sleep better
with all this Lakeland air.'

Alice sat on the terrace and thought through what was
to come next. There was work to be done, tasks to complete.
Many, many tasks. But while Tom was upstairs with Jo, she
chose Kay.

She wrote her a message.

Hi. How's tricks?

Kay replied right away.

Fine. More importantly how are you?

Not great. Can you call?

Her phone rang seconds later.

'Hi,' she said.

'What's happening?' Kay said. 'Are you OK?'

'Yeah,' she said, in a low voice. 'More or less.'

'Why are you whispering? Are you hiding?'

'No,' Alice said. 'But there's not great coverage at the house so I'm outside on the terrace. Tom's inside, but I'd rather he didn't hear me.'

'OK. So what's going on?'

'It's strange, Kay. Now that I'm with him all the time I can see it more clearly. It's like I knew it all along, but I couldn't see it.'

'See what?'

'Who he really is.'

'Jesus,' Kay said. 'What do you mean?'

'He's crazy, Kay.' She lowered her voice further. 'He paces the room, talking to himself, and not just talking – having these heated arguments in two different voices. When I speak to him, he has this kind of fixed smile and glazed look. We went for a walk on the lake shore and he was asking me if my memories of this place make me sad and nostalgic, but I've never been here! It's like he's in an alternative world. And then there's Jo.'

'What about her?'

'Another bruise.'

There wasn't one, but she'd add one later.

'On her left arm, this time.' She paused, for dramatic effect. 'He's hurting her, Kay.'

'You need to get out of there,' Kay said.

'I know, but I can't leave him,' Alice said. 'What if he hurts himself? Or worse?'

'You can't think like that. You have to go.'

'I need to get him some help. Professional help.'

'There's no doubt about that,' Kay said. 'But this has gone too far, Alice. You have to do something now.'

Alice took a deep breath. 'OK,' she said. 'I'll look into it tomorrow.'

* * *

She had one more call to make. She dialled the number and waited for someone to answer.

It was a man's voice, gruff and deep and thick with a Cumbrian accent.

'Hello?'

'Hi there,' she said. 'I was calling about the boat on Craigslist?'

'The dinghy?'

'That's right.'

'Are you interested?'

'I am. My husband and I are staying near Wast Water for a while. He's keen on having something simple to mess about on the lake with.'

'This 'un's pretty small,' the man said. 'My kids learned to sail in it thirty years ago.'

'It's a sailing boat?' Alice said. The listing had not specified that, and she did not know how to sail.

'Used to be. The mast and rigging's long gone. I used it for rowing out to my yacht on Windemere until I sold it.'

'And it works?'

'If you mean floats, yes. It's pretty beaten up, but it's fibreglass, so it'll be around a while yet. There's rowlocks and oars, so she's ready to go.'

'What, sorry?' Alice said. 'There's something and oars?'

'Rowlocks. Don't worry. I'll show you, if you're interested.'

'I am,' Alice said. 'Although let me confirm with my husband. It's really him that wants the boat.'

'I'm here tomorrow,' the man said. 'You can come and look then, if you'd like. And if he's interested.'

'I'll tell you what,' Alice said. 'Let's assume he's OK with it. I'll let you know if not. What's your address?'

The man gave her an address in Ambleside. 'Do you have transport?' he said. 'You'll need a towbar.'

She paused. She didn't have a towbar on her car. 'Damn,' she said. 'I don't. But maybe I can get one fitted at a garage?'

'Don't bother,' the man said. 'If you agree not to haggle, I'll follow you back with it and drop it off for you.'

'That's OK,' Alice said. 'Really. I don't want to be an inconvenience.'

'No inconvenience. I don't get out much these days. I'll be glad to do it.'

DI Wynne

The call was from a foreign number. She didn't know which country the code represented, but she had a good guess. There was only one country she had called recently.

Australia.

'Detective Inspector Wynne,' she said, glancing at the clock. It was just past 9.30 in the evening.

'Hi, my name's Tony Munro. I'm a detective in Perth, Western Australia.'

'Tony,' she said. 'Jane Wynne.'

'Nice to meet you. It's not too late, is it?'

'No. What time is it for you?'

'Too bloody early. 5.30 a.m. But I thought you'd want to hear this as soon as possible, and I'm an early riser. Or a crap sleeper. Same difference.'

'Thank you for calling so early,' Wynne said. 'I take it this is about the request I made?'

'Yeah, about the serial killer. It came my way overnight. First thing I saw in my inbox this morning. Which is why I'm on the blower now. Thing is' – he paused – 'we had the same thing happen here in Perth.'

Wynne felt a surge of adrenaline, then a prickling feeling

on her skin. It was often this way on a case. Nothing, no leads, no progress, and then something. 'When?'

'In 2012 and 2013. Six murders, four women, two guys, which is unusual all by itself. Then there's the method. It's a lot like yours – ambushed late at night, blow to the head with a large hammer, body abandoned. We had no letters and no crucifixes, but other than that – it all looks the same.'

'Did you catch the perp?'

'No. The last victim was murdered in May 2013, and then the killings stopped.'

'Any suspects?'

'None that mattered.'

'And you think those murders might be linked to the ones I'm investigating?'

'Hard to say,' Munro said. 'But it's possible. Especially with that Australian accent.'

'This is very helpful, Detective Munro,' Wynne said. 'Would you be able to share your files? Case notes? Photos?'

'No worries.' There was a sound like someone slurping a drink. Coffee, probably. 'There was one other thing at the time. Probably unrelated, but it's worth a mention.'

'What was that?'

'There was a family killed in late May of that year. Both parents were murdered in the house, and their daughter – she was in her early twenties – disappeared. We had her down as a suspect, but she never showed up again.'

'How is this linked?' Wynne said.

'The method. The parents were killed by blows to the head.'

'But not late at night. In their house?'

'That's right. It seemed possible there was a link because of the hammer, but that's hardly the most original choice of murder weapon.'

'And the daughter disappeared?'

'That was a mystery,' Munro said. 'It seemed like either she was killed too, or she did it and ran away, or her disappearance was totally unrelated. But I thought I'd mention it.'

'What was her name?' Wynne said. 'The daughter.'

'Andrea Petersen. I'll ship those files over, too.'

'Thank you,' Wynne said. 'I appreciate the call.'

Ambleside, July 2013

Brenda

Brenda took a mirror and a pair of scissors from her day pack. There, at the bottom of the pack, were the envelopes of cash. Fucking Alice had seen them; they had almost given her away. They were a sign of the precariousness of her existence.

Thankfully she wouldn't need them any more. Her existence was about to become a lot more secure.

She propped the mirror against a rock and studied her reflection. She'd be glad to get rid of this hair; she only kept it so long so that when she cut it short she'd be totally unrecognizable.

And in this case, so she'd look like Alice. Her hair was close-cropped and dark; Brenda liked it, so she was glad she would soon be wearing the same hairstyle.

She took the scissors in one hand, and a fistful of hair in the other. She held it close to the roots and cut a length of blonde hair from her head.

She threw it in the lake and watched as the strands slowly separated and drifted away from the shore, then grabbed another fistful and lifted the scissors to her head.

When she'd finished she took a baseball cap from Alice's rucksack and put it on her head. She'd have to dye her hair, but for now the cap was enough. She took off her shorts and tank top and pulled a shirt and jeans from Alice's rucksack. Alice was a similar size to her, although her clothes were looser fitting.

It would have to do, and it would be enough. Anyone seeing Brenda in Alice's cap and clothes would assume it was Alice, unless they got up close, which Brenda had no intention of letting them do.

She packed everything away and stood up, heaving the rucksack onto her shoulders. She looked out over Wast Water. It was silent and ancient. It was not the type of place that gave up its secrets easily.

But it was the kind of place that had them.

Near the shore, her hair slowly drifted away. Brenda nodded, a small sign of satisfaction at a job well done, then set off along the rocky path.

On the train she sat by the window, scrolling through Alice's phone. She had watched her unlock it enough times to know the code; it was the same as the PIN she had used to withdraw money the first night they had gone to the pub.

She read through her emails and messages, familiarizing herself with the conversations she and her friends had had and cross-referencing them to photos in her photo roll. She imagined Alice replying to them, hearing her voice in her head, perfecting her tone. Over time – but soon – she would need to phase these friends out. Reply to fewer of their messages, ignore their invitations, not react to their social media posts.

In a week or so, she'd tell a few of them she was going away on her own for a month or two, travelling in Europe. They'd assume she was busy, or had met someone, and gradually she would drift from their consciousness. It was surprising how flimsy friendships could be, how easily jobs and boyfriends and other people replaced the friends you thought were so important. Very few relationships survived one person neglecting them; the other party had to be very committed.

Like Ned. He'd already sent four messages since she'd boarded the train.

HI. Are you home today?

You're booked on the train this evening, right?

Did you get the train?

I could meet you at Nottingham station and take you to your house, if you like?

She had been planning to ignore him, but she had to stop this happening, so she typed a reply.

It's fine. I have a taxi booked. And I need some alone time

Tomorrow, then? We need to talk.

We don't. I said everything I wanted to, Ned.

No. This is too important to throw away. I'll come tomorrow. I'm at my house in Nottingham, clearing out my stuff. Even if it's only for 5 minutes. I have to see you.

Shit. It was clear this guy was not going to leave her alone. Obviously she couldn't see him, which left only one way to deal with the situation.

So soon after Alice. Her pulse quickened in anticipation.

OK. But not at the house. We can meet somewhere neutral.

Where? And when?

In the evening. I have things to do in the day. I'll be in touch tomorrow.

She sent the text and sat back in her seat, looking out of the window. They pulled into a station and a handful of people boarded the train. One, a young man in a blue cap and loose-fitting jeans, sat next to her.

'OK if I sit here?' he said.

She was about to reply *No worries, mate*, but then she remembered.

She'd been working on her English accent for a reason.

'Of course,' she said. 'Feel free.'

Sunday, 29 August 2021

Roland

Roland opened the photos on his mum's iPad. 'Look,' he said. 'Here's Alice at university.'

'She's changed,' she said. 'A lot. Look, Don.'

She handed the iPad to his dad. He rested it on his knees; even the light weight of the tablet was becoming difficult for him to hold.

'She does look different,' he said. He wagged his head from side to side. 'I wouldn't say this to Tom or Alice – so keep this to yourselves – but I'm not sure the change is for the better. There's a spark in her eyes when she was younger which I haven't seen much of lately.'

'That's youth,' his mum said. 'We all had a spark in our eyes back in the day.'

'You still do,' his dad said. 'Not changed at all. That's not what I'm talking about. I love Alice, but she's very reserved. That girl' – he pointed at the screen – 'looks more open.'

'I think if there was a photo of me when I was eighteen I'd look like a different person than I do now,' Roland said. 'People do change, Dad.'

'They do. But the inner person stays the same,' his dad said. 'And I'm just saying that it's almost like there are two versions of Alice. You *haven't* changed, by the way. Not when I see you. I still see the fat little baby I held the day you were born. Did you make a mess of some things? Yes. Did you learn some lessons? I bloody hope so. But you're still you, Roland, at the core.'

'Sometimes I wonder about that,' Roland said. 'Sometimes I wonder whether I corroded myself so badly that there's not much left.'

'You didn't. And I'm glad you're building bridges with your brother.'

'I am too,' his mum said. She put her hand on his forearm, her fingers tracing the scars. 'I'm so happy he asked you to help with this album. It shows he trusts you.'

'A bit,' Roland said. 'He trusts me a bit. Which is a start.'

His dad closed his eyes. He was getting tired even more quickly these days. One day – soon – he would close his eyes for the last time. Roland pushed the thought away; it brought with it the urge – the craving – for self-oblivion, and the reminder that it was all very well staying clean on the good days, but it was how you reacted on the bad days that mattered.

And the day his dad died would be a very bad day indeed.

He leaned over and kissed his dad's head.

'Love you, Dad,' he said.

While he waited for the kettle to boil he checked his emails. He'd applied for a series of jobs doing basic office work, but with his record – he had several convictions for petty theft – work was hard to come by.

There was one from a temporary agency.

Dear Mr Sark
Thank you for registering with our agency. We have a potential opening for you at Rodela Autos, in Widnes.

The owner likes to offer people who need it a second chance and he would like to meet you this afternoon at 4 p.m. The job involves working in the car parts distribution warehouse.

Please let me know whether you are interested and available this afternoon.

Yours

Archie Turner

Was he interested? This was perfect. He would have gone to any interview, taken any work on offer. He replied that he was free and would be there that afternoon.

After he sent it, he noticed another email. This one was from Nellie. He opened it.

Hi Roland

I found one more photo you might use. It's from the summer after we graduated. Mads and I went travelling. Alice was going to come, but in the end she went away with her boyfriend at the time (a guy called Ned). They broke up and she went travelling by herself around Europe but she did send a photo of her and an Australian she met – called Brenda, I think – from when she was in the Lake District. In fact, now I think about it, it was more or less the last time I heard from her. She went to live in Warrington after that summer and we all drifted apart. Fortunately now we're back in touch!

Nellie

He opened the photo. Alice was sitting beside a blonde woman, next to a river. It was a good one; he'd definitely get it printed and give it to Tom.

He was about to close it, when something caught his eye. He studied the photo, then froze.

This couldn't be right. He couldn't be seeing what he was seeing.

He zoomed in on the Australian woman, Brenda.

'What the *fuck*?' he said.

Nottingham, July 2013

Brenda

She spent the morning going through Alice's affairs. Birth certificate, GCSEs, A Levels. Bank statements, a password jotted on the corner of one. Passport, National Insurance card.

All the accoutrements of a life.

A life that was now hers.

Alice had been perfect for this. She was at a transitional point so she could easily move somewhere new and lose touch with her friends. She had no parents or siblings, and a boyfriend she had recently dumped.

She was poised on the cusp of a new life, a life that would soon be Brenda's.

Plus – if what she had said was anything to go by – she had money from her inheritance.

She opened Alice's laptop. She had had it with her in the youth hostel, and Brenda had watched her enter the password on two occasions. She tried it now; it worked.

She went to the website of Alice's bank.

User name. That would be her email, most likely. And her password – if she was like most people – would be the same as the one for her email and laptop.

She typed it in.

Bingo.

Her account details came up, and Brenda giggled. She actually *giggled*. It was not something she did normally, but this was not normal. This was extraordinary.

She had over half a million pounds in her current account, along with some investment accounts, adding up to nearly a million pounds.

Alice was rich. *Brenda* was rich.

The whole world had opened up in front of her. She could take any path she wanted, do anything, go anywhere. There was only one obstacle.

Ned. She could not ever see him again, but it was clear he would not leave her alone. Eventually he would show up, which was a problem.

But, like all problems, there was a solution.

She spent the afternoon looking at Google Maps of the area. She needed a place with specific characteristics. She found it ten miles outside the city.

Ned's student house in Nottingham was about four hundred yards from a pub, the Dirty Duck. On the map it looked like the quickest path for him was along a road that ran between two industrial units, before emerging onto the main road.

Presumably he would come on foot, and presumably he would take the shortest route.

The route between two industrial units, both closed for the day.

She sent him a message.

Can we meet at the Dirty Duck at 7?

The reply came instantly.

Why there? Can we meet earlier?

Because I don't want to run into anyone. And I'm tied up until then

OK. See you then

She parked where she could see the road between the industrial units and waited. Just before seven a man turned into it.

She recognized Ned from the pub in Ambleside and the photos on Alice's phone.

She started the engine and followed him. When he was about twenty yards away she beeped her horn – the horn on Alice's Polo – and pulled to a halt behind him. When he turned to look at her, she beckoned him to get in on the passenger side.

She kept her head down, looking at her phone as he got in, her face hidden by the baseball cap.

He sat in the passenger seat.

'Hi,' he said, his voice nervous. 'Thanks for stopping.'

She raised a finger as though she was too busy to reply, then glanced around, checking there was no one in the area who could see them.

It was deserted. She took off the baseball cap, and he frowned in confusion.

'You're not Alice,' he said.

'No shit, Sherlock,' she said, in her normal, Australian voice.

The confusion deepened. 'Who are you?'

She laughed, but there was no smile. She let him look into her eyes and see what she was. It was the moment she most relished, the moment they realized it was over, the moment they saw that evil was real, and that it lived in her.

It gave her an intense surge of pleasure, the release of a deep tension.

'It doesn't matter, Ned. Not to you, anyway.'

She groaned, then swung the hammer, claw first, into his disbelieving eye.

After that it was over quickly. She cleaned his face with a towel and then jammed the cap onto his head and pushed his chin onto his chest so it appeared he was sleeping. Satisfied it would fool any casual observer, she drove to the pub and parked in a corner of the car park.

In the pub she ordered a glass of white wine and sat by a window so she could see the car. If anyone got too near she'd have to find a way to stop them.

No one did. After five minutes had passed, she sent a text.

Hey. Are you late?

He wouldn't be replying. Even if he had somehow been resurrected, his phone was in the canal by the industrial units. Ten minutes later she sent another.

Give me a call. Let me know if you're still coming.

At 6.30 she sent another.

I get it. You want to show me who's boss. Enjoy your life, Ned

She finished her wine and took the empty glass to the bar. The barman gestured at it.

'Another?'

'No thanks,' she said, in her best Alice voice. 'I've been stood up.'

Sunday, 29 August 2021

Tom

Tom sat by the lake, his back against a sun-warmed rock. On the far shore the slope of a mountain loomed over the surface of the water. It was really quite spectacular – not the type of scenery he associated with England. No rolling hills and sheep-dotted fields here; this was grand and imposing and utterly indifferent.

Jo was sitting opposite him, picking up a small, smooth pebble and then putting it down. Each time she did she gave a little giggle, contemplated the stone, and then promptly picked it up again. After a few seconds it was back on the ground, and she was giggling at her work.

He wondered what she was thinking, or if she was even thinking at all, at least in the way he understood it. There was no doubt she wasn't thinking in words – she wasn't wondering where the rocks had come from or marvelling at the grandeur of the jagged peaks that surrounded them – but there was something causing her to smile and laugh.

Maybe she just liked rocks. Well, there were plenty here. She could take her pick.

She dropped the stone and he picked it up. It was smooth, worn by centuries – maybe millennia – of gentle erosion. He hefted it in his palm, then threw it up and caught it.

'Listen,' he said, and tossed it into the lake. It vanished with a satisfying *plop*.

Jo frowned, then her eyes screwed up and she started to cry.

'I'm sorry,' he said, and grabbed a similar looking stone. He handed it to her, but she batted it away.

'It's as good,' he said, and tried again.

She did not want it. She wanted the particular pebble she had been playing with.

Which was now in the lake.

'Don't worry, Jo,' he said. He took off his shoes and stepped into the frigid water. 'I can get it.'

He walked out to where – roughly – the stone had entered the lake and made a show of searching for it, peering into the water. After a moment he reached down and picked up a similar sized stone and examined it.

'No,' he said, and let it drop. 'Not that one.'

He repeated this a few times, then, eventually, nodded.

'This is it,' he said. 'Here's your pebble.'

He walked out of the lake and placed it on the ground in front of her. She stared at it for a second, then picked it up and, with a giggle, dropped it on the ground. Evidently it was close enough.

Tom smiled and took out his phone. He checked his emails. There was a new one from Roland.

Tom. Check out this photo. You need to see this.

He clicked on it, but the photo didn't load. There was no signal here; the phone must have picked up the email earlier but not had time to download the attachment. He could get it when he was back at the house. No doubt it was something for the album.

There was a noise behind him and he turned around.

The gate at the side of the house was open. He saw Alice's back, walking away towards the drive. A minute later, she reappeared, pulling a small trailer, on top of which was a rowing boat.

There was an old man next to her. She waved, and beckoned for Tom to come over.

'Well, Jo,' he said. 'What on *earth* is Mummy up to?'

Alice

Tom walked up from the lake, Jo in a sling against his chest. The boat – a pale blue fibreglass dinghy about eight feet long with *Annelise* stamped on the side – was light, and the trailer, rusty as it was, wheeled easily enough. The slope down to the lake was steep in parts, though, and she did not want it to run away with her.

And Eric was no help. He was in his late eighties and very frail; she'd been worried he wouldn't survive the drive, especially given the dirt caked on the windscreen of his ancient Land Rover.

'Tom,' she said. 'This is Eric. He helped me bring the boat.'

Eric held out his hand. It was still uncommon for people to shake hands – some pandemic anxiety lingered – but Eric clearly didn't share it.

'How do,' he said. 'Eric Widdop.'

'Tom Sark. Is this your boat?'

'It's yours now. It's what you wanted, I hear.'

'Yes,' she said. 'Tom really likes boats.' Alice caught Tom's eye and raised an eyebrow. 'Don't you, Tom?'

'Oh,' he said. 'I love them. Always wanted one.'

'Well,' Eric said. 'Take care of her. Nice to meet you both.' He looked at Jo. 'And you.'

'Thank you,' Alice said. 'I'll walk you to your car.'

When she got back to the boat, Tom was smiling.

'You bought a boat?'

'Something for us to enjoy. I thought we could go out on the water. Have a picnic.'

He smiled. 'Sounds fun. Eric seemed to think I wanted it?'

'He's a bit confused,' Alice said. 'I tried to explain that it was a surprise for you, but it didn't sink in. So I just said you wanted it.'

'Where did you find it?'

'I saw a sign in the supermarket in Ambleside.'

He laughed. 'So you're buying boats on a whim now? When out getting some groceries? That's not like you.'

'It wasn't expensive. It's seen better days.' She squeezed his hand. 'But it floats. It'll be fun. Come on. Let's take her on her maiden voyage.'

'She doesn't exactly look like a maiden to me,' he said. 'But I know what you mean.'

Tom

The boat *was* fun. Alice had bought a life jacket for Jo; she and Tom didn't have them, but they stayed close to shore, enjoying the sounds of the water lapping against the fibreglass.

'Well,' Tom said. 'I think I'll go on an adventure tomorrow. Maybe cross the entire lake.'

'You can leave Jo here,' Alice said. 'I'm not sure she's ready for a sea voyage yet.'

'Agreed.' He looked at his watch. 'Four p.m. You want to go and start getting dinner ready? I'm starving. Must be all this fresh air.'

'OK,' she said, and grabbed the oars. 'I'll row us in.'

They beached gently on the rocky shore and Tom climbed out. Alice handed Jo to him.

'I'll drag her onto the beach and tie her up,' she said. 'You take Jo and get her something to eat.'

'Got it.'

He carried Jo up to the house and settled her in her high-chair on the terrace, then went into the kitchen to grab a jar of baby food and a spoon. When she saw it she banged her fists on the plastic tray in front of her; she was hungry too.

He spooned the food into her mouth and she ate it quickly.

When the jar was empty she settled down, and he picked up his phone. There was a text from Roland.

Did you get my email earlier?

Checking now. Didn't have a signal by the lake.

He opened the email.

Tom. Check out this photo. You need to see this.

Attached, there was a message from Nellie and a photo.

Hi Roland
   I found one more photo you might use. It's from the summer after we graduated. Mads and I went travelling. Alice was going to come, but in the end she went away with her boyfriend at the time (a guy called Ned). They broke up and she went travelling by herself around Europe but she did send a photo of her and an Australian she met – called Brenda, I think – from when she was in the Lake District. In fact, now I think about it, it was more or less the last time I heard from her. She went to live in Warrington after that summer and we all drifted apart. Fortunately now we're back in touch!
   Nellie

He opened the photo. Alice was sitting next to a blonde woman – Brenda, presumably – beside a river. Again, he was struck by how different she looked to the woman he had married.

Weirdly, Brenda resembled Alice now, at least facially. She had the same sharp features and muscular frame. At a glance, they could have been sisters.

He took a closer look. His back tightened and he felt a dryness in his mouth.

They could have been more than sisters.

They could have been *twins*.

But that was impossible. He read the message from Nellie again. Brenda – the blonde woman in the photo – was some Australian that Alice had met when she was in the Lake District after she graduated.

But she did look a lot like Alice.

Identical, in fact.

He heard footsteps on the terrace and lifted his head from the screen. Alice was standing there, holding the oars.

He glanced at the photo, then at her, then back at the photo.

It was impossible to miss.

Alice was in the photograph, but she was not the woman on the left, the woman with short, dark hair who was in all the other photos of Alice that Nellie had sent.

She was the woman on the right.

The long, blonde-haired Australian called Brenda.

Alice

Tom was looking at her in an odd way. His mouth was slack, as though he was in deep thought. He kept looking at her and then at his phone.

'Alice,' he said, after a moment. 'Can I show you something?'

'Of course.'

He seemed shocked. Scared, almost. She tensed. What the hell did he have on his phone?

Possibilities flashed through her mind. The message she had sent to Eric asking about the boat, maybe. Or her text messages to Nadia and Kay about his moods.

Whatever it was, it wasn't good.

He held up his phone so she could see the screen.

It was worse than she could have imagined. It was the photo Alice Barnes – stupid, stupid, Alice – had taken by the side of the river. She had lifted her phone and snapped it before Brenda could get out of shot.

That was all it took. One photo. One mistake.

'Where did you get that?' she said, fighting to keep her voice even and calm.

'That doesn't matter,' he said. 'I got it, is all that matters.'

'It does. I'm interested.' She needed to stall for some time to think of a way to deal with this, and she needed as much information as she could get.

He shrugged. 'Nellie sent it to me.'

'Nellie? Why did she send you a photo of me?'

Alice Barnes must have sent it to her friends, Nellie and Maddie.

Fuck.

'That doesn't matter,' he said. 'What matters is what's going on in this photo.'

Alice looked at the photo again, and it came to her. The way out was obvious.

'What do you mean?' she said.

'I mean, why are you Brenda?'

She frowned. 'I'm not Brenda,' she said.

He pointed to the blonde-haired woman.

'That's you,' he said.

'I know,' she replied. She pointed at the other woman. 'And that's Brenda.'

'That's Brenda?' he said. 'No. That's Alice. That's supposed to be you. But the other woman is you.'

'You've got it all wrong,' she said. 'That summer I grew my hair out and dyed it blonde. When I was away I met Brenda – that's her – and I liked her look. She cut it short for me and dyed it the same colour as hers – we had quite a bit of fun telling people we were sisters, separated at birth in Australia, with me sent here to live with an English family. This was our big reunion.'

He didn't reply, his face expressionless.

'All these questions,' she said. 'There's really nothing to it.'

He shook his head.

'Alice,' he said. 'Why are you lying?'

Nottingham, July 2013

Brenda

She left the pub and sat in the car. In the passenger seat Ned was dozing – or looked like he was – the cap over his eyes obscuring the gaping hole the claw of the hammer had left where his right eye had been.

She felt fantastic. She always did, afterwards. In the run-up the anticipation was almost unbearable, everything sharper, all her senses heightened. It was as though she saw more colours, in sharper relief, heard more sounds, her body primed and ready to do *anything*.

But afterwards: the release was the most wonderful drug there was.

And she wanted more and more of it.

She took out Alice's phone and selected Ned's mum's number.

Hi. Is Ned at home? We were supposed to meet up but he didn't show.

Then she started the engine and pulled out into the road.

She drove home – to Alice's house – and unlocked the door. The phone pinged with a reply.

> No. He left to meet you earlier. He took the bus. Have you called him?

> I tried. He didn't answer.

> I'll try him. He wanted to see you.

She could only imagine what Ned's mum had put up with. The moodiness, the tears, the pathetic, heartbroken, lovelorn wet blanket of a son. No doubt she was worried he would never find another girlfriend.

Well, he wouldn't now. She was better off without him.

> Don't worry. I'll call him tomorrow. I'm home now.

She put the phone on the table – she didn't need any tracking data showing where she was about to go – and headed back to the car.

She had found the place earlier on Google Maps. In Perth she'd wanted the bodies to be found. She enjoyed reading about them in the press, enjoyed the thrill of seeing her work displayed for the world.

But not this time. This time she needed the body to be gone for ever.

No body, no crime. Just another missing person.

She'd had no choice but to kill him. He'd brought it on himself. She could have ignored his phone calls, refused to see him, told him a thousand times it was over. But he would have kept coming. She could have moved to London, Paris, Bangkok, and one day he would have showed up on her doorstep.

Or maybe not. Maybe he would have found some pride and walked away. It was a risk she couldn't take.

And then there was the thrill of it. Once she had started to plan to kill him, once she had started to anticipate the moment, imagine the swing of the hammer – well, once the idea was in her head there was no getting it out.

Once the needle was in the addict's hand and the vein was raised, the outcome was fixed. There was no turning away.

So here she was.

Calm. Centred. In control.

Satiated, for now.

She had memorized the route. A slag heap next to a deep, toxic pool of sludge from a long-ceased mining operation. It was due to be filled in in the coming years, tons of dirt poured into it in an attempt to hide the scars.

A toxic legacy, buried.

That was fine by her. It could bury her toxic legacy too.

There was no one there when she arrived.

No one to see her cut a hole in the wire fence.

No one to see her drag his body to the edge of the pit of sludge.

No one to hear the pop and hiss as it sank into the filth.

She waved as his body disappeared.

'Bye Ned,' she said.

Sunday, 29 August 2021

DI Wynne

Wynne had been sceptical when she first spoke to Tony Munro, the Australian detective – she was glad he had called, but how likely was it that a series of murders nearly a decade ago on the other side of the world were linked to what was happening in South Warrington right now?

Not very, was the answer, and in her experience long shots rarely paid off.

It was, though, the only thing she had to go on. There were no other leads. No CCTV, no DNA that they could trace, no witnesses. That was the thing with detective work that most people misunderstood – they thought cases were solved by high tech forensics or images from satellites or sudden, Sherlockian flashes of inspiration, but the truth was much more prosaic. Most cases were solved because someone saw something and told the authorities, or because the criminal made a stupid mistake and left their wallet at the scene. Most often of all was the humble confession; under questioning, few people could hold out.

And in this case she had none of those things. Not even a suspect.

So the Perth murders were all she had to go on, and although she wasn't hopeful at first, the more she thought about them, the more she became convinced they were linked.

A savage blow from a hammer to the head. Late at night, in a deserted location. No pattern, and nothing at the scene that spoke of a ritual element to the killings.

Just a random, efficient murder in the dead of night.

Untraceable, inexplicable, and, without some stroke of luck, unsolvable.

She read the notes she had made. Six killings, terminating abruptly in mid 2013. The detectives on the case had speculated as to why they had stopped: perhaps the murderer moved away or was hurt or went to prison for some other offence. It was impossible to know.

She paused and tried to put her thoughts in order. She had no more evidence, no new suspects, but she had learned – potentially – that there was a link to the earlier murders. It wasn't much, but it was something.

She scrolled through the files on the screen. There were hundreds. Each detective had been assigned a group of them to review; if they found nothing, they would swap their group with another detective so that two sets of eyes saw each file. It was tedious, but it was the only way.

She had her files to review, too. She clicked on one, and began to read.

There was a knock on the door. It opened and DS Alexander stepped inside. She was holding a mug of tea and a piece of paper.

'Here,' she said, and put the tea on the table. 'I just had one.'

'Thank you,' Wynne said. 'I appreciate it.'

'That's not the only reason I'm here,' DS Alexander said. 'There's this.'

She handed the paper to Wynne.

'I found it in the files, and printed it out. I thought it was really interesting. Certainly a new perspective.'

'What is it?' Wynne said.

'Forensic psychiatrist's report. Take a read. I've highlighted the interesting part in yellow.'

Wynne scanned down to the highlighted section.

All of the murders have been committed in 'cold blood', by which I mean there is no evidence that the killer was in a heightened emotional state. It is probable they were in some way more focused than usual, but there are no signs of frenzied behaviour. Often in serial killer cases there are significant injuries inflicted post-mortem as, with the victim at their mercy, the killer indulges their wilder fantasies. These can include butchery and /or sexual assault. Of course, these things can also occur pre-mortem; what is striking in this case is their absence.

Wynne looked up at DS Alexander. 'It is striking,' she said. 'We should have noticed that these killings are so dispassionate. Almost like assassinations.'

'There's more,' DS Alexander said. 'Read the note at the bottom.'

Note, added by Det. Tony Munro following conversation with forensic psychiatrist, Sandy Newell.

Dr Newell indicated that she had suspicions the killer might be a woman. She was clear that this was specu-lation on her part based on no more than an intuition, and hence not in her report. However, the absence of the elements of frenzied and / or sexual assault pre-or post-mortem leads her to question the gender of the killer.

Wynne picked up the mug of tea and took a sip.

'You know,' she said. 'Dr Newell may have a point.'

'That's what I thought,' DS Alexander said.

'But I'm not sure it helps us. It simply means we have twice as many suspects. And what about the voice? Australian, and male.'

'Could be a simple mistake,' DS Alexander said. 'Or a piece of mis-direction. The killer said a few words in a deep voice and an Australian accent to put us off.'

'Maybe,' Wynne said. 'Although if there *is* a link to the Perth murders, all they were faking was the deep voice.'

'So what's next?' DS Alexander said.

'I don't know. Keep looking. But' – Wynne paused for more tea – 'we are making – finally – some progress.'

Wynne looked at the clock – 2 p.m., so 10 p.m. in Perth.

Munro would be awake.

Maybe.

She dialled his mobile phone number. It rang for a while – she was expecting it to go to voicemail – and then he answered.

'G'day,' he said. 'You just caught me. Another ten minutes and I'd have been dead to the world.'

'Sorry to bother you so late. But I wanted to talk something through while it's fresh in my mind.'

'No worries, mate,' Detective Munro said. 'If it helps with this case I'm all yours. It's been on my mind for nearly ten years now. What is it?'

'The forensic psychiatrist's report,' Wynne said. 'There's a note to the effect that she wondered if the killer was a woman.'

'Yeah,' he said. 'We talked about it. As you know, more often that not it's men in these cases, but not always. And she said she had a feeling this was a woman. Or might be.'

'What did you think?'

'I thought that it could be either. Women can be equally as vicious as men. But I saw her point. Often the assumption is that a bloke did it – and often it's the right assumption.'

'Did you do anything with the information?'

'Not really. I did wonder though about the woman who disappeared after her parents were killed. The theory there was that she was killed too – but I wondered. Never found a trace of her, though, so the trail went cold.'

'What was her name again?' Wynne said.

'Petersen. Andrea Petersen. I sent the notes on that, too.'

'Great,' Wynne said. 'I'll look them over. And apologies, once again, for the late call.'

'Don't mention it,' Munro said. 'But keep me posted, all right?'

Nottingham, July 2013

Brenda

Ned's mum kept calling, but there was no way she could talk to her. She would realize instantly it wasn't Alice on the line.

She typed a message.

Hi. I'm tied up. Can I call later?

Please do. I'm worried about Ned. He didn't come home last night.

No, she thought. *He didn't, and he won't be any time soon. Not unless he comes back to life and crawls out of that sludge pit.*

Really? I haven't seen him. He probably crashed at a friend's house.

Maybe. But he's not answering his phone, and you know Ned. He's pretty responsible.

He is. Let me know if you find him.

She put the phone aside and opened Alice's laptop. She had to get away for a while. That was no problem; she had plenty of money.

She sent Nellie and Maddie a message – *Hey, going to travel in Europe for a while, get a break from Ned – he's been pretty relentless* – and started looking for flights.

Sunday, 29 August 2021

Tom

Alice stared at him, her eyes hard and unreadable. Then her expression softened.

He got the impression it took some effort.

'I'm not lying,' she said.

'You are. I know you are.'

'Tom,' Alice said. 'You don't know what I looked like back then. I had long hair, and I cut it short. Plenty of people change their appearance.'

'That's not what I'm saying,' he replied. 'I'm agreeing that's you.'

'What *are* you saying?' she said.

He pointed to the woman on the left of the photos. 'She,' he said. 'Is Alice Barnes.' He pointed to the woman on the right. 'She is you. Brenda, according to the email.'

Alice shook her head. 'No. She' – she pointed to Alice Barnes – 'is Brenda.' She gave a huff of exasperation. 'The other woman is me. I don't know why you don't believe me. It's obvious she's me – with blonde hair and a decade younger – but she's me.'

Tom's vision swam. He wanted to believe her – it would make everything much simpler – and for a moment he almost did.

'No,' he said. 'I don't know what's going on, but you're lying.'

'Don't call me a liar.'

'Alice—'

'No. Don't call me a liar.'

'Do you want to know why I have this photo?'

She nodded.

'I'm putting together an album for your birthday. Old-fashioned paper one. And so I asked your friends for photos of you from before I knew you. Nellie and Maddie. They sent me plenty, including this one.'

'OK.' She folded her arms. 'I need a beer. You want one?'

He did, desperately. 'Sure.'

She walked into the kitchen. A few minutes later – no doubt she was taking some time to compose herself – she came out with two bottles of beer. She passed one to him.

'So, you were saying. You went behind my back to get photos from my friends.'

'I was doing something nice. Nellie wants to get back in touch by the way. Anyway, here are the photos she sent.'

He handed her the phone and watched her scroll through the photos. The beer was cold and necessary and he took a long swig, then another.

'Well,' she said, and put the phone on the table. 'I see what you mean. Their friend – Alice Barnes – is in the photo with me, which means I'm the other woman.'

She caught his gaze and held it. Her eyes were different, hollow and empty. A chill ran through him.

'I'm Brenda,' she said. 'You got me, tiger.'

He couldn't process what he was hearing; since he'd seen the photo he'd known something was wrong, but he'd been sure there was an explanation of some sort.

A long lost sister. A name change. Mistaken identity.

But to hear her confirm she was not Alice Barnes, that she was someone else entirely – it wasn't possible.

But it was happening.

'You're *Brenda*?' he said.

'Damn straight, mate,' she said. Her voice had changed. She had an Australian accent.

'But,' he paused, 'I don't get it.'

'No, you don't.'

On the table his phone started to ring. She picked it up.

'Roland,' she said. 'Your fucking idiot brother.'

'Give it to me.'

'I don't think so.' She touched the screen and the call ended.

'Hey. That's my phone.'

She threw it onto the grass. 'Go and get it.'

He started to get to his feet, but his legs felt heavy and he slumped back into his chair. His hands were starting to go numb and his vision was fading.

'What?' he said. 'What's going on?'

320

Alice

Fuck.

Typical fucking Tom. Some stupid romantic gesture and he'd come *this* close to ruining her plans.

What if he'd found out a day earlier, when she wasn't ready? It would have been a *disaster*.

But he hadn't. He'd found out today, when she *was* ready. She'd been planning to wait another day or two, but no matter. Everything was in place now.

He tried to get up and fell back in his chair. Idiot had drunk the beer. It had a sedative in it – a powerful one she kept in her washbag, and which she had sprinted upstairs to get.

And now he had drunk it, it was time. Time to get rid of him. Time to get rid of this damn baby.

She couldn't even think about the baby without her stomach clenching in anger and regret. How had she let it happen? She'd been on the pill and she'd fucked up somehow. She still wasn't sure how. Maybe it was a faulty batch. That could happen. By the time she found out it was too late. Tom was deliriously happy. She couldn't have got rid of it.

So she'd gone through with it. She'd thought it would maybe be OK.

It was the worst mistake of her life.

But she was going to fix things.

She glanced up at Tom. His eyes were closed and he was slumped in the chair, his chin on his chest. He reminded her of Ned after she had caved his skull in with the hammer.

His phone buzzed. It was face down on the grass. She picked it up. There was a message from Roland.

Give me a call, when you get a moment.

Fucking Roland. He wasn't that dissimilar to Tom. They were both weak, although in different ways. That was why she knew she could do this; it would take someone a lot stronger than Roland or Tom to stop her. That had been the case all her life: she was simply better and stronger than the people she encountered.

In part because they couldn't even *imagine* what she would do. Someone upset her, or got in her way? They might think she would be annoyed and try to take some petty, harmless revenge.

The idea that she would crush their skull would barely – if at all – even enter their minds.

Which was the source of her advantage.

She typed a reply.

Maybe tomorrow. I'm tied up tonight.

She switched the phone off and put it down on the table. This was another stroke of luck; when tomorrow came this message would take on a new, more sinister meaning.

A meaning that would only add credence to the story she would tell the world.

Roland

He read the last message again.

Maybe tomorrow. I'm tied up tonight.

There was something odd about it. It didn't make sense that he would brush him off, not when he'd seen the photo. He'd want to talk it through, and he'd want to know how Dad was.

And what was he tied up with? He had nothing to do.

Fuck it. He'd call him. He needed to talk to him, find out what was going on. If nothing else, he needed peace of mind before his interview. He couldn't blow it because he was worried about his brother.

The call went to voicemail.

He tried again. Voicemail, again.

Tom had just been texting him, so he was there and he had a signal, but now he was ignoring the calls? It was weird.

This was not right at all. He needed to find out what was happening, and soon.

So never mind his interview, he was heading up to the Lake District.

323

DI Wynne

Detective Inspector Wynne read the files on the Petersen family murders. There had never been an explanation or resolution. A suburban couple killed in their house for no apparent reason, and then, on top of it, the disappearance of their daughter.

She studied the photos of the crime scene.

Both were killed by vicious hammer strikes to the head. The mother had been hit on the temple; the father in the eye.

They were a lot like the murders she had seen in the last few months. The creeping feeling that these were linked grew.

But she simply couldn't see how.

She opened a file directory called *Andrea Petersen_Missing Person Enquiry*. The first file was called *poster photo* and she clicked on it.

It was a photo of a smiling woman in her early twenties. She had long, reddish hair and an angular face. There was something familiar about her; perhaps it had been circulated in the UK at the time.

No, that wasn't it. It was something else. She reminded Wynne of someone, but she couldn't put her finger on who. It was like when you were watching a film and one of the actors resembled someone you knew, but you couldn't figure it out.

Then she saw it.

'No,' she muttered. 'No.'

She studied the image more closely, and her pulse sped up. She grabbed the laptop and walked into the corridor. DS Alexander was coming out of the bathroom.

Wynne beckoned to her and held up the laptop.

'This remind you of anyone?' she said.

DS Alexander looked at the photo. 'Yes. I didn't know she had red hair when she was younger.'

'You know who this is?'

DS Alexander frowned. 'Of course.'

'Let me tell you who this person is, and we can see if we have the same name.'

'I know who it is.'

'You think you do.'

'What's this about, boss?' Nadia said.

'What would you say if I told you this person' – she nodded at the laptop screen – 'is Andrea Petersen?'

DS Alexander shook her head. 'I'd say, no, it isn't.'

'Why?'

'Because I know who it is. It's Alice.' She paused. 'That's Alice Sark.'

Nadia

Wynne nodded slowly. 'It is Alice Sark. It's also Andrea Petersen.'

It took a few moments for the name to sink in.

'Andrea Petersen? Who disappeared from Perth?'

'The same.'

'No. That's a young Alice.'

'I don't doubt it,' Wynne said. 'This is the photo they issued when she disappeared. It took me longer than you to see it, but it's plain enough. That's Alice Sark. It's also Andrea Petersen.'

'What the fuck is going on?'

'I don't know everything,' Wynne said. 'But here's what I'm starting to piece together. Andrea Petersen killed those people in Perth. For some reason – maybe they discovered what she was up to – she then killed her parents and skipped town. One way or another, she pitched up here and somehow created an identity for herself.'

'Or stole one,' Nadia said.

'Or stole one. And I think she started doing what she'd been doing in Perth.'

'She's the Crucifix Killer?'

Wynne nodded. 'She is.'

Nadia's legs weakened. She pulled a chair out and sat down heavily. Maybe Andrea Petersen was the killer, maybe she'd come from Perth, but the idea she was Alice? It was impossible. Alice was her friend. She'd been working on the case *with* her.

'We've been feeding her information all along,' Wynne said.

'Oh God,' Nadia said. 'This is a lot to take in. I mean, she's my *friend*. Are you sure?'

Wynne held up the laptop. 'You tell me.'

Nadia looked again. There was no doubt. If that was Andrea Petersen, then Andrea Petersen and Alice Sark were the same person.

'We need to get to her,' Nadia said. 'Now.'

'They went away, right?'

'Somewhere in the Lake District. We can track the phone.'

Wynne shook her head. 'Takes too long. We need the address. Did they give it to anyone?'

Nadia paused. 'Not to my knowledge. I advised Alice not to tell anyone where they were going.'

'But maybe Tom told a family member? In case something happened?'

'It's possible. Tom's dad is very ill, so probably not him. His mum, perhaps, or Roland.'

'Call them.'

'I don't have their number.'

Wynne shrugged. 'Get it.'

Stockton Heath, September 2013

Brenda

Brenda sat in the back yard of the small, terraced house she had bought with Alice's inheritance. She had moved in a few weeks after returning from her trip around Europe. She had found it quite boring, if she was honest – a load of ancient cities and pompous resorts – but it had been useful. Europe – in particular the south – would be an easy place to disappear into, if she ever needed to.

For now, though, she was safe. As soon as she got back she had started to search for somewhere to live. There was an internet list of up-and-coming villages; she had picked Stockton Heath, which was halfway up the list at number five. It was as good a place as any, so she viewed a few houses and bought the one that was available soonest.

She lit a fire in the fire pit and watched the flames catch on the kindling. When it was burning well, she laid a pair of logs on top and watched until they were glowing red.

She reached into her day pack and took out her two

Australian passports. She had travelled as Alice Barnes – she didn't want any trace of Brenda Yates travelling through Europe. Brenda had disappeared after visiting Ambleside in July.

Although the real Brenda Yates was buried in a forest outside Perth. She had needed her identity to get out of Australia.

She could never have travelled as Andrea Petersen. There were too many people looking for her.

She opened the first passport. Poor Brenda Yates. With her hair dyed blonde and a cap on, Andrea had been able to pass as her, which was why she had been killed. For no other reason than that.

She had kept them both in case she ever needed them, but it was too risky to keep them. She was Alice Barnes now.

She tore the pages from Brenda Yates's passport and dropped them into the flames. Then she took Andrea Petersen's and did the same. The flames curled around the pages, turning them to ash.

The next day she started looking for jobs. A local newspaper was advertising a journalist internship; it was perfect. Alice had wanted to go into journalism, so it fit with her back story, and it was the kind of job that would give her the freedom she was going to need.

She had no intention of getting an office job; she needed reasons to be on the move, reasons to be in different places, researching stories.

Because the hunger was still there. It was greater than ever. She dreamed at night of picking up some boy or girl, man or woman, offering them a ride, an innocent young woman doing them a favour.

She dreamed of the anticipation as they climbed into the car. Dreamed of the look on their face as they saw the hammer and understood – at the last second – that their life was over.

She would have to do it soon. Find someone nobody would miss. Someone from the streets.

God, she needed it.

Maybe even that night.

That night.

Now the thought was there she couldn't fight the urge. She couldn't stop it.

But first, she had to apply for the job. She started to write her letter.

I am a graduate of Nottingham University, with a first-class honours degree in English.

There was a knock on the door. She got to her feet and walked down the hallway.

A man and a woman, both about her age, were standing on the doorstep.

'Hi,' the woman said. 'I'm Mandy. This is Nick. We live next door. We noticed you'd moved in, so we thought we'd come and introduce ourselves.'

'Oh,' Alice said. 'Thanks. I'm Alice.'

'It's nice to meet you,' Nick said. 'Welcome to the neighbourhood.'

There was an awkward silence.

'Would you like to come in?' Alice said. 'I've not really got any furniture yet. I do have a kettle though. I could make some tea?'

'That's OK,' Mandy said. 'We were on our way to the village to pick up some breakfast. One of the best things about the weekend – you can get out in the day for some fresh air!'

'Right,' Alice said. 'No work.'

'Do you work locally?' Mandy asked.

'No. I'm looking for a job.'

'What field?' Nick said.

'Journalism.'

'Oh,' he replied. 'I don't know any journalists. I work in Engineering. A Swedish company has an office nearby.'

'I just saw an ad for a job,' Alice said. 'I was about to send in an application.'

'Don't let us keep you,' Mandy said.

'It's fine. There's no hurry.'

'OK,' Mandy said. 'Well, it was great to say hi. By the way – a few of us are going out tonight to the local pub – the London Bridge – if you wanted to, you could come along? Meet some people?'

It was the last thing she wanted to do. She had other plans, plans that involved feeding the hunger inside her.

But she had to act normally. And that meant agreeing.

'That would be lovely,' she said.

The pub was packed, the drinkers spilling onto the terrace beside the canal. She spotted Mandy and Nick standing with a large group and headed over.

'Hey,' Mandy called. Her face was flushed from the alcohol. 'So glad you came. Everybody, this is our new neighbour, Alice.' She went around the group, name by name. There were three other couples, all about her age.

'Nice to meet you all,' Alice said. 'I'm going to get a drink. Anyone need anything?'

'I think we're all OK,' Mandy said. 'But I'll come with you. Show you the way.'

'Great,' Alice replied.

They walked into the pub and headed to the bar. As they waited to be served, Mandy took out her phone.

'What's your number?' she said.

Alice told her, and she typed it in.

'I'll call you now so that you have mine.'

'It's very kind of you to include me,' Alice said.

'Not at all! It's hard moving to a new place on your own.'

331

'Not with great neighbours like you!'

'What brings you here?' Mandy said. 'If not work?'

'Honestly?' Alice said. 'This sounds weird, but I searched or cool places to live and found Stockton Heath, so I came here.'

Mandy laughed. 'That's as good a reason as any.'

When they returned to the terrace another person had joined the group. He was tall and thin and had long, floppy hair and a soft smile. He was standing next to Nick, and as they approached, Nick glanced at her and said something to the new guy.

'Alice,' he said. 'I'd like to introduce you to someone. A friend from work.'

The new guy smiled and held out his hand.

'Hi,' he said. 'Alice?'

'Yes.' She shook his hand. 'What's your name?'

'I'm Tom,' he said. 'Tom Sark.'

Sunday, 29 August 2021

Roland

It was thirty-five minutes past six, and he had missed his interview.

He had not met the guy who gave people like him second chances. He had not explained how he had made mistakes, but he understood them and was determined not to make them again. He had not got to say that he knew it wouldn't be easy, but he was going to give it everything he had and that was the best he or anyone could do.

Instead, he was in the Lake District, not too far from the house Tom and Alice had rented, The app on his phone told him he had a little under half an hour to go.

Thirty minutes until he'd find out if he'd wasted his interview for nothing. He was worried he'd blown his chances for good. The guy from the agency had sounded pretty pissed off when he called to say he wouldn't make it.

I'm sorry. Something came up. A family emergency.

It came up thirty minutes before your interview?

It's been bubbling away for a while, but yes. It came to a head right now.

Fine, the guy said. *I'll let them know.*

I don't want to lose the opportunity, Roland replied. *Can I postpone? Maybe tomorrow?*

I'll ask.

It had been obvious what the guy was thinking from the tone of his voice. *Yeah, right. I'm going to go out on a limb for some unreliable junkie? No way, mate.*

He'd decided to tackle it straight on. There was no other way.

Look, he said. *I know this is bad and I know what it looks like. It looks like I'm an addict who's off trying to score when I should be at this interview, so I'm making up some bullshit about a family emergency. But that's not what's happening. If you don't believe me, I get it. But for the record – I'm gutted to have to do this, but the situation I have to deal with is real. And I want you to know that.*

The guy paused before he answered. *OK, we'll see.* He hadn't sounded convinced.

Roland just hoped it was worth it.

Was it? Had he blown this on a whim, on a ridiculous suspicion? Was this one more thing in the long list of things he'd messed up?

No. He knew Tom. Despite all their differences, he knew his brother, and something didn't feel right.

It was worse than that. Something felt *wrong*.

His phone started to ring. It was not a number he recognized, and normally he would have ignored it, but these were not normal times.

'Hello?' he said.

A woman's voice came on the line. 'Is that Roland?'

'Yes. Who's this?'

'My name's Nadia Alexander. I'm a detective sergeant with—'

'Alice's friend?'

'That's right.'

'How can I help?'

'It's kind of a long story,' she said. 'Can you talk?'

Nadia

Nadia put her phone on the table and switched it to speaker.

'You're on speaker phone,' she said. 'Detective Inspector Jane Wynne is with me.'

'Hello, Mr Sark,' Wynne said.

'Hi. Call me Roland. What's this about?'

'We need an address,' Wynne said. 'We're hoping you know where your brother and sister-in-law are staying.'

'Why do you want to know?'

'We're investigating the recent murders,' Nadia said. 'And we need to talk to Alice.'

'What does she have to do with them?' Roland said. There was a guarded tone in his voice and she glanced at Wynne.

'Just questions,' she said. 'But it is quite urgent.'

'OK,' Roland said. 'I have the address. But there's something else. Something a bit odd. I don't think it's really a police matter, but—'

'We can judge that,' Wynne said. 'Anything is of interest at the moment.'

'The thing is,' Roland said. 'I'm actually on my way there now.'

'Why?' Nadia asked.

'Because of what happened.'

'And what is that?' Wynne said.

'Tom's putting together a photo album for Alice's birthday. He asked some of her university friends to send pictures from those days, then he asked me to print them out and bring them up to him so he can get the album ready. He doesn't have a printer where they're staying. Anyway, the friends sent some pictures of Alice when she was eighteen, nineteen, and she looks quite different to how she is now. Similar – same hair and stuff like that – but only superficially. Tom noticed it too, but we put it down to the fact people change. Lose weight, that kind of thing.'

Wynne looked up, her eyes wide.

'Mr Sark,' she said, 'this is very interesting information.'

'There's more,' Roland said. 'Another photo came today, of Alice and an Australian she met when she was travelling in the Lake District after she graduated.'

'An Australian?' Nadia said. 'How do you know that?'

'Alice sent the photo to her friends and said the other girl in the photo was an Aussie. She's called Brenda.'

'Not Andrea?' Wynne said.

'No. Definitely Brenda. Who's Andrea?'

'Someone we're seeking in connection with the case,' Wynne said. 'I need to tell you—'

'Wait,' Roland said. 'That's not all. The really weird thing is that Alice is the girl in the photos her friends sent, but Brenda – well, *she's* Alice.'

'I don't understand,' Nadia said. 'How is Brenda Alice?'

'You know I said Alice didn't look like the Alice we know? Well, she does look like Brenda. It's unmistakeable. Alice – the Alice Tom is married to – is really Brenda.'

Nadia muted the phone.

'Holy fucking shit,' she said. 'That's what Andrea Petersen

337

did. She took another identity from someone – Brenda – and then ran into the real Alice Barnes.'

'And took her identity too,' Wynne said. 'Probably violently.'

'Hello?' Roland said. 'Are you there?'

Nadia unmuted her phone. 'Yes. We were talking for a moment.'

'I sent it to Tom and asked him what was going on, but he brushed me off. It felt weird, so I decided to go up and see for myself. It cost me a job interview, so I hope it's worth it.'

'A what?' Wynne said.

'Never mind. It doesn't matter.'

'Can you send the email?' Nadia said.

'I'm driving.'

'That's OK,' Wynne said. 'Just this once.'

'OK. Hang on.'

A few moments later the email arrived. Nadia opened the photo, and muted the phone again.

'Brenda' was a blonde-haired version of Andrea Petersen.

'That confirms it,' Wynne muttered. 'Andrea is Brenda is Alice. We have to get there now.'

'Where are you now, Mr Sark?'

'I'm close to the house. Maybe thirty—' his phone cut out.

'Mr Sark?' Wynne said. 'Hello? Can you hear me?'

There was no reply, then, a moment later, he was back on the line.

'Are you there?' he said. 'I'm cutting out. Reception's not great up here.'

'Mr Sark,' Wynne said. 'I don't think it's a good idea for you to go to the house.'

'Why? Is something wrong?'

'Something's very wrong,' Wynne said. 'Alice Sark is not who you think she is. She's very dangerous.'

'Dangerous? How's she—' His voice cut out again, then a few moments later, he was back.

'How's she dangerous?' he said.

'That doesn't matter for now,' Wynne said. 'Can you give us the address? That's the most important piece of information.'

'Of course. It's—'

The line went quiet.

'Mr Sark?'

There was no reply.

'Try him again,' Wynne said.

Nadia dialled the number. It went straight to voicemail.

'Shit,' she said. 'We lost him.'

Stockton Heath, December 2013

Brenda

It was the eve of Christmas Eve, and she was meeting Mandy in Manchester to do some final Christmas shopping.

What a fucking *torture* that was. But it was what people did, and she had to fit in.

She grabbed her car keys and phone. Her phone buzzed. It was a message from Mandy.

Going to be a bit late. Maybe half an hour?

No problem. Take your time

As she pressed send there was a knock on the door. She didn't get many visitors, and she didn't want them. The last ones had been some kind of religious group offering salvation. If it was them again, she'd give them short shrift.

She opened the door. There was a woman standing there, thin, pale and drawn.

She did not look well.

'Hello?' Alice said.

'Alice,' she replied, and Alice realized who it was. She had never met her, but she had spoken to her, and she recognized her voice.

It was Ned's mum.

This was bad. Very bad.

'Hi,' she said, and turned away to hide her face. 'I suppose you'd better come in.'

As she walked back into the house her mind was racing. She could have slammed the door, but now Ned's mum had found her – and how had she found her? – she would be here again and again.

The same as her useless son. Dogged persistence seemed to run in the family.

No, she had to deal with this, whatever that meant.

'Tea?' she said, over her shoulder.

'No,' Ned's mum said, her voice cold and broken. 'I want nothing from you.'

'OK.' She opened the door to the living room and waved her inside. 'I'll make one for myself. I'll be back in a sec.'

She went into the kitchen and filled the kettle. While it boiled she tried to think this through.

Ned's mum – whose name she could not remember – was going to see very soon that she was not Alice. It was unlikely she would figure out what had happened, but that didn't matter. She'd start asking questions, and pretty soon it would become clear what was going on, and Alice would be in deep shit.

So she had to stop that happening. And there was only one way.

Alice's mouth dried up in anticipation. A Christmas bonus. Unexpected, and very welcome.

As she left the kitchen she sent Mandy a message.

Change of plans. I'm going shopping alone. Get your special present! See you at 5 at the pub?

She set her phone down on the counter, and went to deal with Ned's mum.

She closed the door behind her, keeping her face hidden, then went to stand in front of the window so she was silhouetted against the light.

'Been a while,' she said. 'How did you find me?'

'With difficulty,' Ned's mum said. 'But then I have little else to do.'

'Did Ned ever show up?'

'You know he didn't. You know what happened to him.'

'Don't be ridiculous.'

'You sound different,' Ned's mum said.

'I've got a cold. Can't seem to shake it.'

'Hmm.' She shifted on the couch. 'Ned came to see you that night and something happened. He told you what he was planning, or where he was going, or you did something to him.'

'I don't know what you're talking about. He never showed up.'

'You do. Ned would *never* have stood you up. All he'd wanted to do since he got back from your holiday was see you. It was all he talked about. So he showed up, all right, and something happened. I want you to tell me what it was.' Her voice rose to a plaintive wail. 'I'm his *mum*, for Christ's sake! I deserve to know what happened to my son. He's my only child, Alice! Have some pity, please.'

Alice stepped forward and leaned towards her, her hands buried in the deep pockets of her winter cardigan.

342

Have some pity? Alice had no pity.

'You're right,' she said. 'I *do* know what happened.'

She stared at the old woman, letting all of her true self be revealed. There was no smile on her face, no light in her eyes, nothing human about her at all.

She knew the effect her stare had on people.

Ned's mum recoiled, her face creased in fear.

'You're not – you're not Alice,' she whispered.

'No.'

'Oh God,' she said. 'Who – what – are you?'

'You want to know what happened to your son?'

The woman nodded, her eyes wide.

'I smashed his head in with a hammer.'

Her hand shot out and she grabbed Ned's mum's neck. The woman whimpered.

'But that's not what I've got in mind for you, you old bitch.' She clamped her hand over her mouth and nose. 'I've got something much more creative in store for *you*.'

Ned's mum's hands started to flap as the oxygen ran out.

'You should have stayed home, old woman,' Alice said. 'You should have stayed the fuck away from me.'

Sunday, 29 August 2021

Alice

Tom had been hard to move, but she needed him in the boat before he woke up. Breathing heavily, she studied him, his head against the gunwale, his limbs loose. Joanna – that useless, wailing little animal – was asleep, for once, upstairs.

She opened her day pack and took out the things she'd need. He'd come around any moment, if she'd got the dose right, and then she could finish this for good.

A group of ducks circled on the lake. The water was dark and deep and cold. Bad things could happen here. Secrets could be hidden.

They could remain hidden.

Alice – the original Alice – was proof of that.

His hand twitched. She watched, waiting for any more signs that he was waking up.

His hand moved again, and then his eyes flickered open. They were unfocused and glazed, but gradually he came around. He groaned, and tried to sit up, but his muscles wouldn't cooperate.

'Alice,' he said. 'Alice. What's happening? What are you doing?'

Tom

That was the question that came first to him.

What was she doing?

There was a why, too, but that could wait. For now he needed to know what she was trying to accomplish.

'What am I doing?' she said. 'It's obvious, isn't it? I'm arranging your suicide.'

Through his brain fog one word registered above all the others.

'Suicide?'

'Yes. Poor Tom, too many sleepless nights, the stress of fatherhood, the worry about his wife's involvement with the serial killer: he's been behaving erratically. Aggressive, some days. Depressed, others. Hurting his baby. Bruising her. And now – well, now he's – tragically – taken his own life.'

'No one will believe it,' Tom said. 'No one will believe I did *any* of that.'

'Really? That's not what Kay thinks. Or Nadia. I've been explaining to them for a while how worried I am. When you finally go through with it, they won't be surprised at all. All the evidence will be there, in plain sight.'

'What evidence? I didn't do anything!'

345

'As I said. I've been telling them the opposite. How you've been threatening me – that message you sent saying you'd do whatever it took to protect Joanna was perfect, by the way, I managed to make that look like a threat, and I told them how scared I was that you were falling apart, that you wanted to hurt me and Jo. That there was a new bruise, since we arrived here. Who else could it be?'

'I'd never hurt Jo.'

'*I* know that,' she said. 'But no one else does. The picture I painted told the opposite story. And the picture is what people see. Whether it is real or not is irrelevant.'

'But I didn't do anything.'

'This isn't sinking in, is it Tom? I know you didn't, but so what? It was *me*, but no one will ever know that.'

His head spun. He couldn't get a grasp on what she was saying. None of it made sense. 'It was *you*? You hurt our baby?'

'Yes. I wanted a way to show how you'd been gradually losing it, got frustrated at her for not letting you sleep, until you lost control and started pinching her. So I gave her the bruises and started to make it look like you were the guilty one.' She paused, her head tilted as though she was deep in thought. 'I must say, I enjoyed it.'

'How? How could you enjoy hurting a baby?'

'It was interesting.'

'*Interesting*?'

'Yes. Seeing whether they feel pain.'

'Of course babies feel pain!'

'In the way animals do, yes. But do they really *understand* it?'

'Oh God,' he said. 'What's wrong with you?'

'With me? Nothing. But with you? *Everything*.' She drew out the last word. 'I mean, you tried to drown Jo in the bath—'

'That was an accident!'

'So you say. But that's not what the world thinks. That's where I got the idea, by the way, of how to get rid of you both – by drowning.'

He shook his head. 'What do you mean, both?'

'Did I forget to mention that? In your agony, you're going to take your daughter with you. A beautiful – but tragic – final daddy-daughter moment.'

'No,' he said. 'Please, no. Don't hurt her, Alice. She's your child!'

She laughed. 'My child? I don't have children, Tom. I can't have them.'

'You did! You gave birth to her.'

'I can give *birth* to them, but I don't have children. When I look at her I feel nothing. She's the same as any other person. Nothing. And that's the problem. I'm tethered to her *for ever*. And I can't do that, Tom. You can't expect me to do that. She's ruining my life. So she has to go.'

He looked at his wife and he saw nothing that he recognized. Her eyes were empty pools. This was impossible to believe.

But it was happening. That was the one fact he had to cling to. This was happening, and he somehow had to stop it.

'You're insane,' he said. 'You're totally insane.'

'You would call me that. But it's you – and all the rest of you – who are insane. You have this gift of a life and you choose to waste it on a fucking baby?' She laughed again. 'It's not me who's lost their mind. The funny thing is, I would have stayed with *you*. I would have let you live. You're harmless, a nonentity. You're a useful disguise. But once she arrived I had to get rid of her, and the only way I could was by having it be *you* who did it. Under pressure, you lost your mind. The evidence was all there – I should have seen it.'

'A disguise? We're married.'

347

She laughed. 'You're weak, Tom, and stupid, but I could live with that. Not the baby, though.'

'So you hated our daughter all along? Is that what you're saying? There's nothing about her you like?'

'There was *one* benefit,' she said. 'I had an excuse to be out at night in the car. And when I was, I'd see these people walking, all alone, and it reminded me of someone I used to be, and what *she* used to do.'

As he listened, her words – and their meaning – started to sink in.

'It's you, isn't it? You're the Crucifix Killer.'

She nodded and smiled.

'What about the letters?'

'I wrote them, then posted them, or left them in the house. I made sure my articles were taunting, insulting, personal, so it wasn't a surprise when the killer singled me out.'

'But why? What was the point of sending them?'

'I needed a reason for us to come here. As he got closer – and more threatening – well, we had to flee. To run away to this remote, lonely place. Where the stress – the fear – could easily set off a disastrous psychological breakdown in a vulnerable man.'

He let out a low moan. 'You killed those people. Why?'

'I *have* to, Tom.'

'And the crucifixes? Why them?'

'There have been other killings,' she said. 'In the past. I didn't want anyone to link them, so I came up with the crucifixes. It was a nice touch. Dramatic.'

'It was all you?' he said. He could hardly get his words out. 'You did *all* of it?'

'Yes, Tom. I pulled *all* the strings. Quite brilliant, no?'

It was the first time he'd seen any emotion in her eyes, and what he saw made him feel sick.

He saw pride.

348

He didn't understand any of this, but there was no time to process any of it. He had to get out of this boat and get his limbs working so he could get away from her, from this *monster*.

But he couldn't move. He was trapped in his own body.

'Who are you?' he said. 'Who the hell are you?'

'You really want to know?' She shrugged. 'I guess at this point there's no harm in telling you.'

Perth, Australia, May 2013

Andrea

Andrea Petersen sat at the kitchen table, a ham sandwich in front of her. She was hungry; she'd been for a long swim that morning and hadn't eaten breakfast.

It was not the only thing she was hungry for.

Six times now she had killed. After the first, opportunistic, one, five times she had left her waitressing job and cruised the streets of Perth looking for a victim.

Someone alone, on foot, in a quiet area. There weren't many, at two o'clock in the morning.

But there were some.

She thought back to the first one. That was the best: all her life she had felt an emptiness inside that nothing could fill, but she had never known what it was. And then she had seen the girl, pale and thin and staggering drunkenly as she walked, and she had stopped and opened the door, beckoned her into the car.

Even at that point she had not fully known what she was going to do. She had not planned to kill anyone because she did not truly understand that was what she needed.

At least consciously. Somewhere deep in her brain she knew.

Maybe that was why the hammer was on the back seat. She'd used it two days before to fix the fence at her parents' house – her dad was useless at that kind of thing – and left it in the car when she was done.

Either way, there it was.

It happened almost as though she was in a dream. Everything fell into place. The girl, the hammer, the sudden realization of what she had to do.

And when it was done she finally understood who – what – she was.

She didn't sleep that night. She lay awake, content – satiated – for the first time in her life.

It didn't last. The emptiness came back and the hunger grew. This time, though, she knew what to do about it. The relief was boundless.

The second time was not as good as the first. How could it be? The first was perfection. But it was still blissful. It still *worked*. As had the next, and the others after that.

And now she needed to kill again. Maybe tonight. Maybe tomorrow.

She took a bite of the sandwich. It was good; her hunger abated.

But only her hunger for food. The deeper hunger – the real hunger, the hunger that defined her – remained.

She tidied up the plate, then cleaned the table. She couldn't stand mess; it was why she had hated the dog her parents had brought home when she was a teenager. It wandered around shedding hair and sniffing things and licking her hands.

Fortunately it was stupid, like all dogs, so it happily devoured the meat she had laced with rat poison. She told her parents it had eaten something toxic – mushrooms were the main suspect – and they had held a twee little ceremony for it.

Like she gave a shit about the dog. She didn't understand how anybody cared about an animal. It was ridiculous, and she could barely hide her contempt for her parents as they placed a rock with Allie – the dog's name – on it in a corner of the yard. She had the feeling they were doing it for her, to help her grieve the loss of her beloved pet.

They needn't have bothered.

She checked her work schedule. She was due in at 7 p.m.; her shift would wrap up around midnight, and then – her stomach clenched in anticipation – she would find and kill number seven.

There was a knock on the front door, then it swung open. Her mum walked in.

'Hi,' she said. She seemed tense and nervous. Her eyes were red. She'd been crying, Andrea assumed.

'G'day Mum,' she said. 'I wasn't expecting you.'

'I came because – your dad and I want to talk to you.'

'I was at your place yesterday. Is something up?'

Her mum sniffed. 'Dad found something in your car yesterday. He went out to check the tyre pressure and oil. You know how he's a stickler for that kind of thing. And he found – he found your hammer.'

Andrea nodded. 'So?'

'Why do you have a hammer in your car, darling?'

'In case someone attacks me. Carjacking.'

Her mum gave a sad, soft smile. 'You don't need to lie any more,' she said. 'I know what you are.'

Andrea stared at her.

'What do you mean?'

'Ever since you were a baby, I knew something was wrong. You weren't like the other babies, from the very start. It was

352

obvious. You didn't react like them. You didn't smile at me, you didn't show *any* emotion. At playgroups you weren't interested in the other kids at all. You only sat, and watched. I asked the doctors and they shrugged it off as something developmental, but I knew. A mother always knows.'

'This is crazy,' Andrea said. 'You sound like a madwoman.'

'No, I don't. As you got older it continued. I did some research; I knew what was happening. You didn't care about anyone else. It was obvious. Eventually you learned to smile at the right times and say the right things, but it was an act. It's why we gave you that dog. We wanted you to form a connection with something outside yourself.'

'I liked Allie,' Andrea said.

'You killed Allie,' her mum replied. 'You poisoned her.' She held up her hand. 'But that's all in the past. I hoped you'd find a way to live. I hoped it wouldn't come to this, but I always knew it was a possibility. I wondered if it was you killing those poor people – they were always killed on nights you were working – but there was no proof. I didn't *want* to believe it. But then Dad found the hammer.' She smiled the same sad smile. 'So I know, Andrea.'

There was no point denying it.

'So what's next?' Andrea asked.

'We can get through this,' her mum said.

'Are you going to tell the police?'

Her mum shook her head. 'We should. But you're our daughter. And what good would it do? We can help you. We have a plan, and we won't let you kill again, so there's no point involving the police. It makes no difference.' She looked Andrea in the eyes. 'Unless you tell me you don't want our help?'

'Of course I do.'

'Dad and I want to talk it through with you at the house, but before that I need to know you're committed to fixing this, Andrea.'

There was only one answer she could give.

'I am, Mum. I promise.'

'That's what I hoped to hear. Here's what we want to do. The first step is for you to move back home. One of us will be with you at all times. And then we'll seek help. Find someone who can help fix you.'

It sounded like the closest thing to Hell on Earth that Andrea could imagine. And fix her? She wasn't broken.

But it seemed – for now – she had no choice but to agree.

'You need to pack and come with me, now,' her mum said.

'OK,' she said. 'I'll come.'

Perth was a big enough city to disappear in, at least for a while, and she had a few days before anyone discovered her parents' bodies.

It had been almost as good as the very first time. Her mum had acted betrayed and hurt when she saw the hammer and realized what her daughter was going to do. Her dad had been almost grateful.

What mattered was that they were both dead, and she was free to go anywhere and be anyone.

She sat at a bar, sipping a glass of lemonade, waiting.

It was the second night when she met her. Tall, long, blonde hair, same eye colour, a more than superficial similarity in looks – certainly enough to get through a passport check. She introduced herself with a smile and asked the woman for her name.

She was called Brenda.

And she was going to England in a few days' time. Ticket bought, passport ready.

Perfect.

Stockton Heath, 28 December 2013

Alice

Local Woman Drowned in Boating Lake

The woman drowned in the Highlands Boating Lake has been identified as Marjorie Blundell. Police divers dragged the lake late on Christmas Eve after Mrs Blundell was reported missing by her husband and her car was found near the water.

A police spokesperson said they believed the tragedy to be the result of a suicide. Mrs Blundell's son, Ned, disappeared in the late summer and she had been suffering with depression since then. It is not uncommon for feelings of loneliness and loss to intensify during the holiday period.

'What are you reading?'

Mandy was in her living room, a mug of tea in each hand.

'The news,' Alice said.

Mandy looked over her shoulder.

'Local Nottingham news. Keeping up with events in your old stomping grounds? A drowning, huh? Exciting stuff.'

'Kind of,' Alice said. 'I knew the woman who killed herself.'

'Really? Who was she?'

'I had a boyfriend at university. A guy called Ned. It was his mum.'

'Jesus,' Mandy said. 'I'm sorry to hear that.'

'Don't be,' Alice said. 'We weren't close.'

Sunday, 29 August 2021

Tom

She finished telling him the story of who she was, where she had come from, how she had met the real Alice Barnes, whose body was somewhere in the lake underneath them.

Whose body he would soon be joining. He shook the thought away. He had to concentrate, although it was nearly impossible to do so. He couldn't believe what he was hearing, or the flat, emotionless way she spoke. What she was saying was momentous, but it was as though she was reading a memo outlining a dry legal argument.

He tried to piece it together.

Her real name was Andrea Petersen, but she had killed a woman called Brenda, before doing the same to Alice Barnes, and assuming her identity.

In the meantime, she had killed her own parents, and the real Alice's boyfriend and his mum, as well as God knew how many other people. Six in Perth, and four in Warrington at least, but there would be other victims, scattered around the places she had travelled to as a journalist, searching for stories.

He felt sick and dizzy. His whole world had been pulled

from under him, but he would have to deal with all that later.

For now he had only one focus. Getting out of here. Getting *Jo* out of here.

That, though, was not as simple as it sounded. He needed time for whatever she had given him to wear off, and then he could maybe move again. She would have to believe he was still drugged, so it was crucial he didn't move.

Which would make it hard to test whether he could or not.

'What are you going to do?' he said.

She held up a vial and a needle. 'Heroin.'

'You're going to give me heroin?'

She nodded. 'At least you'll die happy.'

'Why would you give me heroin?'

'It's the last act of a desperate man. Inject himself, drift out onto the water – in the boat he asked his wife to buy, Eric will confirm that story – his baby in his arms, and slip over the side to his death, leaving behind a grieving, pitiful wife.'

'You don't have to do this,' he said. 'If you want rid of me and Jo you can have that. I'll take her. You don't have to see us ever again. You've started again before. You can do it now.'

She shook her head. 'No. If I wanted to do that, I could have. I could have left you any time, gone somewhere new, but I didn't want to. And it isn't that easy. I thought about it, of course. But I'd have to leave everything behind, and I'd never find another Alice Barnes. She was perfect: on the cusp of a new life, no family, lots of money. I could simply slip into her life. But now? To find someone my age in that position? Almost impossible.' She gave a cold laugh. 'So I have no choice, Tom. And I like my life. But I don't want you – or that baby – to be part of it.'

'You could still go. Leave now. I won't follow you.'

'Too late. You know the truth. You'd go straight to the police.'

'I wouldn't! You could disappear and you'd never hear from me again.'

'I can't take that risk.'

'You can. I promise. We must mean something to you. There must be some shred of maternal feeling deep ins—'

She laughed.

'There is nothing,' she said. 'Nothing at all, other than hatred. You, I find annoying, in the way a lion is annoyed by the flies buzzing around its kill. Irrelevant, but irritating. The baby is different. I *hate* her, Tom. I want to *destroy* her.'

She leaned over, her eyes fixed on his. They were the eyes of a predator, hungry and cruel.

'And besides,' she said. 'I've been looking forward to this. I have a need, Tom, and it has to be met. I must have my fill.'

'No,' he said. 'No. Please.'

Nadia

Nadia banged the steering wheel in frustration. She and Wynne had just pulled onto the M6, heading north.

'I can't believe we didn't get the address. I called the parents but they don't have it. He only gave it to Roland.'

'It's frustrating,' Wynne said. 'But we have to move on and work with what we've got.'

'Which isn't much,' Nadia said. 'I feel so *stupid*. I should have asked immediately.'

'A lesson learned.' Wynne looked out of the window. 'They're in the Lake District,' she said. 'Which is a start.'

'It's a big place,' Nadia replied. 'But agreed. It's a start.'

'We informed the local police? So they're ready when we get an address?'

'Yes. They're expecting us at Kendal Police Station.'

'And we have a call into the phone companies, I presume? To get the last known location of Mr Sark's phone?'

'Yeah. But it's late on a Sunday, and they don't like handing out people's personal data.'

'Did DSI Ryan talk to them?'

'She did. And they're on it. But it takes time.'

'Yes,' Wynne said. 'It does. There's also the house. They

took it on a long-term rental. Almost certainly through Vrbo or AirBnb. Even if not, there's only so many ways to rent a house at short notice. So we ask those companies to look at recent long-term rentals to see if Alice or Tom Sark show up.'

'That's great,' Nadia said. 'But it's the same as with the phones. Roland's there *now*. And he's going to tell her she's been found out, at which point she's going to try to kill him, or get the fuck out of there. The only hope we have is if he stops her somehow. But she's not going to be stopped easily. She's a psychopath, boss. And the thing with psychopaths is that they will stop at nothing to get what they want. If he takes her on thinking she's anything like a normal woman, she'll tear him apart.'

'I think that's a fair assessment,' Wynne said. 'But I'm not sure what options we have. Like you said, the Lake District is a big place.'

'So what do we do?'

Wynne shrugged. 'We wait. And hope. This one's in the lap of the gods now, Nadia.'

Alice

She'd had enough. She knew what he was doing. He was playing for time, trying to stall her to see if anything showed up, if any opportunity arrived.

He was probably hoping the sedative would wear off and he could jump up and overpower her. She almost sighed at the thought. He may have been bigger and heavier and even stronger than her, but she fought with a ferocity that he couldn't even imagine. She'd bite his throat and rip out his larynx and spit it in his face if need be.

She'd enjoy it. It would be an interesting experience.

And she didn't want to hear any more of his drivel. He should die with some dignity. Accept his fate. Accept she was the better person. This *begging* was unseemly.

She'd explained her position. She didn't care about him. She didn't hate him, she wasn't angry at him. She didn't feel she needed revenge on him. She felt nothing. He was an inconvenience, and so he had to be removed. She no more felt animosity to him than she did to the trash when she was taking it out to the bins.

The fucking baby was different. That thing was a parasite,

sucking the very life out of her. She was looking forward to pushing its face under the water and watching it drown.

Maybe he didn't understand it, but that wasn't her fault.

'Alice,' Tom said. 'Or Andrea. Whatever your name is. Please. Stop this. There must be some part of you that wants to let me – me and Jo – go? So please, just leave. Leave here and you'll never hear from me or anyone I know again. I'll tell the police anything you want. You went for a swim and drowned. We had a big argument and you left. Anything at all. Please, Alice. The years we spent together must mean something?'

'No,' she said. 'They mean nothing at all. You mean nothing at all.'

She filled the syringe and took a rubber hose from the day pack. She tied it around his upper arm and waited for the vein on the inside of his elbow to pop up.

'No,' he said. 'Don't do this.'

The tip of the needle pierced his skin and a small bead of blood formed where it had entered. She pressed the plunger and emptied the drug into his arm.

For a few seconds nothing happened, then his jaw slackened and his mouth fell open. His tongue lolled out of it.

He moaned and a look of ecstasy came over his face, then his eyes, already heavy-lidded, started to close.

'Jo,' he mumbled. 'Jo.'

She wiped the vial and the syringe clean of her prints, then pressed them against his fingers and laid them on the bottom of the dinghy. They would follow him to the bottom of the lake – she had an image of them drifting slowly down and settling on Alice Barnes' corpse, but that was ridiculous as she was on the other shore – but it paid to be cautious.

Then she stood up and turned to the house.

All of a sudden the moment was here. Get the baby, put her on her daddy's chest, and push the boat out into the water. She'd take it out until it was maybe twenty feet deep, and then tip it over.

Then, in the morning, a panicked phone call to the police.

I woke up and my husband's not here. I went to bed early last night and he put our daughter to bed. But neither of them are here. I can't get him on his mobile phone.

Then, after they found the body, back home to take care of the last piece of the puzzle.

Roland. She had to find out what – if anything – he knew. If he knew too much there'd be another overdose. It would be easy enough to explain – a recovering addict falling apart under the stress of his brother's suicide.

Two brothers dead so close together. An unthinkable tragedy.

Then she heard something. The sound of a car engine. The crunch of tyres on the gravel drive at the front of the house.

Who was this? Who *could* it be? She ran through who knew they were here. The owner of the house come to say hello? Eric? There was no one else. Whoever it was, she had to get rid of them, and quickly.

Roland

Roland pulled up outside a stone cottage. He had lost the GPS signal in the last few miles and had to slow down outside each drive he passed to check the house names.

The cottage was dark, which was odd as the light was fading. There was a gate at the side and he could see the lake about fifty yards away. On the far side the high screes loomed over the water, their reflections giving the lake the appearance of a bottomless black hole.

He shuddered. There was a stark beauty here, but this was a cold and eerie place. He pulled his jacket tight around himself.

The gravel crunched under his feet as he walked to the front door. No possibility of a surprise entrance, then. He knocked on the door and held his breath. He wondered what he was going to find, and what he was going to do. The police had said she was dangerous, but at the end of the day it was Alice – or Brenda – and she was unlikely to be able to overpower him, never mind both him and Tom together.

All he wanted to do was tell Tom what was happening, tell him Alice was not who she said she was, and then make sure he was safe. She wouldn't be expecting him, so it was likely that things were as they had been for years – there was no reason for her to have chosen today to do anything sinister.

But still. The police had said she was dangerous. His hackles rose.

He sensed there was something not right here, and he had to be careful.

He knocked again, but there was no answer. He tried the door handle, a large iron circle, and it turned with a creak. The door opened, and he stepped inside.

It was cool and quiet. There was a smell of ash, as if there'd been a fire in the grate recently. He listened for any noise – footsteps, voices, television.

Nothing. The house felt deserted. He looked out of the window at the drive. Alice's car was there.

'Hello?' he called, softly. 'Tom? Alice?'

He was in a living room, dark beams lowering the ceiling. Through the living room were the stairs; past those was a dining room, and then a kitchen. Outside he could see a terrace with four seats around a table.

He heard a noise behind him and spun around. Alice was standing in the doorway to the dining room. She was staring at him, her eyes dark, emotionless pits.

Then she smiled.

'Roland,' she said. 'What a pleasant surprise.'

Alice

What the *fuck* was he doing here?

How did he even have the address? Tom – the fucking idiot – must have told him for some reason. And now he was here. But why? What could he want?

She didn't know, but it didn't really matter. He was going to have to die, one way or another.

But that presented a problem. Two brothers in the same place, on the same night? If he'd come an hour or two earlier it would have been fine. She could have postponed killing Tom, but now there was no way of backing out of that. He knew *everything*, so he couldn't live.

And now Roland was here, neither could he.

Which left her right back at the same problem. Two brothers dead in one night? It was too much of a coincidence. Questions would be asked. Questions would be answered. Emails would be read.

Her true identity would be uncovered.

Unless she made it *work* for her. A coincidence would raise eyebrows, but what if there was no coincidence? What if one death caused the other?

She smiled.

Yes. That was the answer. And she had the perfect way to make it happen.

'How was the drive?' she asked. 'And what brings you here?'

Roland

Her smile reminded him of a doll his grandmother – his mum's mum – had had when he and Tom were kids. It was porcelain, and the smile was painted on. The rest of the face was expressionless and the red lips were out of place, almost sinister.

'I had to run something by Tom,' he said. 'That's all. I tried to phone but it didn't ring. I guessed you had no service up here.'

'It must be quite urgent,' she said. 'To come all this way.'

'It is,' he said.

'What is it?'

He could hardly tell her, but what could be so urgent he would drive this far to tell his brother?

Of course. The answer was obvious.

'It's Dad.'

'What about him? Has something happened?'

He nodded, glad of a lie that made sense. 'He's taken a turn for the worse.'

The smile morphed into an open-mouthed look of shock. It was no more genuine.

'My God. How bad is he?'

'Worse,' Roland said. 'Not critical, but worse. Tom might want to come and see him.'

It really was the perfect excuse for him being here. Believable, and even better, it was a reason for Tom to leave immediately. He might not have to discuss the photo – and what the police had said – until they were on their way home.

They could bring Joanna, too. Say she needed to see her grandad.

And then he would tell the police where she was and they could come and deal with her. Something was very wrong here, but he, Tom, and Joanna would be safe, and that was all that Roland cared about.

'That's awful,' she said. 'And he's going to want to see him, for sure. But he's out on a walk with Jo at the moment. He left minutes before you arrived, so he may be a while.'

'I didn't see him as I drove in.'

'There's a path by the lake. He went that way.' She gestured to the terrace. 'Do you want to wait out there? Take a seat. I'll make you a cup of tea.'

He didn't want to spend any more time there than he had to, but there was no sign of Tom, and it was possible he was out walking.

And he had no choice.

'OK,' he said. 'That would be lovely.'

Alice

It was clear from his demeanour that he was lying about their father. She had seen the look of relief on his face when the lie came to him; if he had thought of it earlier it might have been more convincing, but she had seen exactly what was happening.

He was here for another reason entirely, and she knew what it was.

There was only one thing it could be.

He knew about the photo. Somehow he had found out.

She bit her lip hard in frustration. She should have figured that out earlier, maybe gone through Tom's emails. But things had moved too quickly, and now here Roland was, fucking up her plans.

Well, it didn't change anything. He was going to die anyway. This just meant she'd have to find out whether he'd told anyone else before she killed him. And if he had, she would have even more to deal with.

But she was calm. She would find a way. She always found a way.

She looked out of the kitchen window. He was sitting at the table, facing the lake. The boat wasn't visible from that angle; the lawn was flat and then there was a sudden dip. You had to be much closer to the lake shore before you could see anything on it.

The kettle whistled and she poured the water onto a teabag. As it steeped she opened her day pack and pulled out what she needed.

She smiled. This was going to be a fun warm-up to the main event.

And she couldn't *wait*.

She put milk in the tea and went outside.

Roland

This was not right at all. There was a chill in the air and the sun was setting. At this time Tom should have been home, eating with his wife and daughter before getting ready to put her to bed, not wandering around the shores of a lake.

He forced himself to keep calm. It was possible Tom was out walking. Perhaps the fresh air helped Joanna to get to sleep. Perhaps it helped Tom clear his mind and relax.

Perhaps.

But none of that could change the feeling that something was wrong. It was the whole situation. The photograph, the lack of a response from Tom, the police phone call. There was something going on with Alice, something long-standing and very bad that was not going to end well.

And he was worried that whatever it was, was coming to a head. Maybe Tom had confronted her with the photo and they'd had a huge row. Maybe he had stormed out and was out there now, unwilling to come back. Maybe he'd left her for good. That would certainly explain the strained atmosphere she gave off.

He glanced down at the table. Tom's phone was lying on it, face down.

He would have taken it if he had stormed out or gone for a walk.

The kitchen door opened and Alice came out holding a mug of tea. She put it on the table and sat opposite him.

'He forgot his phone,' she said. 'No surprise. There's no signal anyway. And I think he enjoys the quiet time with Jo.'

'Does she like the walks?'

Alice shrugged. 'Seems to. She's too young to know where she is.'

'It goes in, though. One way or another.'

'So people say.'

'Did he say when he'd be back?'

'I don't think it'll be too long.'

There was a cry from upstairs. They both glanced up at the open window.

The cry came again, then turned into a wail.

'I thought you said he took Jo with him?' Roland said.

'Oh,' Alice said. 'I must have got mixed up. She was probably asleep and he didn't want to wake her.'

The tension between them rose. He caught her eye and held her gaze.

'Alice,' he said. 'There's something we need to talk—'

Her left hand snaked out and grabbed his wrist. She slammed it down onto the tabletop, palm upwards, then jerked him forwards. Her right hand curled into a fist and she slammed it into his temple.

His head swam and stars danced in front of his eyes. He blinked to clear them, and then he saw what she had done.

'No,' he said. 'No. Not that.'

Alice

It was surprisingly easy, but then his body was used to it.

After she hit him she reached into her pocket for the things she had taken from her day pack. Two syringes, both full of heroin.

This was how it would end for the Sark brothers: Roland, having fallen off the wagon, came to see his brother and, while there, overdosed in spectacular fashion. While Alice tried unsuccessfully to revive him, Tom – already on the ragged edge of sanity – finally collapsed and, in a grotesque imitation of his brother, took his own and his daughter's life.

No coincidence here, but one all too predictable death – she'd read once that a lot of overdoses happened when a junkie fell off the wagon and couldn't hold themselves back – and one caused by it.

A tragedy she would never recover from. A poor, devoted wife and mother grieving at the savage loss of her husband and child.

She pushed the needle into his vein and pressed the plunger, but only a fraction of the way. She wanted to watch him succumb, wanted to extract the maximum satisfaction from this.

He blinked, shaking away the fog the punch had left in his brain, and looked down at his arm. His eyes widened in alarm. He knew what this meant.

She pushed the plunger a little deeper. His pupils enlarged as the drug ran through his body, coursing along all the pathways it had carved over the years and lighting them up.

She could *see* the bliss spread over him. She could feel her own body respond as her craving for the drug she needed was satisfied.

She groaned, then laughed and took her hand off the syringe. It toppled sideways and he grabbed it to stop it falling from his arm.

She put a second syringe on the table. Either he'd inject it himself after the first one, unable to resist, or she'd wait for him to pass out and inject it herself.

What a night this was turning out to be. It was thrilling beyond anything she could have imagined.

Roland

Oh God. Oh God, not this. This was the one thing he could not resist.

He could feel it in his body. It was *wonderful*, better than anything. And he wanted more.

Then she took away her hand and he grabbed the syringe. It was so familiar, so comforting, blissful. Just a little more, and all this would go away. Not that he cared any more, not now, not with the drug, his best friend, his one and only true friend, running riot in his body and taking away all his worries.

She stared at him, her eyes boring into his soul.

'Go on,' she said. 'It's yours. All yours. You know what to do.'

The smile was back, but this time it was not forced. It was real. It was her true self.

And it was demonic. She was inhuman, a force of pure evil without any shred of compassion or love or human feeling at all.

He was terrified. He knew he was going to die at her hands, be consumed by her hellish fire.

And that made him want – need, crave – the release of the drug even more. What was death when you felt this good?

His thumb went over the plunger. This was it. This was the end.

Then he heard a sound. It was like a baby crying.

It *was* a baby crying.

It was Jo. His niece.

And he understood. It wasn't only him who would die at her hands. It was Jo and Tom and countless others.

The cry came again, louder this time.

'No,' he said. 'No.'

He pulled the syringe from his arm and threw it as far away as he could.

'Where's Tom?' he said. 'Where's my brother?'

Alice

Well, fuck that.

It turned out he had a spine after all. Never mind. She'd have to do this the old-fashioned way.

She reached into her day pack and took out her hammer. She had no idea how she'd explain this, but she'd come up with something.

And then he lifted the table and slammed it into her. Her chair tipped over backwards and she fell, her legs up at a weird angle and her head against the stone terrace. He leaned on the table, his weight pinning her to the ground.

'It's over,' he said. 'It's finished. Where's Tom?'

She shook her head. It was hard to breathe and the words came slowly. 'Not saying.'

'I know,' he said. 'You're not who you say you are. Right, Brenda?'

'Andrea,' she gasped. 'For what it's worth.'

'Andrea?'

'Yeah. I can tell you because I'm going to kill you.'

'No,' he said. 'You're not. The police know about you too. They'll be here soon enough. And I'll lie like this until they do.'

Idiot, she thought. He shouldn't be telling her all this.

Because it changed everything again.

She felt her clarity of thought return. The police were on their way. So she had only one option.

Tom would get what he wanted after all. She would have to disappear, and start again somewhere else.

She shifted so that her hips were against the ground and her knees were on the tabletop.

'Don't try anything,' he said. 'It won't work.'

What was he? Five ten and skinny? She'd leg pressed much more.

'I'm not trying—' she began, and then twisted so her feet were against the lip of the table and shoved as hard as she could. It wasn't the perfect position, but it was enough to spin the table and put him off balance so the pressure lessened for a moment and she was able to wriggle free.

She jumped to her feet. She had to get out of here. There was time, but not much. Every second counted now. She had to get in her car and get out of here.

But he would follow her.

Shit.

She could kill him with the hammer. But he would fight, so there was no guarantee it would work, and then she would have used her time, and he would still follow her. It could make the situation worse.

But there *was* a way to stop him from following her. An easy way.

Roland

She held the hammer raised and ready to strike. She was tense, coiled like an animal, and he could see she was weighing up what to do, cold and calculating.

He glanced at the second syringe she had left on the table. The taste he had had was nowhere near enough. God, he wanted to grab it and shove it in his arm, vanish into the abyss.

No. He had Jo and Tom to think about, not to mention the fact she was going to attack him. She was going to lunge at him and swing the hammer at his head. He'd be ready. He'd been in his fair share of fights down the years. You couldn't mix with the people he had mixed with unless you could look after yourself.

But then she licked her lips and turned away and ran into the house.

He saw immediately where she was going. She was going to get Jo.

She was going to hurt his niece. To bash her brains out with that hammer.

He ran after her. She turned out of the kitchen and into the dining room and he heard her footsteps on the stairs. Good. He could trap her upstairs.

He walked up the stairs. When he was near the top she walked out of a bedroom door and onto the landing. In one hand she was holding Jo. In the other, she was holding the hammer.

'Hand her to me,' he said. 'You don't need to do this.'

'Move,' she said. 'Now.'

'No. I can't let you hurt her.'

'I said move.' She lifted the hammer close to Joanna's head. 'I'm going to count to three, and then I'm going to kill her.'

'You won't do that.'

'One.'

'I know you won't.'

'Two.'

She was perfectly still, her eyes trained on his. They had the same emotionless, inhuman look as before.

There was no doubt she would do it, then try to do the same to him. He could run away, but it would be too late for Jo.

He took a step down.

'Good,' she said. 'Keep going. All the way.'

He backed away and she followed, keeping a few steps' distance between them. When he was at the bottom of the stairs she nodded towards the terrace. 'Outside, back to me.'

He went out, looking forward, all too aware she was behind him.

'Lie down,' she said.

He lay on the terrace, next to the scattered furniture. This was it. He braced himself for the sharp blow from the hammer.

It never came.

Instead, she set off at a jog towards the lake, Jo bouncing in her arms.

Alice

He would follow her, no doubt, but that was part of the plan. He would think she was going to drown the infant, and he would run after them.

She glanced over her shoulder. He was on his feet, looking at them. As she watched, he started in their direction.

Good. She sped up. She needed to reach the water before he caught them.

She ran down the slope that led to the rocky beach. Tom lay sprawled in the dinghy, his head lolling over the side of the boat. She ran into the lake until she was waist deep in water.

Roland appeared at the top of the slope.

'Tom,' he said. 'Is he alive?'

'For now.'

'What did you do to him?'

'Heroin.'

His eyes widened. 'You gave him heroin?'

'To knock him out. Then I was going to push him out on the lake with Jo and capsize them. It'd look like a murder-suicide. But you showed up.'

'So what now?'

'This,' she said, and dropped Jo into the lake.

Roland

Jo splashed into the water and sank. Alice sprinted out of the lake and up towards the house.

Roland understood her plan, but there was nothing he could do to stop her.

She was making him choose between rescuing his niece or chasing her. And there was only one choice.

He ran into the lake. The water was bitterly cold and dark. He reached the spot where she had dropped Jo and searched for her. For a moment he couldn't find her, and then he saw a flash of white and plunged his hands into the water, grasping for his niece.

He felt an arm or a leg and grabbed it, then yanked her out of the water. She was pale and faintly blue and he didn't think she was breathing, but he slapped her back and then she frowned and opened her mouth and started to cry.

It was the best sound he had ever heard. He clutched her to his chest. She was cold, and her clothes were wet, and he was going to have to warm her up, but first he had to check on Tom.

He ran to the boat, with Jo in one arm, and pressed his fingers to Tom's neck.

There was a pulse. It was faint, but it was there. He needed to call an ambulance, and get the police here. He ran up to the house. His phone had no signal. Tom's was on the terrace; he picked it up, but it was off and he didn't know the passcode.

He went inside. Maybe he could find the router and get the password.

It was in the living room.

And next to it was an old rotary phone. He picked up the handset, and lifted it to his ear. There was a dial tone.

He rang 999. As he did, he looked out of the window.

Alice's car was gone. But she couldn't have got too far.

Alice

She was calm as she drove away. She had always known it might come to this. She put her hand on her day pack. It was why she kept it packed.

Australian dollars. Lots of them. As well as pounds, now. She had all the money she'd need.

As well as different coloured contact lenses. A couple of wigs. Some glasses with non-prescription lenses. A couple of ID cards.

She thought through her escape. It would be maybe ten or twenty minutes before the police got to the cottage. Then another few minutes before they understood what was going on. Which meant she had, at forty or so miles an hour, about ten or fifteen miles' distance she could put between her and them.

Quite a radius.

She would head west, to the port towns of Whitehaven and Workington, then north to Carlisle. There were plenty of cars and people there, and plenty of places to hide.

And then, she could start again.

Start *everything* again.

Roland

He undressed Jo and wrapped her in a towel. She was unhappy, mewling and crying – maybe she was hungry, although she'd have to wait, as he had no idea how to feed her – but she was safe.

He held her to his chest and ran down the lawn to Tom.

He was still in the boat, passed out. Roland had seen two of his friends, if friends was the right word, die from overdoses, and he knew what an overdose looked like.

And Tom was in a similar state to them, his skin sallow and his lips tinged with blue. Roland felt for a pulse again.

It was weaker.

How much had she given him? Tom had never taken heroin before and his tolerance would be low. Even a small amount could be fatal. At the very least it could make him vomit and he would, in the position he was in, likely choke.

Roland sat Joanna on the grass and turned Tom onto his side. It was ironic: him, of all people, helping his brother into the recovery position.

He heard the sound of an engine approaching. A car door closed, then another, and he heard a man's voice call out.

'Down here,' he shouted. 'Come in the side gate.'

Two paramedics – a man and a woman – appeared at the side of the house and walked down to meet him.

'What's going on?' the woman said.

He pointed at Tom, sprawled in the boat. 'He's taken heroin. Well, someone injected him, but either way, he needs help. I don't think he's OD'd yet, but he's close.' He held out his forearm to show them the scars. 'I've had a bit of experience of this kind of thing.'

'Right,' the woman said. She looked at Joanna. 'The baby?'

'I rescued her from the lake,' Roland said. 'She was cold, but I think she's OK for now. She might be hungry. I have no idea what to do with babies.'

'I take it the baby is not your child?' the woman said.

'No. Her dad's in the boat. The heroin guy.'

The woman frowned. 'What the hell is going on here?'

'It's a long story,' Roland said. 'I don't know all of it myself.'

DI Wynne

Wynne cut the call.

'They're there,' she said. 'Medics arrived first, then two uniforms.'

'What's the situation?' DS Alexander said.

'She's gone. Every officer in the county's looking for her car.'

'Fuck.'

'We have the car details. We'll find her.'

'And the others?'

'Joanna and Roland are fine. Mr Sark's gone to Whitehaven hospital. He's stable but suffering from a possible heroin overdose.'

'Heroin? Tom's not a user.'

Wynne nodded. 'I know.'

'What happened there?'

'We'll find out shortly, I imagine.'

When they arrived, Roland was sitting at the kitchen table, feeding a jar of baby food to Jo. The two uniforms – a pair of burly men in their twenties called Dave and Steve – were leaning against the wall.

'Roland,' DS Alexander said. 'I'm glad you're safe.'

'Did you hear anything about Tom?' he said.

'He's stable. I suspect they'll keep him in overnight. But I think he'll be OK.'

'Do you feel up to talking, Mr Sark?' Wynne said.

'Of course,' Roland replied. 'No problem.'

'Then why don't you take us through what happened?'

'And then what?'

'Then DS Alexander and I will take you and Joanna home. The forensics teams will come in and look over this place. And we'll find Mrs Sark.'

'I don't want to go home,' Roland said. 'I want to be there when Tom comes around.'

DS Alexander put her hand on his forearm. 'I think that's a great idea,' she said. 'We'll take Joanna to your parents. Do they have stuff for her?'

'Yes,' Roland said. 'She's stayed over quite often.'

'Then you can go to Whitehaven hospital,' Wynne said.

Tom

He was a long time coming round, and when he did he had no idea where he was. Not that it mattered. He felt an overwhelming sensation of nausea. When he was ten they had gone on a ferry to France and he had suffered horribly from seasickness; this was like that, turned up by a factor of ten.

He tried to sit up but his head throbbed and he lay back down. He was in a bed of some kind; through the nausea he could make out an antiseptic smell which brought something to mind.

A hospital.

He was in a hospital.

What had happened? Had he had an accident?

And then he started to remember.

Alice was Brenda was Andrea. The Crucifix killings. More in Perth, and others besides.

And then him. He was supposed to be next. But he was alive. Somehow he had escaped Alice's plan.

Which left Joanna next in line. His eyes snapped open. The room was empty.

Joanna. He had to find out what had happened to his daughter.

He started to scream.

Roland

A nurse tapped him on the shoulder. 'Your brother's awake. We told him you're here and you're coming along now. Be quick, if you could. He's a little agitated.'

Tom was sitting up in his bed, his face pallid, his fists clenched into balls.

'Roland,' he said. 'Where is she? Where's Jo?'

'She's with Mum and Dad. At their house.'

'Is she safe?'

He nodded. 'She's fine.'

His brother's hands unclenched and he fell back on the bed.

'Thank *God*,' he said. 'Alice was going to – she was going to—'

'I know,' Roland said. 'I was there.'

'You were there? Why?'

'Your emails were weird. Something seemed off and I got worried, so I drove up. Alice – or whatever her name is – told me you were out walking with Jo, but then I heard Jo crying. Alice threw her in the lake—'

'She what?'

'To occupy me so she could get away.' He sat on Tom's

bed. 'It's a long story. But once I was there she figured out that her only option was to run. The police were on their way.'

'Roland,' Tom said. 'If you hadn't come—' His voice faltered at the magnitude of what he was saying.

Roland nodded. 'I know. But I did.'

'Thank God,' Tom said. 'Thank *you*. What happened to Alice?'

'She got away.'

Tom's eyes closed. 'The police didn't catch her?'

'They arrived too late. They're looking for her. They'll find her soon enough.'

'I hope so. I don't like the thought of her out there.'

'Me neither. How are you feeling?'

'Tired. A bit nauseous. But I'm OK, I think. I want to go home. I want to see Jo.'

'I'll ask,' Roland said. 'Sit tight. And don't worry. This is over now, Tom.'

DI Wynne

Wynne sat opposite DSI Marie Ryan. Ryan was tapping her desk with the eraser on the end of a yellow pencil.

'So,' Ryan said. 'We lost her.'

'We're still looking. We know what vehicle she's in.'

'For now.'

Wynne nodded. 'For now.'

'And she has a track record of disappearing.' Ryan winced. 'This isn't great, Jane.'

'Far from it,' Wynne said. 'We were very close. But not close enough.'

'She's going to pop up somewhere,' Ryan said. 'And start killing again. The public know that. They're scared, and we need her behind bars.'

'We'll get her.'

'If we don't, we'll have to hold a press conference,' Ryan said. 'Tell people what happened. What should we say?'

Wynne shrugged. 'The truth.'

'Which would be?'

'That we learned the identity of the Crucifix Killer – Alice Sark – and that she was really Andrea Petersen. And all the rest of it. We need to get out in front of this. It'll come out eventually anyway, so it's better if it comes from us.'

'And that she got away.'

Wynne nodded. 'And that.'

'Jesus,' Ryan said. 'This story's going to run and run.'

'Unless we apprehend her.'

'Yes,' Ryan said. 'You work on that. I'll deal with the rest.'

Monday, 30 August 2021

Tom

It was midday when they arrived at their parents' house. The doctors had let him leave after breakfast. It was the first time they had arrived there together in more than a decade. Roland pulled up and switched off the engine.

'I can't believe this,' Tom said. 'Any of it. Who Alice was, what she did . . .' His voice tailed off. 'I don't know how it happened. Or what's next.'

'There's not much from my life which is of use to you,' Roland said. 'But in a weird way I know what you mean. I've gone over what I did and wondered how it came to that. How it went so wrong. And here's what I learned: it doesn't matter. You have to move forward.'

Tom smiled at his brother. 'Thanks,' he said. 'And thanks for being there. If you hadn't showed up Jo and I would be dead.'

'I just did what I could,' Roland said.

'You did great.'

They got out of the car and walked to the house. As Roland put the key in the front door it opened. His mum hugged them both.

'Thank God,' she said. 'Thank God you're safe.'

'I'm sorry, Mum. I'm sorry this—' Tom started to say.

'Shhh. You have no reason to apologize. This is all on her. On Alice, or whatever she was called.'

'Is Jo here?' Tom said. 'I want to see her.'

'She's sleeping upstairs.'

Tom walked up to his old bedroom, which was where Joanna slept when she was here. She was in her crib, lying on her back, her arms above her head, her mouth parted. She looked utterly peaceful. She would have no memory of any of this.

She would have no memory of her mother.

She resembled Alice, there was no mistaking it. She had the same grey-green eyes. A shiver ran through him.

One day you're going to find out who your mum was, he thought, *which is going to be an interesting conversation.*

He pushed the thought away. He was too tired to worry about it now. There'd be people with expertise in this kind of thing – how they got it he had no idea – who could help them deal with it when the time came. Maybe he would lie and say she died. A boating accident, perhaps.

He kissed Jo on the forehead, her skin soft and warm against his lips, then went downstairs. His mum and dad and Roland were talking in the kitchen and he paused by the door.

'Poor Tom,' his mum was saying. 'This is going to be terrible for him.'

'In the short term, yes,' Roland said. 'But he's better off without her. There was something wrong with her. When she'd stopped pretending to be like a normal person it was like looking into the eyes of an animal. There was nothing there. Nothing human, at any rate.'

'I wonder what made her like that.'

'Who knows,' his dad said. 'But I don't think people like that are made. I think they're born. It's in them, somehow.'

Tom paused. He pictured Joanna in her crib, pictured her grey-green eyes. She was Alice's daughter, as well as his. He tried to ignore the thought, but it was impossible to push away. What if she was like Alice?

He walked into the kitchen. His dad was sitting at the table. He put his hands on the arms of his chair and levered himself to his feet, wincing with pain.

'Sit down,' Tom said. 'It's OK.'

His dad waved his objection aside. 'Come here.'

He held out his arms and Tom hugged him. It was years since he had hugged his dad.

'I'm glad you're OK, son,' his dad said. 'And Jo, too. I couldn't have taken it if anything had happened to her. To *either* of you.'

'We're OK now.' His dad sat down and Tom took the seat next to him. 'I heard you talking,' he said. 'About how Alice was. And it made me wonder about Jo.'

'Wonder what?' his dad said. 'If she's like Alice?'

He nodded. 'Exactly.'

His dad stuck out his bottom lip and shook his head. 'Not a chance,' he said. 'I know that girl, and she's a superstar. She's nothing like Alice.'

'You could be right,' he said. 'After she drugged me, Alice told me about her life. She told me that her mum knew what she was when she was very young. She never cried, never played with the other kids, never seemed interested in her mum.'

'That's nothing like Jo,' his mum said. 'Nothing at all. She's a sweet little thing.'

Upstairs, Jo began to wail.

His mum smiled.

'I think she's going to be fine, Tom. You both are.'

DI Wynne

Wynne settled her phone on the table. She had just heard from the local police force.

They had found Andrea Petersen's car on a side street in Carlisle, about a hundred yards from the bus station. Wynne was fairly certain what she had done. Dumped the car, and caught a bus to destinations unknown.

Andrea Petersen had done this before, so she knew the drill. She'd have had a stash of cash, travel documents, and something to change her appearance. Every cop in the area was looking for a woman with short, dark hair, but she might now have long blonde or short red hair. She could also be anywhere. Points north led her to Scotland. Points south to Leeds or Manchester or Liverpool. Places with ports and airports and millions of people to disappear into.

And Petersen knew how to disappear.

Wynne would keep looking. She had nothing if not perseverance.

But she knew, in her bones, that Andrea Petersen – Alice Sark – was gone.

For now.

Because – like DSI Ryan had said – one day she'd turn up again. And when she did, Wynne would be waiting for her.

EPILOGUE

Barrow, Maine, USA, October 2021

A young woman – maybe early thirties – with close-cropped, metallic red hair, sat at the desk in the house lettings agency. The woman opposite smiled.

'So, what did you think of the house?' she said.

'I love it,' the woman replied. 'It's perfect for me. If it's available, I'll take it.'

'It is. We'll need first month, last month, and one month's rent as a security deposit. Could I see your ID?'

The young woman handed over a driver's licence. It was issued in Ohio, in the name of Dana Sand.

'You're from Ohio, Dana?' the woman said.

'That's right.'

'What brings you to Barrow, Maine? It's quite a ways from Ohio.'

'My job.'

'What is it that you do?'

'I'm a journalist.'

'And you chose to come to Maine?'

Dana Sand nodded. 'I was travelling in Scotland this

summer,' she said. 'And I realized that I enjoyed the change of scene. So I decided to move somewhere different when I came home. I read an article about cool small towns, and Barrow came up.'

'Well,' the woman said, as she handed back her driving licence. 'We're glad to have you here. I hope I hear about some of your handiwork!'

'I think you will,' Dana Sand said. 'I'm pretty sure of that.'

Acknowledgements

The more I write, the more I understand what a team effort it is to get a book out into the world, and the more grateful I am to all those who work on doing so.

My warmest thanks, therefore, to:

The team at HarperCollins for everything they do.

Charlotte Webb, for her copy-editing skills but also her intimate knowledge of the geography of Wast Water.

Kathryn Cheshire, for her patience, dedication and unerring editorial insight.

And to Becky Ritchie, for her guidance and unwavering support – they are greatly appreciated.

MORE FROM

A girl is missing. Five years old, taken from outside her school.

The police are at a loss; her parents are beyond grief.

But the biggest mystery is yet to come: one week later, their daughter is returned.

And this is just the beginning of the nightmare.

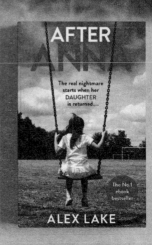

Kate returns from a holiday to news of a serial killer in her home town – and his victims all look like her.

It could, of course, be a simple coincidence. Or maybe not.

She becomes convinced she is being watched.

Is she next?

One day, Sarah Havenant discovers that there are two Facebook profiles in her name. One is hers. The other, she has never seen.

Whoever has set up the second profile has been waiting for Sarah to find it. And now that she has, her life will no longer be her own...

ALEX LAKE

For Claire, life is good. She has a career she loves, friends she can rely on and a husband who dotes on her.

For Alfie, it couldn't be more different. His life with Claire is built on a lie.

And when the truth comes out, the consequences threaten to destroy *everything*.

In seven days, Maggie's son, Max, turns three. And she's dreading it.

For the last twelve years Maggie has been imprisoned in a basement. She gave birth to two sons before Max, and on their third birthdays her captor came and took them from her.

The clock is ticking...

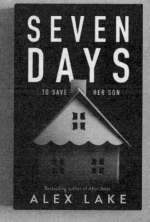

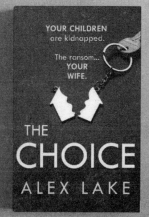

Matt only turned his back for a moment. But when he looks around, his car – with his three young children inside – has vanished.

Then he receives a message: *This is a kidnap. If you want to see your children again, you will exchange them for your wife.*

He has just hours to make the decision...